PENGUIN

THE SEEDS

John Wyndham was born in 1903. Until 1911 he lived in Edgbaston, Birmingham, and then in many parts of England. After a wide experience of the English preparatory school he was at Bedales from 1918 till 1921. Careers which he had tried include farming, law, commercial art, and advertising, and he first started writing short stories, intended for sale, in 1925. From 1930 till 1939 he wrote stories of various kinds under different names, almost exclusively for American publications. He also wrote detective novels. During the war he was in the Civil Service and afterwards in the Army. In 1946 he went back to writing stories for publication in the U.S.A. and decided to try a modified form of what is unhappily known as 'science fiction'. He wrote *The Day of the Triffids* and *The Kraken Wakes* (both of which have been translated into several languages), *The Chrysalids*, *The Midwich Cuckoos* (filmed as *The Village of the Damned*), *Trouble with Lichen*, *The Outward Urge* (with Lucas Parkes), *Consider Her Ways and Others* and his last book, *Chocky*, all of which have been published as Penguins. John Wyndham died in March 1969.

JOHN WYNDHAM

THE SEEDS OF TIME

———

PENGUIN BOOKS
IN ASSOCIATION WITH
MICHAEL JOSEPH

PENGUIN BOOKS

Published by the Penguin Group
Penguin Books Ltd, 27 Wrights Lane, London w8 5TZ, England
Viking Penguin, a division of Penguin Books USA Inc.
375 Hudson Street, New York, New York 10014, USA
Penguin Books Australia Ltd, Ringwood, Victoria, Australia
Penguin Books Canada Ltd, 2801 John Street, Markham, Ontario, Canada L3R 1B4
Penguin Books (NZ) Ltd, 182–190 Wairau Road, Auckland 10, New Zealand

Penguin Books Ltd, Registered Offices: Harmondsworth, Middlesex, England

First published by Michael Joseph 1956
Published in Penguin Books 1959
25 27 29 30 28 26

Printed in England by Clays Ltd, St Ives plc
Set in Linotype Baskerville

Contents

Foreword

THE best definition of the science-fiction story that I know is Mr Edmund Crispin's: that it 'is one which presupposes a technology, or an effect of technology, or a disturbance in the natural order, such as humanity, up to the time of writing, has not in actual fact experienced'.

The disposition of something like ninety per cent of science-fiction to use this definition only in conjunction with the adventure-narrative form of story is primarily an accident of commercial exploitation, and an unfortunate one that makes it difficult to see the trees for the wood.

When, a good many years ago now, I first happened upon magazines that specialized in stories of the kind, their proprietors had already concocted the formula which they *knew*, with that conviction that sustains minor showmen everywhere, to be the only one that the public would stand for and pay for; and almost the only reason for not dismissing their productions forthwith was the occasional discovery of the different story that had somehow got under their guard.

In general, the formula has been preserved so that even now, after twenty-five years, the bulk of science-fiction, and its adaptations to film and broadcast serial form, has been determinedly kept in the cliff-hanger class.

Nevertheless, there came a time when certain editors grew mildly mutinous with the perception that the terms of reference did not truly restrict them to the adventures of galactic gangsters in space-opera, and they began, some by stealth, others by declaration, to encourage their authors to do a bit more exploration within the definition.

With that, the field became open to experiments, and the nine stories I have chosen here are (or were) virtually experiments, made at intervals during fifteen years, in adapting the science-fiction motif to various styles of short story.

The earliest, *Meteor*, is closest to the usual adventure-narrative, and was written to suit a pre-war editor (though

its beginning was later adapted a little for post-war repub-
lication).

Taking a look at science-fiction again after a wartime
interval, one seemed to see indications that it was trying
to change its spots. This idea set off the somewhat pastoral
Time to Rest. It was swiftly returned by an American
agent with the hurt reproof that it wouldn't do at all: this
kind of thing, as I ought to know, hadn't a chance unless it
was packed full of adjectives and action. However, it did
later on appear in four periodicals and two anthologies, so
I felt better about it.

Meanwhile, *Pillar to Post*, written to suit, I hoped, the
policy of a newly arisen American magazine, came near
enough to it to be accepted and afterwards anthologized.

After that, I rather gave up other people's policies, and
tried various styles. The intention of *Chronoclasm*, in the
comedy-romantic, was to entertain the general reader and
break away from the science-fiction enthusiast. *Pawley's
Peepholes* is satirical farce. *Opposite Number* attempts,
with perhaps qualified success, the light presentation of a
somewhat complicated idea. For *Dumb Martian* and
Survival I tried to use the pattern of the English short-story
in its heyday. *Compassion Circuit* is the short horror-story.
A neo-Gothick trifle, could one say? And finally there is
Wild Flower where one has encouraged science-fiction to
try the form of the modern short-story.

In the careers of these stories my debts have become too
widely spread to be acknowledged here with the detail one
could wish, and since it would be invidious to mention only
some editors and their periodicals, I must have recourse to
the collective (and the order of the alphabet). Thus, with a
great deal more gratitude than adequacy, I fear, I take this
opportunity of thanking those editors, a number of whom
I can never hope to meet, in Australia, France, Great
Britain, Holland, Italy, South Africa, Sweden, and the
U.S.A. who have so much encouraged me by printing one
or more of these experiments on the theme: 'I wonder
what might happen if ... ?'   J. W.

Chronoclasm

I FIRST heard of Tavia in a sort of semi-detached way. An elderly gentleman, a stranger, approached me in Plyton High Street one morning. He raised his hat, bowed, with perhaps a touch of foreignness, and introduced himself politely:

'My name is Donald Gobie, Doctor Gobie. I should be most grateful, Sir Gerald, if you could spare me just a few minutes of your time. I am so sorry to trouble you, but it is a matter of some urgency, and considerable importance.'

I looked at him carefully.

'I think there must be some mistake,' I told him. 'I have no handle to my name – not even a knighthood.'

He looked taken aback.

'Dear me. I *am* sorry. Such a likeness – I was quite sure you must be Sir Gerald Lattery.'

It was my turn to be taken aback.

'My name *is* Gerald Lattery,' I admitted, 'but Mister, not Sir.'

He grew a little confused.

'Oh, dear. Of course. How very stupid of me. Is there –' he looked about us, '– is there somewhere where we could have a few words in private?' he asked.

I hesitated, but only for a brief moment. He was clearly a gentleman of education and some culture. Might have been a lawyer. Certainly not on the touch, or anything of that kind. We were close to *The Bull*, so I led the way into the lounge there. It was conveniently empty. He declined the offer of a drink, and we sat down.

'Well, what is this trouble, Doctor Gobie?' I asked him.

He hesitated, obviously a little embarrassed. Then he spoke, with an air of plunging:

'It is concerning Tavia, Sir Gerald – er, Mr Lattery. I think perhaps you don't understand the degree to which the whole situation is fraught with unpredictable conse-quences. It is not just my own responsibility, you understand, though that troubles me greatly – it is the results that cannot be foreseen. She really must come back before very great harm is done. She *must*, Mr Lattery.'

I watched him. His earnestness was beyond question, his distress perfectly genuine.

'But, Doctor Gobie –' I began.

'I can understand what it may mean to you, sir, nevertheless I do implore you to persuade her. Not just for my sake and her family's, but for everyone's. One has to be so careful; the results of the least action are incalculable. There has to be order, harmony; it must be preserved. Let one single seed fall out of place, and who can say what may come of it? So I beg you to persuade her –'

I broke in, speaking gently because whatever it was all about, he obviously had it very much at heart.

'Just a minute, Doctor Gobie. I'm afraid there is some mistake. I haven't the least idea what you are talking about.'

He checked himself. A dismayed expression came over his face.

'You – ?' he began, and then paused in thought, frowning. 'You don't mean you haven't met Tavia yet?' he asked.

'As far as I know, I do. I've never even heard of anyone called Tavia,' I assured him.

He looked winded by that, and I was sorry. I renewed my offer of a drink. But he shook his head, and presently he recovered himself a little.

'I am so sorry,' he said. 'There has been a mistake indeed. Please accept my apologies, Mr Lattery. You must think me quite light-headed, I'm afraid. It's so difficult to explain. May I ask you just to forget it, please forget it entirely.'

Presently he left, looking forlorn. I remained a little puzzled, but in the course of the next day or two I carried out his final request – or so I thought.

The first time I did see Tavia was a couple of years later, and, of course, I did not at the time know it was she.

I had just left *The Bull*. There was a number of people about in the High Street, but just as I laid a hand on the car door I became aware that one of them on the other side of the road had stopped dead, and was watching me. I looked up, and our eyes met. Hers were hazel.

She was tall, and slender, and good-looking – not pretty, something better than that. And I went on looking.

She wore a rather ordinary tweed skirt and dark-green knitted jumper. Her shoes, however, were a little odd; low-heeled, but a bit fancy; they didn't seem to go with the rest. There was something else out of place, too, though I did not fix it at the moment. Only afterwards did I realize that it must have been the way her fair hair was dressed – very becoming to her, but the style was a bit off the beam. You might say that hair is just hair, and hairdressers have in-finite variety of touch, but they haven't. There is a kind of period-style overriding current fashion; look at any photo-graph taken thirty years ago. Her hair, like her shoes, didn't quite suit the rest.

For some seconds she stood there frozen, quite unsmil-ing. Then, as if she were not quite awake, she took a step forward to cross the road. At that moment the Market Hall clock chimed. She glanced up at it; her expression was suddenly all alarm. She turned, and started running up the pavement, like Cinderella after the last bus.

I got into my car wondering who she had mistaken me for. I was perfectly certain I had never set eyes on her before.

The next day when the barman at *The Bull* set down my pint, he told me:

'Young woman in here asking after you, Mr Lattery. Did she find you? I told her where your place is.'

I shook my head. 'Who was she?'

'She didn't say her name, but . . .' he went on to describe her. Recollection of the girl on the other side of the street came back to me. I nodded.

'I saw her just across the road. I wondered who she was.' I told him.

'Well, she seemed to know you all right. "Was that Mr Lattery who was in here earlier on?" she says to me. I says yes, you was one of them. She nodded and thought a bit. "He lives at Bagford House, doesn't he?" she asks. "Why, no Miss," I says, "that's Major Flacken's place. Mr Lattery, he lives out at Chatcombe Cottage." So she asks me where that is, and I told her. Hope that was all right. Seemed a nice young lady.'

I reassured him. 'She could have got the address anywhere. Funny she should ask about Bagford House – that's a place I might hanker for, if I ever had any money.'

'Better hurry up and make it, sir. The old Major's getting on a bit now,' he said.

Nothing came of it. Whatever the girl had wanted my address for, she didn't follow it up, and the matter dropped out of my mind.

It was about a month later that I saw her again. I'd kind of slipped into the habit of going riding once or twice a week with a girl called Marjorie Cranshaw, and running her home from the stables afterwards. The way took us by one of those narrow lanes between high banks where there is barely room for two cars to pass. Round a corner I had to brake and pull right in because an oncoming car was in the middle of the road after overtaking a pedestrian. It pulled over, and squeezed past me. Then I looked at the pedestrian, and saw it was this girl again. She recognized me at the same moment, and gave a slight start. I saw her hesitate, and then make up her mind to come across and speak. She came a few steps nearer with obvious intention. Then she caught sight of Marjorie beside me, changed her mind, with as bad an imitation of not having intended to come our way at all as you could hope to see. I put the gear in.

'Oh,' said Marjorie in a voice that penetrated naturally, and a tone that was meant to, 'who was that?'

I told her I didn't know.

'She certainly seemed to know you,' she said, disbelievingly.

Her tone irritated me. In any case it was no business of hers. I didn't reply.

She was not willing to let it drop. 'I don't think I've seen her about before,' she said presently.

'She may be a holiday-maker for all I know,' I said. 'There are plenty of them about.'

'That doesn't sound very convincing, considering the way she looked at you.'

'I don't care for being thought, or called, a liar,' I said.

'Oh, I thought I asked a perfectly ordinary question. Of course, if I've said anything to embarrass you –'

'Nor do I care for sustained innuendo. Perhaps you'd prefer to walk the rest of the way. It's not far.'

'I see, I am sorry to have intruded. It's a pity it's too narrow for you to turn the car here,' she said as she got out. 'Goodbye, Mr Lattery.'

With the help of a gateway it was not too narrow, but I did not see the girl when I went back. Marjorie had roused my interest in her, so that I rather hoped I would. Besides, though I still had no idea who she might be, I was feeling grateful to her. You will have experienced, perhaps, that feeling of being relieved of a weight that you had not properly realized was there?

Our third meeting was on a different plane altogether.

My cottage stood, as its name suggests, in a coombe which, in Devonshire, is a small valley that is, or once was, wooded. It was somewhat isolated from the other four or five cottages there, being set in the lower part, at the end of the track. The heathered hills swept steeply up on either side. A few narrow grazing fields bordered both banks of the stream. What was left of the original woods fringed between them and the heather, and survived in small clumps and spinneys here and there.

It was in the closest of these spinneys, on an afternoon when I was surveying my plot and decided that it was about time the beans came out, that I heard a sound of small branches breaking underfoot. I needed no more than a glance to find the cause of it; her fair hair gave her away. For a moment we looked at one another as we had before.

'Er – hullo,' I said.

She did not reply at once. She went on staring. Then: 'Is there anyone in sight?' she asked.

I looked up as much of the track as I could see from where I stood, and then up at the opposite hillside.

'I can't see anyone,' I told her.

She pushed the bushes aside, and stepped out cautiously, looking this way and that. She was dressed just as she had been when I first saw her – except that her hair had been a trifle raked about by branches. On the rough ground the shoes looked even more inappropriate. Seeming a little reassured she took a few steps forward.

'I –' she began.

Then, higher up the coombe, a man's voice called, and another answered it. The girl froze for a moment, looking scared.

'They're coming. Hide me somewhere, quickly, please,' she said.

'Er –' I began, inadequately.

'Oh, quick, quick. They're coming,' she said urgently.

She certainly looked alarmed.

'Better come inside,' I told her, and led the way into the cottage.

She followed swiftly, and when I had shut the door she slid the bolt.

'Don't let them catch me. Don't let them,' she begged.

'Look here, what's all this about. Who are "they"?' I asked.

She did not answer that; her eyes, roving round the room, found the telephone.

'Call the police,' she said. 'Call the police, quickly.' I hesitated. 'Don't you *have* any police?' she added.

'Of course we have police, but –'

'Then call them, please.'

'But look here –' I began.

She clenched her hands.

'You must call them, please. Quickly.'

She looked very anxious.

'All right, *I'll* call them. You can do the explaining,' I said, and picked up the instrument.

I was used to the rustic leisure of communications in those parts, and waited patiently. The girl did not; she stood twining her fingers together. At last the connexion was made:

'Hullo,' I said, 'is that the Plyton Police?'

'Plyton Police –' an answering voice had begun when there was an interruption of steps on the gravel path, followed by a heavy knocking at the door. I handed the instrument to the girl and went to the door.

'Don't let them in,' she said, and then gave her attention to the telephone.

I hesitated. The rather peremptory knocking came again. One can't just stand about, not letting people in; besides, to take a strange young lady hurriedly into one's cottage, and immediately bolt the door against all comers ... ? At the third knocking I opened up.

The aspect of the man on my doorstep took me aback. Not his face – that was suitable enough in a young man of, say, twenty-five – it was his clothes. One is not prepared to encounter something that looks like a close-fitting skating-suit, worn with a full-cut, hip-length, glass-buttoned jacket, certainly not on Dartmoor, at the end of the summer season. However, I pulled myself together enough to ask what he wanted. He paid no attention to that as he stood looking over my shoulder at the girl.

'Tavia,' he said. 'Come here!'

She didn't stop talking hurriedly into the telephone. The man stepped forward.

'Steady on!' I said. 'First, I'd like to know what all this is about.'

He looked at my squarely.

'You wouldn't understand,' he said, and raised his arm to push me out of the way.

I have always felt that I would strongly dislike people

who tell me that I don't understand, and try to push me off my own threshold. I socked him hard in the stomach, and as he doubled up I pushed him outside and closed the door.

'They're coming,' said the girl's voice behind me. 'The police are coming.'

'If you'd just tell me –' I began. But she pointed.

'Look out! – at the window,' she said.

I turned. There was another man outside, dressed similarly to the first who was still audibly wheezing on the doorstep. He was hesitating. I reached my twelve-bore off the wall, grabbed some cartridges from the drawer, and loaded it. Then I stood back, facing the door.

'Open it, and keep behind it,' I told her.

She obeyed, doubtfully.

Outside, the second man was now bending solicitously over the first. A third man was coming up the path. They saw the gun, and we had a brief tableau.

'You there,' I said. 'You can either beat it quick, or stay and argue it out with the police. Which is it to be?'

'But you don't understand. It is most important –' began one of them.

'All right. Then you can stay there and tell the police how important it is,' I said, and nodded to the girl to close the door again.

We watched through the window as the two of them helped the winded man away.

*

The police, when they arrived, were not amiable. They took down my description of the men reluctantly, and departed coolly. Meanwhile, there was the girl.

She had told the police as little as she well could – simply that she had been pursued by three oddly dressed men and had appealed to me for help. She had refused their offer of a lift to Plyton in the police car, so here she still was.

'Well, now,' I suggested, 'perhaps you'd like to explain to me just what seems to be going on?'

She sat quite still facing me with a long level look which had a tinge of – sadness? – disappointment? – well, unsatisfactoriness of some kind. For a moment I wondered if she were going to cry, but in a small voice she said:

'I had your letter – and now I've burned my boats.'

I sat down opposite to her. After fumbling a bit I found my cigarettes and lit one.

'You – er – had my letter, and now you've – er – burnt your boats?' I repeated.

'Yes,' she said. Her eyes left mine and strayed round the room, not seeing much.

'And now you don't even know me,' she said.

Whereupon the tears came, fast.

I sat there helplessly for a half-minute. Then I decided to go into the kitchen and put on the kettle while she had it out. All my female relatives have always regarded tea as the prime panacea, so I brought the pot and cups back with me when I returned.

I found her recovered, sitting staring pensively at the unlit fire. I put a match to it. She watched it take light and burn, with the expression of a child who has just received a present.

'Lovely,' she said, as though a fire were something completely novel. She looked all round the room again. 'Lovely,' she repeated.

'Would you like to pour?' I suggested, but she shook her head, and watched me do it.

'Tea,' she said. 'By a fireside!'

Which was true enough, but scarcely remarkable.

'I think it is about time we introduced ourselves,' I suggested. 'I am Gerald Lattery.'

'Of course,' she said, nodding. It was not to my mind an altogether appropriate reply, but she followed it up by: 'I am Octavia Lattery – they usually call me Tavia.'

Tavia? – Something clinked in my mind, but did not quite chime.

'We are related in some way?' I asked her.

'Yes – very distantly,' she said, looking at me oddly. 'Oh,

dear,' she added, 'this is difficult,' and looked as if she were about to cry again.

'Tavia ... ?' I repeated, trying to remember. 'There's something ...' Then I had a sudden vision of an embarrassed elderly gentleman. 'Why, of course; now what was the name? Doctor – Doctor Bogey, or something?'

She suddenly sat quite still.

'Not – not Doctor Gobie?' she suggested.

'Yes, that's it. He asked me about somebody called Tavia. That would be you?'

'He isn't here?' she said, looking round as if he might be hiding in a corner.

I told her it would be about two years ago now. She relaxed.

'Silly old Uncle Donald. How like him! And naturally you'd have no idea what he was talking about?'

'I've very little more now,' I pointed out, 'though I can understand how even an uncle might be agitated at losing you.'

'Yes. I'm afraid he will be – very,' she said.

'Was: this was two years ago,' I reminded her.

'Oh, of course you don't really understand yet, do you?'

'Look,' I told her. 'One after another, people keep on telling me that I don't understand. I know that already – it is about the only thing I do understand.'

'Yes. I'd better explain. Oh dear, where shall I begin?' I let her ponder that, uninterrupted. Presently she said: 'Do you believe in predestination?'

'I don't think so,' I told her.

'Oh – no, well perhaps it isn't quite that, after all – more like a sort of affinity. You see, ever since I was quite tiny I remember thinking this was the most thrilling and wonderful age – and then, of course, it was the time in which the only famous person in our family lived. So I thought it was marvellous. Romantic, I suppose you'd call it.'

'It depends whether you mean the thought or the age ...' I began, but she took no notice.

'I used to picture the great fleets of funny little aircraft during the wars, and think how they were like David going out to hit Goliath, so tiny and brave. And there were the huge clumsy ships, wallowing slowly along, but getting there somehow in the end, and nobody minding how slow they were. And quaint black and white films; and horses in the streets; and shaky old internal combustion engines; and coal fires; and exciting bombings; and trains running on rails; and telephones with wires; and, oh, lots of things. And the things one could do! Fancy being at the first night of a new Shaw play, or a new Coward play, in a real theatre! Or getting a brand-new T. S. Eliot, on publishing day. Or seeing the Queen drive by to open Parliament. A wonderful, thrilling time!'

'Well, it's nice to hear somebody think so,' I said. 'My own view of the age doesn't quite –'

'Ah, but that's only to be expected. You haven't any perspective on it, so you can't appreciate it. It'd do you good to live in ours for a bit, and see how flat and stale and uniform everything is – so deadly, deadly dull.'

I boggled a little: 'I don't think I quite – er, live in your *what*?'

'Century, of course. The Twenty-Second. Oh, of course, you don't know. How silly of me.'

I concentrated on pouring out some more tea.

'Oh dear, I knew this was going to be difficult,' she remarked. 'Do you find it difficult?'

I said I did, rather. She went on with a dogged air:

'Well, you see, feeling like that about it is why I took up history. I mean, I could really *think* myself into history – some of it. And then getting your letter on my birthday was really what made me take the mid Twentieth Century as my Special Period for my Honours Degree, and, of course, it made up my mind for me to go on and do postgraduate work.'

'Er – my letter did all this?'

'Well, that was the only way, wasn't it? I mean there simply wasn't any other way I could have got near a history-machine except by working in a history laboratory, was there? And even then I doubt whether I'd have had a chance to use it on my own if it hadn't been Uncle Donald's lab.'

'History-machine,' I said, grasping a straw out of all this. 'What is a history-machine?'

She looked puzzled.

'It's well – a history-machine. You learn history with it.'

'Not lucid,' I said. 'You might as well tell me you make history with it.'

'Oh, no. One's not supposed to do that. It's a very serious offence.'

'Oh,' I said. I tried again: 'About this letter –'

'Well, I had to bring that in to explain about history, but you won't have written it yet, of course, so I expect you find it a bit confusing.'

'Confusing,' I told her, 'is scarcely the word. Can't we get hold of something concrete? This letter I'm supposed to have written, for instance. What was it about?'

She looked at me hard, and then away. A most surprising blush swept up her face, and ran into her hair. She made herself look back at me again. I watched her eyes go shiny, and then pucker at the corners. She dropped her face suddenly into her hands.

'Oh, you *don't* love me, you *don't*,' she wailed. 'I wish I'd never come. I wish I was dead!'

'She sort of – sniffed at me,' said Tavia.

'Well, she's gone now, and my reputation with her,' I said. 'An excellent worker, our Mrs Toombs, but conventional. She'll probably throw up the job.'

'Because I'm here? How silly!'

'Perhaps your conventions are different.'

'But where else could I go? I've only a few shillings of your kind of money, and nobody to go to.'

'Mrs Toombs could scarcely know that.'

'But we weren't, I mean we didn't –'

'Night, and the figure two,' I told her, 'are plenty for our conventions. In fact, two is enough, anyway. You will recall that the animals simply went in two by two; their emotional relationships didn't interest anyone. Two; and all is assumed.'

'Oh, of course, I remember, there was no probative then – now, I mean. You have a sort of rigid, lucky-dip, take-it-or-leave-it system.'

'There are other ways of expressing it, but – well, ostensibly at any rate, yes, I suppose.'

'Rather crude, these old customs, when one sees them at close range – but fascinating,' she remarked. Her eyes rested thoughtfully upon me for a second. 'You –' she began.

'You,' I reminded her, 'promised to give me a more explanatory explanation of all this than you achieved yesterday.'

'You didn't believe me.'

'The first wallop took my breath,' I admitted, 'but you've given me enough evidence since. Nobody could keep up an act like that.'

She frowned.

'I don't think that's very kind of you. I've studied the mid Twentieth very thoroughly. It was my Special Period.'

'So you told me, but that doesn't get me far. All historical scholars have Special Periods, but that doesn't mean that they suddenly turn up in them.'

She stared at me. 'But of course they do – licensed historians. How else would they make close studies?'

'There's too much of this "of course" business,' I told her. 'I suggest we just begin at the beginning. Now this letter of mine – no, we'll skip the letter,' I added hastily as I caught her expression. 'Now, you went to work in your uncle's laboratory with something called a history-machine. What's that – a kind of tape-recorder?'

'Good gracious, no. It's a kind of cupboard thing you get into to go to times and places.'

'Oh,' I said. 'You – you mean you can walk into it in 21something, and walk out into 19something?'

'Or any other past time,' she said, nodding. 'But, of

course, not anybody can do it. You have to be qualified and licensed and all that kind of thing. There are only six permitted history-machines in England, and only about a hundred in the whole world, and they're very strict about them.

'When the first ones were made they didn't realize what trouble they might cause, but after a time historians began to check the trips made against the written records of the periods, and started to find funny things. There was Hero demonstrating a simple steam-turbine at Alexandria sometime B.C.; and Archimedes using a kind of napalm at the siege of Syracuse; and Leonardo da Vinci drawing parachutes when there wasn't anything to parachute from; and Eric the Red discovering America in a sort of off-the-record way before Columbus got there; and Napoleon wondering about submarines; and lots of other suspicious things. So it was clear that some people had been careless when they used the machine, and had been causing chronoclasms.'

'Causing – what?'

'Chronoclasms – that's when a thing goes and happens at the wrong time because somebody was careless, or talked rashly.

'Well, most of these things had happened without causing very much harm – as far as we can tell – though it is possible that the natural course of history was altered several times, and people write very clever papers to show how. But everybody saw that the results might be extremely dangerous. Just suppose that somebody had carelessly given Napoleon the idea of the internal combustion engine to add to the idea of the submarine; there's no telling what would have happened. So they decided that tampering must be stopped at once, and all history-machines were forbidden except those licensed by the Historians' Council.'

'Just hold it a minute,' I said. 'Look, if a thing is done, it's done. I mean, well, for example, I am here. I couldn't suddenly cease to be, or to have been, if somebody were to go back and kill my grandfather when he was a boy.'

'But you certainly couldn't be here if they did, could

you?' she asked. 'No, the fallacy that the past is unchange-able didn't matter a bit as long as there was no means of changing it, but once there was, and the fallacy of the idea was shown, we had to be very careful indeed. That's what a historian has to worry about; the other side – just *how* it happens – we leave to the higher-mathematicians.

'Now, before you are allowed to use the history-machine you have to have special courses, tests, permits, and give solemn undertakings, and then do several years on proba-tion before you get your licence to practise. Only then are you allowed to visit and observe on your own. And that is all you may do, observe. The rule is very, very strict.'

I thought that over. 'If it isn't an unkind question – aren't you breaking rather a lot of these rules every minute?' I suggested.

'Of course I am. That's why they came after me,' she said.

'You'd have had your licence revoked, or something, if they'd caught you?'

'Good gracious. I could never qualify for a licence. I've just sneaked my trips when the lab has been empty some-times. It being Uncle Donald's lab made things easier because unless I was actually caught at the machine I could always pretend I was doing something special for him.

'I had to have the right clothes to come in, but I dared not go to the historians' regular costume-makers, so I sketched some things in a museum and got them copied – they're all right, aren't they?'

'Very successful, and becoming, too,' I assured her. '– Though there is a little something about the shoes.'

She looked down at her feet. 'I was afraid so. I couldn't find any of quite the right date,' she admitted. 'Well, then,' she went on, 'I was able to make a few short trial trips. They had to be short because duration is constant – that is, an hour here is the same as an hour there – and I couldn't get the machine to myself for long at a time. But yesterday a man came into the lab just as I was getting back. When he saw these clothes he knew at once what I was doing, so the only thing I could do was to jump straight back into the machine – I'd never have had another chance. And they came after me without even bothering to change.'

'Do you think they'll come again?' I asked her.

'I expect so. But they'll be wearing proper clothes for the period next time.'

'Are they likely to be desperate? I mean would they shoot, or anything like that?'

She shook her head. 'Oh, no. That'd be a pretty bad chronoclasm – particularly if they happened to kill somebody.'

'But you being here must be setting up a series of pretty resounding chronoclasms. Which would be worse?'

'Oh, mine are all accounted for. I looked it up,' she assured me, obscurely. 'They'll be less worried about me when they've thought of looking it up, too.'

She paused briefly. Then, with an air of turning to a more interesting subject, she went on:

'When people in your time get married they have to dress up in a special way for it, don't they?'

The topic seemed to have a fascination for her.

*

'M'm,' mumbled Tavia. 'I think I rather like Twentieth-Century marriage.'

'It has risen higher in my own estimation, darling,' I admitted. And inded, I was quite surprised to find how much higher it had risen in the course of the last month or so.

'Do Twentieth-Century marrieds always have one big bed, darling?' she inquired.

'Invariably, darling,' I assured her.

'Funny,' she said. 'Not very hygienic, of course, but quite nice all the same.'

We reflected on that.

'Darling, have you noticed she doesn't sniff at me any more?' she remarked.

'We always cease to sniff on production of a certificate, darling,' I explained.

Conversation pursued its desultory way on topics of personal, but limited, interest for a while. Eventually it reached a point where I was saying:

'It begins to look as if we don't need to worry any more about those men who were chasing you, darling. They'd have been back long before now if they had been as worried as you thought.'

She shook her head.

'We'll have to go on being careful, but it is queer. Something to do with Uncle Donald, I expect. He's not really mechanically minded, poor dear. Well, you can tell that by the way he set the machine two years wrong when he came to see you. But there's nothing we can do except wait, and be careful.'

I went on reflecting. Presently:

'I shall have to get a job soon. That may make it difficult to keep a watch for them,' I told her.

'Job?' she said.

'In spite of what they say, two can't live as cheap as one. And wives hanker after certain standards, and ought to have them – within reason, of course. The little money I have won't run to them.'

'You don't need to worry about that, darling,' Tavia assured me. 'You can just invent something.'

'Me? Invent?' I exclaimed.

'Yes. You're already fairly well up on radio, aren't you?'

'They put me on a few radar courses when I was in the R.A.F.'

'Ah! The R.A.F.!' she said, ecstatically. 'To think that you actually fought in the Second Great War! Did you know Monty and Ike and all those wonderful people?'

'Not personally. Different arm of the Services,' I said.

'What a pity, everyone liked Ike. But about the other thing. All you have to do is to get some advanced radio and electronics books, and I'll show you what to invent.'

'You'll –? Oh, I see. But do you think that would be quite ethical?' I asked, doubtfully.

'I don't see why not. After all the things have got to be invented by somebody, or I couldn't have learnt about them at school, could I?'

'I – er, I think I'll have to think a bit about that,' I told her.

It was, I suppose, coincidence that I should have mentioned the lack of interruption that particular morning – at least, it may have been: I have become increasingly suspicious of coincidences since I first saw Tavia. At any rate, in the middle of that same morning Tavia, looking out of the window, said:

'Darling, there's somebody waving from the trees over there.'

I went over to have a look, and sure enough I had a view of a stick with a white handkerchief tied to it, swinging slowly from side to side. Through field-glasses I was able to distinguish the operator, an elderly man almost hidden in the bushes. I handed the glasses to Tavia.

'Oh, dear! Uncle Donald,' she exclaimed. 'I suppose we had better see him. He seems to be alone.'

I went outside, down to the end of my path, and waved him forward. Presently he emerged, carrying the stick and handkerchief bannerwise. His voice reached me faintly: 'Don't shoot!'

I spread my hand wide to show that I was unarmed. Tavia came down the path and stood beside me. As he drew close, he transferred the stick to his left hand, lifted his hat with the other, and inclined his head politely.

'Ah, Sir Gerald! A pleasure to meet you again,' he said.

'He isn't Sir Gerald, Uncle. He's Mr Lattery,' said Tavia.

'Dear me. Stupid of me. Mr Lattery,' he went on, 'I am sure you'll be glad to hear that the wound was more uncomfortable than serious. Just a matter of the poor fellow having to lie on his front for a while.'

'Poor fellow –?' I repeated, blankly.

'The one you shot yesterday.'

'I *shot*?'

'Probably tomorrow or the next day,' Tavia said, briskly. 'Uncle, you really are dreadful with those settings, you know.'

'I understand the principles well enough, my dear. It's just the operation that I sometimes find a little confusing.'

'Never mind. Now you are here you'd better come indoors,' she told him. 'And you can put that handkerchief away in your pocket,' she added.

As he entered I saw him give a quick glance round the room, and nod to himself as if satisfied with the authenticity of its contents. We sat down. Tavia said:

'Just before we go any further, Uncle Donald, I think you ought to know that I am married to Gerald – Mr Lattery.'

Dr Gobie peered closely at her.

'Married?' he repeated. 'What for?'

'Oh, dear,' said Tavia. She explained patiently: 'I am in love with him, and he's in love with me, so I am his wife. It's the way things happen here.'

'Tch, tch!' said Dr Gobie, and shook his head. 'Of course I am well aware of your sentimental penchant for the Twentieth Century and its ways, my dear, but surely it wasn't quite necessary for you to – er – go native?'

'I like it, quite a lot,' Tavia told him.

'Young women will be romantic, I know. But have you thought of the trouble you will be causing Sir Ger – er, Mr Lattery?'

'But I'm *saving* him trouble, Uncle Donald. They *sniff* at you here if you don't get married, and I didn't like him being sniffed at.'

'I wasn't thinking so much of while you're here, as of after you have left. They have a great many rules about presuming death, and proving desertion, and so on; most dilatory and complex. Meanwhile, he can't marry anyone else.'

'I'm sure he wouldn't *want* to marry anyone else, would you, darling?' she said to me.

'Certainly not,' I protested.

'You're quite sure of that, darling?'

'Darling,' I said, taking her hand, 'if all the other women in the world...'

After a time Dr Gobie recalled our attention with an apologetic cough.

'The real purpose of my visit,' he explained, 'is to persuade my niece that she must come back, and at once. There is the greatest consternation and alarm throughout the faculty over this affair, and I am being held largely to blame. Our chief anxiety is to get her back before any serious damage is done. Any chronoclasm goes ringing unendingly down the ages — and at any moment a really serious one may come of this escapade. It has put all of us into a highly nervous condition.'

'I'm sorry about that, Uncle Donald — and about your getting the blame. But I am *not* coming back. I'm very happy here.'

'But the possible chronoclasms, my dear. It keeps me awake at night thinking —'

'Uncle dear, they'd be nothing to the chronoclasms that would happen if I did come back just now. You must see that I simply *can't*, and explain it to the others.'

'*Can't* —?' he repeated.

'Now, if you look in the books you'll see that my husband — isn't that a funny, ugly, old-fashioned word? I rather like it, though. It comes from two ancient Icelandic roots —'

'You were speaking about not coming back,' Dr Gobie reminded her.

'Oh, yes. Well, you'll see in the books that first he invented submarine radio communication, and then later on he invented curved-beam transmission, which is what he got knighted for.'

'I'm perfectly well aware of that, Tavia. I do not see —'

'But, Uncle Donald, you must. How on earth can he possibly invent those things if I'm not here to show him how to do it? If you take me away now, they'll just not be invented, and then what will happen?'

Dr Gobie stared at her steadily for some moments.

'Yes,' he said. 'Yes, I must admit that that point had not ocurred to me,' and sank deeply into thought for a while.

'Besides,' Tavia added, 'Gerald would hate me to go, wouldn't you, darling?'

'I –' I began, but Dr Gobie cut me short by standing up.

'Yes,' he said. 'I can see there will have to be a postponement for a while. I shall put your point to them, but it will be only for a while.'

On his way to the door he paused.

'Meanwhile, my dear, do be careful. These things are so delicate and complicated. I tremble to think of the complexities you might set up if you – well, say, if you were to do something irresponsible like becoming your own progenetrix.'

'That is one thing I can't do, Uncle Donald. I'm on the collateral branch.'

'Oh, yes. Yes, that's a very lucky thing. Then I'll say *au revoir*, my dear, and to you, too, Sir – er – Mr Lattery. I trust that we may meet again – it has had its pleasant side to be here as more than a mere observer for once.'

'Uncle Donald, you've said a mouthful there,' Tavia agreed.

He shook his head reprovingly at her.

'I'm afraid you would never have got to the top of the historical tree, my dear. You aren't thorough enough. That phrase is *early* Twentieth Century, and, if I may say so, inelegant even then.'

The expected shooting incident took place about a week later. Three men, dressed in quite convincing imitation of farmhands, made the approach. Tavia recognized one of them through the glasses. When I appeared, gun in hand, at the door they tried to make for cover. I peppered one at considerable range, and he ran on, limping.

After that we were left unmolested. A little later we

began to get down to the business of underwater radio – surprisingly simple, once the principle had been pointed out – and I filed my applications for patents. With that well in hand, we turned to the curved-beam transmission.

Tavia hurried me along with that. She said:

'You see, I don't know how long we've got, darling. I've been trying to remember ever since I got here what the date was on your letter, and I can't – even though I remember you underlined it. I know there's a record that your first wife deserted you – "deserted", isn't that a dreadful word to use: as if I would, my sweet – but it doesn't say when. So I must get you properly briefed on this because there'd be the most frightful chronoclasm if you failed to invent it.'

And then, instead of buckling down to it as her words suggested, she became pensive.

'As a matter of fact,' she said, 'I think there's going to be a pretty bad chronoclasm anyway. You see, I'm going to have a baby.'

'No!' I exclaimed delightedly.

'What do you mean, "no"? I *am*. And I'm worried. I don't think it has ever happened to a travelling historian before. Uncle Donald would be terribly annoyed if he knew.'

'To hell with Uncle Donald,' I said. 'And to hell with chronoclasms. We're going to celebrate, darling.'

The weeks slid quickly by. My patents were granted provisionally. I got a good grip on the theory of curved-beam transmission. Everything was going nicely. We discussed the future: whether he was to be called Donald, or whether she was going to be called Alexandria. How soon the royalties would begin to come in so that we could make an offer for Bagford House. How funny it would feel at first to be addressed as Lady Lattery, and other allied themes....

And then came that December afternoon when I got back from discussing a modification with a manufacturer in London and found that she wasn't there any more....

Not a note, not a last word. Just the open front door, and a chair overturned in the sitting-room. . . .

Oh, Tavia, my dear . . .

I began to write this down because I still have an uneasy feeling about the ethics of not being the inventor of my inventions, and that there should be a straightening out. Now that I have reached the end, I perceive that 'straightening out' is scarcely an appropriate description of it. In fact, I can foresee so much trouble attached to putting this forward as a conscientious reason for refusing a knighthood, that I think I shall say nothing, and just accept the knighthood when it comes. After all, when I consider a number of 'inspired' inventions that I can call to mind, I begin to wonder whether certain others have not done that before me.

I have never pretended to understand the finer points of action and interaction comprehended in this matter, but I have a pressing sense that one action now on my part is basically necessary: not just to avoid dropping an almighty chronoclasm myself, but for fear that if I neglect it I may find that the whole thing never happened. So I must write a letter.

First, the envelope:

To my great, great grandniece,
Miss Octavia Lattery.

   (To be opened by her on her 21st birthday.
   6 June 2136.)

Then the letter. Date it. Underline the date.

My sweet, far-off, lovely Tavia,
   Oh, my darling . . .

Time to Rest

I

THE view was not much. To eyes which had seen the land-scapes of Earth it was not a view at all so much as just an-other section of the regular Martian backdrop. In front and to the left smooth water spread like a silk sheet to the horizon. A mile or more to the right lay a low embankment with yellow-red sand showing through rush-like tufts of skimpy bushes. Far in the background rose the white crowns of purple mountains.

In the mild warmth of noon Bert let his boat carry him along. Behind him, a fan of ripples spread gently and then lapsed back into placidity. Still further back the immense silence closed in again, and nothing remained to show that he had passed that way. The scene had scarcely changed for several days and several hundred miles of his quietly chugging progress.

His boat was a queer craft. There was nothing else like it on Mars – nor any other place. For he had built it himself – and without knowing anything about the building of boats. There had been a kind of plan – well, a rough idea – in his head, at first, but he had had to modify that so many times that most of it had grown empirically from the plates and materials he had been able to find. The result had some-thing of sampan, punt, and rain-water tank in its ancestry, but it satisfied Bert.

He sprawled in comfortable indolence at the stern of his craft. One arm in a tattered sleeve hung over the tiller, the other lay across his chest. Long legs in patchwork trousers sprawled out to end in strange boots with canvas uppers and soles contrived of woven fibres; he had made those himself, too. The reddish beard on his thin face was trimmed to a point; above it his dark eyes looked ahead with little interest from under the torn, stained brim of a felt hat.

He listened to the phut-phutting of the old engine as he

might to the purr of a friendly cat; indeed, he thought of it as an old friend, bestowing upon it a kindly care to which it responded with grunts of leisurely goodwill as it bore him along. There were times when he talked to it encouragingly or told it the things he thought; it was a habit he did not approve of and which he curbed when he noticed it, but quite often he did not notice. He felt an affection for the wheezy old thing, not only for carrying him along thousands of miles of water, but because it kept the silence at bay.

Bert disliked the silence which brooded over desert and water like a symptom of mortification, but he did not fear it. It did not drive him, as it did most, to live in the settlements where there was neighbourliness, noise, and the illusion of hope. His restlessness was stronger than his dislike of the empty lands; it carried him along when the adventurous, finding no adventure, had turned back or given in to despair. He wanted little but, like a gipsy, to keep moving.

Bert Tasser he had been years ago, but it was so long since he had heard the surname that he had almost forgotten it: everybody else had. He was just Bert – for all he knew he was the only Bert.

'Ought to be showing up soon,' he murmured, either to the patient engine or himself, and sat up in order to see better.

A slight change was beginning to show on the bank; a weed was becoming more frequent among the scrawny bushes, a slender-stalked growth with polished, metallic-looking leaves, sensitive to the lightest breath of wind. He could see them shivering with little flashes in increasing numbers ahead, and he knew that if he were to stop the engine now he would hear not the dead envelope of silence, but the ringing clash of myriads of small hard leaves.

'Tinkerbells,' he said. 'Yes, it won't be far now.'

From a locker beside him he pulled a much-worn hand-drawn map, and consulted it. From it he referred to an equally well-used notebook, and read over the list of names written on one of the pages. He was still muttering them as he returned the papers to the locker and his attention to the way ahead. Half an hour passed before a dark object became visible to break the monotonous line of the bank.

'There it is now,' he said, as if to encourage the engine over the last few miles.

The building, which had appeared oddly shaped even from a distance, revealed itself as a ruin on closer approach. The base was square and decorated on the sides with formal patterns in what had once been high relief, but was now so smoothed that the finer details were lost. Once it had supported some kind of tower; though exactly what kind had to be guessed, for no more than the first twenty feet of the upper structure remained. It, too, bore remnants of worn carving, and, like the base, was built of a dusky red rock. Standing a hundred yards or so back from the bank, it was deceptive in its isolation. The size and the degree of misadventure which time and adaptation had brought it only became appreciable as one approached more closely.

Bert held on his course until he was opposite before he turned his clumsy craft. Then he swung over and headed towards the bank at slow speed until he grounded gently on the shelving shore. He switched off the engine, and the indigenous sounds took charge; the tinny chime of the tinkerbells, a complaining creak from a ramshackle wheel turning slowly and unevenly a little to his left along the bank, and an intermittent thudding from the direction of the ruin.

Bert went forward to the cabin. It was snug enough to keep him warm in the cold nights, but ill lit, for glass was hard to come by. Groping in the dimness he found a bag of tools and an empty sack, and slung them over one shoulder. He waded ashore through the few inches of water, drove in a hook to hold his boat against the unlikely chance of disturbance in the placid water, and turned with a long easy stride towards the building.

To either side of the place and beyond it clustered a few

small fields where neatly lined crops stood fresh and green among narrow irrigation ditches. Against one wall of the stone cube was an enclosure and a shed roughly built of irregular fragments which might have been part of the vanished tower. Despite its inexpert appearance it was neatly kept, and from beyond it came occasionally, the grunt of small animals. In the near face of the cube was a doorway, and to either side of it unsquare holes which, though glassless, appeared to be windows. Outside the door a woman was at work, pounding grain on a shallow worn rock with a kind of stone club which she held in both hands. Her skin was a reddish brown, her dark hair rolled high on her head, and her only garment a skirt of coarse russet cloth stencilled with a complex yellow pattern. She was middle aged, but there was no slackening of muscles or deterioration of poise. She looked up as Bert approached, and spoke in the local patois:

'Hullo, Earthman,' she said, 'we were expecting you, but you've been a long time.'

Bert replied in the same language.

'Late am I, Annika? I never know the date, but it seemed about time I was this way again.'

He dropped the bags, and instantly a dozen little banni-kuks scampered to investigate them. Disappointed, they clustered round his feet mewing inquisitively, and turning their little marmoset-like faces up to him. He scattered a handful of nuts from his pocket for them, and sat down on a convenient stone. Recalling the list of names in the note-book he asked after the rest of the family.

They were well, it seemed. Yanff, her eldest son, was away, but Tannack, the younger, was here, so were the girls Guika and Zaylo; Guika's husband, too, and the children, and there was a new baby since he last came. Except for the baby they were all down in the far field: they would be back soon.

He looked where she pointed, and saw the dark dots moving in the distance among the neat rows.

'Your second crops are coming along nicely,' he said.

'The Great Ones remember,' she said in a matter-of-fact way.

He sat watching her as she worked. Her colouring and that of the setting made him think of pictures he had seen years ago – by Gauguin, was it? – though she was not the kind of woman that Gauguin had painted. Possibly he would not have seen beauty there, as Bert himself had failed to at first. Martians, with their lighter build and delicate bones, had looked frail and skinny to him when he first saw them, but he had grown used to the difference: an Earth woman would look queer and dumpy now, he guessed – if he were ever to see one.

Aware of his gaze upon her Annika stopped pounding and turned to look at him; she did not smile but there was a kindness and understanding in her dark eyes.

'You're tired, Earthman,' she said.

'I've been tired a long time,' said Bert.

She nodded comprehendingly, and returned to her work.

Bert understood, and he knew that in her quiet way she understood. They were a gentle, sympathetic people, and sincere. It was a tragedy, one of a string of similar tragedies that the first Earthman to ground on Mars had seen them as a weak effete race; the 'natives', inferiors, to be kicked about, and exploited whenever convenient. It had stopped now; either they had got to know the Martian people better, as he had, or they lived in the settlements and seldom saw them; but he still felt ashamed for his own people when he thought of it.

After some minutes she said:

'How long is it you've been going round now?'

'About seven of your years: that's nearly fourteen of ours.'

'That's a long time.' She shook her head. 'A long time to be roaming, all by yourself. But then you Earthmen aren't like us.' She gazed at him again as though trying to see the difference beyond his eyes. 'Yet not so very different,' she added, and shook her head slowly again.

'I'm all right,' Bert told her briefly. He pulled the conversation on to another course. 'What have you got for me this time?' he asked, and sat half-listening while she told him of the pans that wanted mending, the new ones she was needing, how the wheel wasn't delivering as much water as usual; how Yanff had tried to rehang the door when it came off its hinges and what a poor job he had made of it. The other half of his attention went wandering – perhaps that was one of the things that happened when you were so much alone.

II

The 'I'm all right' had been a buffer; he knew it, and he knew she knew it. None of the Earthmen was 'all right'. Some of them put up a show, others did not, but there was the same trouble underneath. A number wandered restlessly as he did; most of them preferred to rot slowly and alcoholically in the settlements. A few, grasping at shadows while they dreamed, had taken Martian girls and tried to go native. Bert felt sorry for them. He was used to seeing their faces light up and he knew their eagerness to talk when he met them; and always of reminiscences, nostalgic rememberings.

Bert had chosen the wandering life. The stagnation had shown its effect in the settlement quite soon, and it took no great power of perception to see what was going to happen there. He had spent a whole Martian year in building his boat, equipping her, making pots and pans for trade purposes, and stocking her with tools and supplies; and once he had set out upon a tinker's life restlessness kept him moving. The settlements saw little of him save when he called in for fuel for his engine or stayed awhile in the winter working on pans and other useful trade goods, and at the end of it he was glad to leave. Each time he called the deterioration seemed more noticeable, and a few more of those he had known had sought relief by drinking themselves to death.

But recently he had felt a change in himself. The restlessness still kept him from lingering longer than necessary in the settlements, but it did not drive him as it used to, nor was there the old satisfaction in the rounds and journeys that he planned for himself. He felt no temptation to join the men in the settlements, but he had begun to understand the gregariousness which held them there, and to understand, too, why they found it necessary to drink so much. It made him uneasy at times to realize that he had changed enough to be able to sympathize with them.

Mostly it was age, he supposed. He had been barely twenty-one when he had completed his first and last rocket flight; most of the others had been ten, fifteen, twenty years older: he was catching up now with the feelings they had had years ago, aimlessness, hopelessness, and a longing for things that had vanished for ever.

Exactly what had taken place on Earth, none of them knew, nor ever would know. His ship had been four days out of the Lunar Station, bound for Mars, when it happened. One of his mates, a man a little older than himself had roused him from his bunk and dragged him to the port-hole. Together they had gazed at a sight which was printed for ever on his memory: the Earth split open, with white-hot fire pouring from the widening cracks.

Some had said that one of the atomic piles must have gone over the critical mass and touched off a chain reaction; others objected that if that were so the Earth would not have split, but have flared something like a nebula followed by non-existence. Much ill-informed argument regarding the possibility of a chain reaction limited to certain elements had followed, and occasionally recurred. The truth was that nobody knew. All that was certain was that it had broken up, disintegrating into a belt of innumerable asteroids which continued to scurry round the sun like a shower of cosmic pebbles.

Some of the men had taken a long time to believe what they had actually seen; they were the worst affected when they did understand. Some found that their minds would not grasp and hold it as a fact; for them the Earth went on, ever unattainable, yet somewhere existent. Demoralization had spread through the ship, a few were for turning back, unreasonably convinced that they should be there, and in some way giving help: afterwards it had continually been their grudge that they had not been allowed to, even if it were useless. The skipper had decided that there was nothing to be done but hold on their course for Mars.

The navigators had looked more and more worried as their tables became increasingly inaccurate with orbits changing about them; they had watched with wonder the freed moon leave her path and sail through space guided by incalculable forces until she came eventually within the clutch of the giant Jupiter; but long before that happened the ship had, by a combination of calculation and guesswork, made her successful last drop to Mars.

Other ships, too, had come in; research vessels from the Asteroid Belt and beyond, traders from the Jovian moons diverted from the homeward course. Some that were expected never arrived, but in the end there were a couple of dozen lying idle on Mars with no home port to seek. Several hundreds of men idled with them. As well as crews, there were miners, drillers, refiners, prospectors, explorers, station maintenance men, settlement staff, and the rest, all thrown together on an alien world to make the best of it.

There had also been two women, hostesses or stewardesses. Good enough girls, and amiable at first, though no great beauties. But circumstances were against them, and the pressure was great. They had gone quickly to the astonishing depths of badness good women can reach once they start. It was reckoned they had caused a score of murders each before they were found to be susceptible to the same method of disposal. Things were quieter after that; with drinking as the main amusement.

It might, Bert told himself, have been worse. It *was* worse for those who had had wives and families. He had less personal loss: his mother had died some years before, his

father had been an old man, there had been a girl, a
sweetly pretty girl with hair like red gold and who grew
prettier in his memory as time went by: Elsa her name
was, but there had not really been a lot to it; and though
it was pleasant to recall that she might have married him,
he had never in point of fact seriously tried to find out
whether she would or would not. Then, too, there was a
slender consolation that he was on Mars and at least better
off than those who must have been trapped in the steamy
heat of Venus, or on the cold Jovian moons. Life offered
something beyond perpetual battle to survive, and though
it might not be very much, it had been better to go out
and see what there was rather than soak away youth
and strength with the rest. So he had started to build his
boat.

Bert still thought that the best and wisest thing he had
ever done. The work had kept him too busy to mope, and
then when he had set off it had been as an explorer, a
pioneer along many of the thousands of miles of canals
that he travelled. There had been the business of getting to
know the Martians, and of finding them quite unlike what
he had been told. That had involved learning languages
completely different in structure from his own, and the
local variations of them, and he had kept at it until he
spoke four patois better than any other Earthman he knew,
and could get along comfortably in several more. He found
that he usually thought in one of them nowadays. Along
canals which were sometimes like calm seas sixty or eighty
miles wide, and sometimes less than a single mile, he
chugged slowly from one cultivated site to another. The
more he saw of the huge waterways and their multiplicity,
the greater had grown his first amazement at them; nor
after years of travelling them was he nearer an understanding of how they had been built than when he first set out.
The Martians could tell him nothing when he asked: it
was something which had been done by the Great Ones
long, long ago. He came to accept the canals with the rest

and was grateful to the Great Ones, whoever they might have been, for providing the smooth lanes all over their planet.

He grew fond of the Martian people. Their quietness, their lack of hurry, and their calm, philosophic ways were a soothing antidote to his sense of drive and thrust. He found out quite soon that what his companions had called their laziness and effeteness was a misunderstanding of minds that worked differently in some ways, and certainly saw life differently; whose conception of the virtues was altogether alien, and he found out how his abilities could help their deficiencies in exchange for the foods they knew how to grow.

Thus he had wandered back and forth mending and making in exchange for his keep, never staying long anywhere. It had only been recently that he had gradually become aware that the restlessness which still possessed him was no longer to be assuaged by wandering alone – if by wandering at all.

Bert had not noticed that Annika had ceased to talk when his thoughts went astray. He had no idea how much time passed before she ceased pounding to look up and say:

'They're coming now.'

The two men came first, heads down and deep in conversation. They were lightly, almost weakly, built, to Earth judgement, but Bert had long ceased to apply alien standards; he saw them as well set up and capable. The women followed. Guika was carrying the smallest of three children while the others held on to the hands of her sister who laughed down at them. Guika was now, he thought, about twenty-five by Earth reckoning, her sister Zaylo about four years younger. Like their mother they wore roughly woven bright patterned skirts and their hair was held in its high dressing by silver pins; like her, too, they were smoothly rhythmic in their movements. He scarcely recognized Zaylo at first; she had not been at home on his last two visits and there was change enough for him to be uncertain.

Tannack, the son, saw him and came hurrying forward. His greeting was glad and kindly. The others came up and surrounded him as they always did, looking rather as if they were reassuring their memories about the appearance of an Earthman.

Annika gathered up her flour, and disappeared into the stone pediment of the tower which was their home. The rest of them followed chattering and laughing with Bert, plainly pleased to see him again.

During the meal Tannack told him all over again of all the things that had worn out, got broken, and gone wrong. They didn't sound very serious, nothing that the ordinary handyman could not soon have put right, yet that was one of the directions where his value lay; a fault and its remedy which took him five minutes to perceive and could cost them as many weeks of careful cogitation and then, as likely as not, they would fail in its application. The utterly unmechanical quality in them astonished him yet. It was something they had never developed beyond absolute necessity. He had wondered if it and the passiveness which was also so different a characteristic from the nature of the Earthmen might be due to their never having been the dominant race on the planet until there was little left to dominate. The mysterious Great Ones who had built the canals, the now fallen buildings and cities, and who had in some way vanished, centuries or perhaps thousands of years ago, had been the rulers: it seemed as if under them the idea of warring and fighting had had no chance to develop, and the mechanical sense no need. If so, it was a tradition planted firmly enough never to be lost. At times he felt that there was a lingering subconscious sense of taboo about such things. They still looked for their blessings to the Great Ones who 'remembered'. Bert would have very much liked to know what those Great Ones were and even how they had looked, but no one could tell him.

After they had eaten he went outside to build himself a little fire and lay out his tools. They brought him pans, hoes, and other things to mend, and then disappeared about various jobs. The three children stayed to watch, sitting on the ground playing with the scampering little bannikuks, and chattering to him as he worked. They wanted to know why he was different from Tannack and the others, why he wore a jacket and trousers, what use his beard was. Bert began to tell them about Earth; about great forests and soft green hills, of the huge clouds which floated in summer in skies that were bright blue, of great green waves with white tops, of mountain streams, of countries where there were no deserts, and flowers grew wild everywhere in the spring, of old towns and little villages. They did not understand most of what he said, and perhaps they believed less, but they went on listening and he went on talking, forgetting they were there until Annika interrupted to send them off to their mother. She sat down near him when they had gone.

The sun would soon be down, and he could feel the chill already in the thin air. She seemed not to notice it.

'It is not good to be lonely, Earthman,' she said. 'For a time, when one is young and there is much to see, it seems so, though it is better shared. Later it is not good.'

Bert grunted. He did not look up from the iron pot he was mending.

'It suits me to be on my own. I ought to know,' he told her.

She sat looking far away; beyond the twinkling tinker-bells, and beyond the smooth water behind them.

'When Guika and Zaylo were children you used to tell them tales of the Earth – but they weren't the tales you were telling just now. In those days you talked about huge cities where millions of your people lived, of great ships that were like lighted castles by night, of machines travelling on the ground at unbelievable speeds and others that flew above, even faster; of voices that could speak through the air to the whole Earth, and many other marvellous things. And sometimes you sang queer, jerky Earth songs to make them laugh. You did not talk of any of those things tonight.'

'There are plenty of things to talk about. I don't need to go on telling of the same things each time,' he said. 'Why should I?'

'What you should say matters less than what you do say, but why you say it matters more than either,' she murmured.

Bert blew on his glowing little fire and turned the iron in it. He made no reply.

'Yesterday was never the future. One cannot live backwards,' she told him.

'Future! What future has Mars? It is senile, dying. One just waits with it for death,' he said, with impatience.

'Was not Earth, too, beginning to die from the moment it started to cool?' she asked. 'Yet it was worth building upon, worth raising civilizations there, wasn't it?'

'Well – was it?' he inquired bitterly. 'For what?'

'If it were not, it would be better if we had never been.'

'Well?' he said again, challengingly.

She turned to look at him.

'You don't think that – not really.'

'What else am I to think?' he asked.

The light was growing poor. He covered the fire with a stone and began to pack up his tools. Annika said:

'Why don't you stay here with us, Earthman? It's time for you to rest.'

He looked up at her in astonishment, and started to shake his head automatically, without consideration. He had planted it in his mind that he was a wanderer, and he had no wish to examine the strength of the setting. But Annika went on:

'You could help a lot here,' she said. 'You find things easy that are difficult for us. You are strong – with the strength of two of our men.' She looked beyond the ruin at the neat small fields. 'This is a good place. With your help it could be better. There could be more fields and more stock. You like us, don't you?'

He sat looking into the twilight, so still that an inquisitive bannikuk climbed up to explore his pocket. He brushed the little creature away.

'Yes,' he said, 'I've always liked coming here, but . . .'

'But what, Earthman?'

'That's just it – "Earthman". I don't belong here with you. I don't belong anywhere. So I just keep visiting, and moving on.'

'You could belong here – if you would. If Earth were re-created now, it would be stranger to you than Mars.'

That he could not believe. He shook his head.

'You feel it would be disloyal to think that – but I fancy it is true, nevertheless,' Annika said.

'It can't be.' He shook his head again. 'Anyway, what does it matter?'

'It matters this much,' Annika told him, 'that you are on the verge of finding out that life is not something which can be stopped just because you don't like it. You are not apart from life: you are a part of it.'

'What has all that to do with it?' Bert asked.

'Just that mere existence is not enough. One exists by barter. One lives by giving – and taking.'

'I see,' said Bert, but doubtfully.

'I don't think you do – yet. But it would be better for you to, and better for us, if you were to stay. And there is Zaylo.'

'Zaylo?' Bert repeated, wonderingly.

III

Zaylo came to the bank while he was repairing the wheel the next morning. She settled down a few feet away on the slope, and sat with her chin on her knees watching. He looked up and their eyes met. Something entirely unexpected happened to Bert. Yesterday he had seen her as a child grown up, today it was different. There was a pain in his chest and a hammering, the skin on his temples felt oddly tight, his hand trembled so that he almost dropped the bar he was holding. He leant back against the wheel, staring at her but unable to speak. A long time seemed to pass before he could say anything, and the words sounded clumsy in his own ears.

What they talked about he could never afterwards remember. He could only recall the sight of her. Her expression, the depth of her dark eyes, the gentle movements of her mouth, the way the sun shone on her skin as though there were a mist over polished copper, the lovely line of her breasts, the slim feet in the sand beneath the brightly patterned skirt. There were a host of things he had never noticed before; the modelling of her ears, the way her hair grew, and the ingenuity of coils which could be held firmly on top of her head by the three silver pins, the slenderness of her hands and fingers, the pearled translucence of her teeth, and on through a catalogue of wonders hitherto incredibly unobserved.

It was a day of which Bert recalled very little else but that there seemed to be sections of him being torn slowly and painfully apart, yet still so close that sometimes he looked out from one section, and sometimes from the other. He would see himself in his boat, sliding along the endless canals in the sunlight with vastnesses of desert stretching out on either side, sitting out the sudden dust-storms in his small cabin where the throat-drying sand managed still to penetrate every ingenuity, and then going on as usual to do tinker's work at the next inhabited area. That was the life he had got used to, and life he had chosen – he could go on with it as before and forget Zaylo – yet he knew it would not be quite as before because it was not going to be easy to forget her. There were pictures which he would not be able to leave behind; Zaylo smiling as she played with her sister's babies, Zaylo walking, sitting, standing; Zaylo herself. There were dreams rising inadvertent and beneath his guard, imaginings which swam into his mind in spite of his intention to keep them out; the warmth of Zaylo lying beside him, the light weight of her on his arm, the firmness, the lovely colour of her, the relaxation there would be in having a place to lay one's heart, and a hand to cherish it. It all hurt like a hardened dressing drawing from a wound.

After the evening meal he went away from the rest, and hid himself in his boat. Looking across the table at her it had seemed to him that she saw all that was going on inside him, and knew more about it than he did himself. She made no gesture, no sign, but she was aware of everything with a calmness somehow alarming. He did not know whether he hoped or feared that she might follow him to the boat – but she did not come.

The sun set while he sat, unconscious that he had begun to shiver with the chill of the Martian night. After a time he moved stiffly, and roused himself. He paddled through the few inches of water and climbed the bank. Phobos was shedding a dim light across the fields and the arid land beyond. The ruined tower was a misshapen black shadow.

Bert stood looking out into the great darkness where his home had been. Mars was a trap to hold him alive, but he would not let it pet and tame him. He was not to be wheedled by softness from the harsh grudge he owed providence. His allegiance was to Earth, the things of Earth, the memory of Earth. It would have been better to have died when the mountains and oceans of Earth were burst open; to have become one more mote among the millions memorially circling in the dark. Existence now was not life to be lived; it was a token of protest against the ways of fate.

He peered long into the sky hoping to see one of the asteroids which once was some corner of the loved, maternal Earth: perhaps, among the myriad points that shone, he did.

A wave of desolation swept through him; a hungry abyss of loneliness opened inside him. Bert raised his clenched fists high above his head. He shook them at the uncaring stars, and cursed them while the tears ran down his cheeks.

As the far-off chugging of the engine faded slowly into silence there was only the clinking of the tinkerbells to disturb the night. Zaylo looked at her mother with misty eyes.

'He has gone,' she whispered, forlornly.

Annika took her hand, and pressed it comfortingly:

'He is strong, but strength comes from life – he cannot be stronger than life. He will be back soon – quite soon, I think.' She put up her hand and stroked her daughter's hair. After a pause she added: 'When he comes, my Zaylo, be gentle with him. These Earthmen have big bodies, but inside them there are lost children.'

Meteor

THE house shook, the windows rattled, a framed photograph slipped off the mantel-shelf and fell into the hearth. The sound of a crash somewhere outside arrived just in time to drown the noise of the breaking glass. Graham Toffts put his drink down carefully, and wiped the spilt sherry from his fingers.

'That sort of thing takes you back a bit,' he observed. 'First instalment of the new one, would you think?'

Sally shook her head, spinning the fair hair out a little so that it glistened in the shaded light.

'I shouldn't think so. Not like the old kind, anyway – they used to come with a sort of double-bang as a rule,' she said.

She crossed to the window and pulled back the curtain. Outside there was complete darkness and a sprinkle of rain on the panes.

'Could have been an experimental one gone astray?' she suggested.

Footsteps sounded in the hall. The door opened, and her father's head looked in.

'Did you hear that?' he asked, unnecessarily. 'A small meteor, I fancy. I thought I saw a dim flash in the field beyond the orchard.' He withdrew. Sally made after him. Graham, following more leisurely, found her firmly grasping her father's arm.

'No!' she was saying, decisively. 'I'm not going to have my dinner kept waiting and spoiled. Whatever it is, it will keep.'

Mr Fontain looked at her, and then at Graham.

'Bossy; much too bossy. Always was. Can't think what you want to marry her for,' he said.

After dinner they went out to search with electric lamps. There was not much trouble in locating the scene of the impact. A small crater, some eight feet across, had appeared almost in the middle of the field. They regarded it without learning much, while Sally's terrier, Mitty, sniffed over the newly turned earth. Whatever had caused it had presumably buried itself in the middle.

'A small meteorite, without a doubt,' said Mr Fontain. 'We'll set a gang on digging it out tomorrow.'

Extract from Onns' Journal:

As an introduction to the notes which I intend to keep, I can scarcely do better than give the gist of the address given to us on the day preceding our departure from Forta * by His Excellency Cottafts. In contrast to our public farewell, this meeting was deliberately made as informal as a gathering of several thousands can be.

His Excellency emphasized almost in his opening words that though we had leaders for the purposes of administration, there was, otherwise, no least amongst us.

'There is not one of you men and women † who is not a volunteer,' looking slowly round his huge audience. 'Since you are individuals, the proportions of the emotions which led you to volunteer may differ quite widely, but, however personal, or however altruistic your impulses may have been, there is a common denominator for all – and that is the determination that our race shall survive.

'Tomorrow the Globes will go out.

'Tomorrow, God willing, the skill and science of Forta will break through the threats of Nature.

'Civilization is, from its beginning, the ability to co-ordinate and direct natural forces – and once that direction has been started, it must be constantly maintained. There have been other dominant species on Forta before ours: they were not civilized, they did not direct nature: they dwindled and died as conditions changed. But we, so far, have been able to *meet* conditions as they have changed, and we flourish.

'We flourish, moreover, in such numbers as undirected Nature could never have sustained. In the past we have surmounted problem after problem to make this possible, but

---

* Onns gives no clues to Forta's position, nor as to whether it is a planet, a moon, or an asteroid.

† The terms 'men' and 'women' are not used biologically, but in the sense of the dominant species referring to its own members.

now we find ourselves faced with the gravest problem yet. Forta, our world, is becoming senile, but we are not. We are like spirits that are still young, trapped in a failing body ...

'For centuries we have kept going, adapted, substituted, patched, but now the trap is closing faster, and there is little left to prop it open with. So it is now, while we are still healthy and strong, that we must escape and find ourselves a new home.

'I do not doubt that great-grandchildren of the present generation's great-grandchildren will be born on Forta, but life will be harder for them: they will have to spend much more labour simply to keep alive. That is why the Globes must go now, while we have strength and wealth to spare.

'And for you who go in them – what? Even guesses are vain. The Globes will set out for the four corners of the heavens, and where they land they may find anything – or nothing. All our arts and skills will set you on your courses. But, once you have left, we can do no more than pray that you, our seed, will find fruitful soil.'

He paused, lengthily. Then he went on:

'Your charge you know, or you would not have offered yourselves. Nevertheless, it is one which you will not be able to learn too well, nor teach too often. In the hands of each and every one of you lies a civilization. Every man and woman of you is at once the receptacle and the potential fountain of all that Forta signifies. You have the history, the culture, the civilization of a planet. Use it. Use it well. Give it to others where it will help. Be willing to learn from others, and improve it if you can. Do not try to preserve it intact; a culture must grow to live. For those who cling too fondly to the past there is likely to be no future. Remember that it is possible that there is no intelligence elsewhere in the universe, which means that some of you will hold a trust not only for our race, but for all conscious life that may evolve.

'Go forth, then. Go in wisdom, kindliness, peace, and truth.

'And our prayers will go out with you into the mysteries of space....'

... I have looked again through the telescope at our new home. Our group is, I think, lucky. It is a planet which is neither too young nor too old. Conditions were better than before, with less cloud over its surface. It shines like a blue pearl. Much of the part I saw was covered with water – more than two-thirds of it, they tell me, is under water. It will be good to be in a place where irrigation and water supply are not one of the main problems of life. Nevertheless, one hopes that we shall be fortunate enough to make our landing on dry ground or there may be very great difficulties . . .

I looked, too, at some of the places to which other Globes are bound, some small, some large, some new, with clouded surfaces that are a mystery. One at least is old, and in not much better case than our own poor Forta – though the astronomers say that it has the ability to support life for several millions of years. But I am glad that our group is going to the blue, shining world : it seems to beckon us, and I am filled with a hope which helps to quieten my fears of the journey.

Not that fears trouble me so much now; I have learnt some fatalism in the past year. I shall go into the Globe, and the anaesthetic gas will lull me to sleep without my being aware of it. When I wake again it will be on our shimmering new world. . . . If I do not wake, something will have gone wrong, but I shall never know that. . . .

Very simple, really – if one has faith. . . .

This evening I went down to look at the Globes; to see them objectively for the last time. Tomorrow, in all the bustle and preparation there will be no time for reflection – and it will be better so.

What a staggering, amazing – one had almost said impossible – work they are! The building of them has entailed labour beyond computation. They look more likely to crush the ground and sink into Forta herself than to fly off into space. The most massive things ever built! I find it almost impossible to believe that we can have built thirty of these metal mountains, yet there they stand, ready for tomorrow. . . .

And some of them will be lost. . . .

Oh, God, if ours may survive, let us never forget. Let us show ourselves worthy of this supreme effort. . . .

It can well be that these are the last words I shall ever write. If not, it will be in a new world and under a strange sky that I continue. . . .

•

'You shouldn't have touched it,' said the Police Inspector, shaking his head. 'It ought to have been left where it was until the proper authorities had inspected it.'

'And who,' inquired Mr Fontain coldly, 'are the proper authorities for the inspection of meteors?'

'That's beside the point. You couldn't be sure it was a meteor, and these days a lot of other things besides meteors can fall out of the sky. Even now you've got it up you can't be sure.'

'It doesn't look like anything else.'

'All the same, it should have been left to us. It might be some device still on the Secret List.'

'The Police, of course, knowing all about things on the Secret List?'

Sally considered it time to break in.

'Well, we shall know what to do next time we have a meteor, shan't we? Suppose we all go and have a look at it? It's in the outhouse now, looking quite unsecret.'

She led the way round to the yard, still talking to stave off a row between the Inspector and her father.

'It only went a surprisingly short way down, so the men were soon able to get it out. And it turned out to be not nearly as hot as we'd expected, either, so they could handle it quite easily.'

'You'd not say "quite easily" if you'd heard the language they used about the weight of it,' observed her father.

'It's in here,' Sally said, leading the party of four into a musty, single-storey shed.

The meteor was not an impressive sight. It lay in the middle of the bare board floor; just a rugged, pitted, metallic-looking sphere something over two feet in diameter.

'The only kind of weapon that it suggests to me is a cannon-ball,' said Mr Fontain.

'It's the principle,' retorted the Inspector. 'We have standing orders that any mysterious falling object is to remain untouched until it has been examined by a War Office expert. We have already informed them, and it must not be moved again until their man has had a look at it.'

Graham who had hitherto taken no part, stepped forward and put his hand on it.

'Almost cold now,' he reported. 'What's it made of?' he added curiously.

Mr Fontain shrugged.

'I imagine it's just an ordinary chunk of meteoric iron. The only odd thing about it to me is that it didn't come down with more of a bump. If it were any kind of secret weapon, it would certainly be an exceedingly dull one.'

'All the same, I shall have to give orders that it is not to be moved until the W.O. man has seen it,' said the Inspector.

They started to move back into the yard, but on the threshold he paused.

'What's that sizzling sound?' he inquired.

'Sizzling?' repeated Sally.

'Kind of hissing noise. Listen!'

They stood still, the Inspector with his head a little on one side. Undeniably there was a faint, persistent sound on a note just within the range of audibility. It was difficult to place. By common impulse they turned back to regard the ball uneasily. Graham hesitated, and then stepped inside again. He leaned over the ball, his right ear turned down to it.

'Yes,' he said. 'It is.'

Then his eyes closed, and he swayed. Sally ran forward and caught him as he sagged. The others helped her to drag him out. In the fresh air he revived almost immediately.

'That's funny. What happened?' he asked.

'You're sure the sound is coming from that thing?' asked the Inspector.

'Oh, yes. Not a doubt about it.'

'You didn't smell anything queer?'

Graham raised his eyebrows: 'Oh, gas, you mean. No, I don't think so.'

'H'm,' said the Inspector. He turned a mildly triumphant eye on the older man. 'Is it usual for meteors to sizzle?' he inquired.

'Er – I really don't know. I shouldn't think so,' Mr Fontain admitted.

'I see. Well, in the circumstances I suggest that we all withdraw – preferably to a well-shielded spot on the other side of the house, just in case – while we wait for the expert,' announced the Inspector.

Extract from Onns's Journal:

I am bewildered. I have just woken. But has it happened – or have we failed to start? I cannot tell. Was it an hour, a day, a year, or a century ago that we entered the Globe? No, it cannot have been an hour ago; I am sure of that by the tiredness of my limbs, and the way my body aches. We were warned about that:

'You will know nothing,' they said, 'nothing until it is all over. Then you will feel physically weary because your bodies will have been subjected to great strains. That should pass quite soon, but we shall give you some capsules of concentrated food and stimulants to help you overcome the effects more quickly.'

I have taken one capsule, and I begin to feel the benefit of it already, but it is still hard to believe that it is over.

It seems such a short time ago that we climbed the long passage into the interior of the Globe and dispersed as we had been instructed. Each of us found his or her elastic compartment, and crawled into it. I released the valve to inflate the space between the inner and outer walls of my compartment. As the lining distended I felt myself lifted on a mattress of air. The top bulged down, the sides closed in, and so, insulated from shock in all directions, I waited.

Waited for what? I still cannot say. One moment, it seems, I lay there fresh and strong: the next, I was tired and aching.

Only that, to indicate that one life has ended and a new one is about to begin. My compartment has deflated. The pumps have been exchanging the gas for fresh air. That must mean that we are now on that beautiful, shining blue planet, with Forta only a speck in our new heavens.

I feel different for knowing that. All my life hitherto has been spent on a dying planet where our greatest enemy was lethal discouragement. But now I feel rejuvenated. There will be work, hope, and life here: a world to build, and a future to build it for ...

I can hear the drills at work, cutting a way out for us. What, I wonder, shall we find? We must watch ourselves closely. It may be easier for us to keep faith if we face hardships than if we find ourselves among plenty. But, whatever this world is like, faith *must* be kept. We hold a million years of history, a million years of knowledge, that *must* be preserved.

Yet we must also, as His Excellency said, be ready to adapt ourselves. Who can tell what forms of life may already exist here? One could scarcely expect to find real consciousness on a planet so young, but there may be the first stirrings of intelligence here. We must watch for them, seek them out, cultivate them. They may be quite different from us, but we must remember that it is their world, and help them where we can. We must keep in mind that it would be a wicked thing to frustrate even an alien form of life, on its own planet. If we find any such beings, our task must be to teach, to learn, to co-operate with them, and perhaps one day we may achieve a civilization even greater than Forta's own. ...

'And just what,' inquired the Inspector, 'do you think you're doing with that, Sergeant Brown?'

The police-sergeant held the limp, furry body dangling by its tail.

'It's a cat, sir.'

'That's what I meant.'

'Well, I thought the W.O. gentleman might want to examine it, sir.'

'What makes you think the War Office is interested in dead cats, Sergeant?'

The sergeant explained. He had decided to risk a trip into the outhouse to note developments, if any. Bearing in mind the Inspector's suggestion of gas, he had tied a rope round his waist so that he could be dragged back if he were overcome, and crawled in, keeping as low as possible. The precautions had proved unnecessary, however. The hissing or sizzling had ceased, and the gas had evidently dispersed. He had been able to approach the ball without feeling any effects whatever. Nevertheless, when he had come so close to it that his ear was almost against it he had noticed a faint buzzing.

'Buzzing?' repeated the Inspector. 'You mean sizzling.'

'No, sir, buzzing.' He paused, searching for a simile. 'The nearest thing, to my mind, would be a circular saw, but as you might hear it from a very long way off.'

Deducing from this that the thing, whatever it was, was still active, the sergeant had ordered his constables away to cover on the far side of an earth bank. He himself had looked into the shed from time to time during the next hour and a half, but observed no change.

He had noticed the cat prowl into the yard just as they were settling down to a snack of sandwiches. It had gone nosing round the shed door, but he had not bothered about it. Half an hour later, when he had finished his meal and cigarette, he had gone across to take another look. He had discovered the cat lying close to the 'meteor'. When he brought it out, he had found it was dead.

'Gassed?' asked the Inspector.

The sergeant shook his head. 'No, sir. That's what's funny about it.'

He laid the cat's body on top of a convenient wall, and turned the head to expose the under side of the jaw. A small circle of the black fur had been burnt away, and in the centre of the burn was a minute hole.

'H'm,' said the Inspector. He touched the wound, and then sniffed at his forefinger. 'Fur's burnt, all right, but no smell of explosive fumes,' he said.

'That's not all, sir.'

The sergeant turned the head over to reveal an exactly similar blemish on the crown. He took a thin, straight wire from his pocket, and probed into the hole beneath the jaw. It emerged from the other hole at the top of the head.

'Can you make anything of that, sir?' he asked.

The Inspector frowned. A weapon of minute bore, at point-blank range might have made one of the wounds. But the two appeared to be entrance and exit holes of the same missile. But a bullet did not come out leaving a neat hole like that, nor did it singe the hair about its exit. To all appearances, two of these microscopic bullets must have been fired in exactly the same line from above and below the head – which made no kind of sense.

'Have you any theories?' he asked the sergeant.

'Beats me, sir,' the other told him.

'What's happened to the thing now? Is it still buzzing?' the Inspector inquired.

'No, sir. There wasn't a sound from it when I went in and found the cat.'

'H'm,' said the Inspector. 'Isn't it about time that W.O. man showed up?'

Extract from Onns's Journal:

This is a terrible place! As though we were condemned to some fantastic hell. Can this be our beautiful blue planet that beckoned us so bravely? We cannot understand, we are utterly bewildered, our minds reel with the horror of this place. We, the flower of civilization, now cower before the hideous monstrosities that face us. How can we ever hope to bring order into such a world as this?

We are hiding now in a dark cavern while Iss, our leader, consults to decide our best course. None of us envies him his responsibility. What provisions can a man make against not only the unknown, but the incredible? Nine hundred and sixty-four of us depend on him. There were a thousand: this is the way it happened.

I heard the drill stop, then there was a clanking as it was dismantled and drawn from the long shaft it had bored. Soon after that came the call for assembly. We crawled out of our compartments, collected our personal belongings, and met in the centre hall. Sunss, our leader then, himself called the roll. Everyone answered except four poor fellows who had not stood the strain of the journey. Then Sunss made a brief speech.

He reminded us that what had been done was irrevocable. No one yet knew what awaited us outside the Globe. If it should somehow happen that our party was divided, each group must elect its leader and act independently until contact with the rest was re-established.

'We need long courage, not brief bravery,' he said. 'Not

heroics. We have to think of ourselves always as the seed of the future; and every grain of that seed is precious.'

He hammered home the responsibility to all of us.

'We do not know, and we shall never know, how the other globes may have fared. So, not knowing, we must act as though we alone had survived, and as if all that Forta has ever stood for is in our hands alone.'

It was he who led the way down the newly-bored passage, and he who first set foot in the new land. I followed with the rest, filled with such a conflict of feelings as I have never known before.

And this world into which we have emerged: how can I describe it in all its alien qualities?

To begin with; it was gloomy and shadowed – and yet it was not night-time. Such light as there was came from a vast, grey panel hanging in the dusky sky. From where we stood it appeared trapezoid, but I suspect that was a trick of perspective, and that it was in fact a square, bisected twice, by two dark bars, into four smaller squares. In the murk over our heads it was possible to make out dimly-faint darker lines intersecting at strange angles. I could not guess at their significance.

The ground we stood on was like nothing I had known. It was a vast level plain, but ridged, and covered with small, loose boulders. The ridges were somewhat like strata that had been laid side by side instead of one on another. They lay all one way, disappearing into gloomy distance before and behind. Close beside us was a crevasse, as wide as my own height, also running either way, in a perfectly straight line. Some considerable distance beyond it was another, similar crevasse running exactly parallel to it, and beyond that a third, and an indication of a fourth.

The man beside me was nervous. He muttered something about a geometrical world lit by a square sun.

'Rubbish!' I told him shortly.

'Then how do you explain it?' he asked.

'I do not rush into swift, facile explanations,' I told him. 'I observe, and then, when I have gathered enough data, I deduce.'

'What do you deduce from a square sun?' he asked, but I ignored him.

Soon we were all assembled outside the Globe, and waiting for Sunss to give directions. He was just about to speak when we were interrupted by a strange sound – a kind of regular soft padding, sometimes with a rasping scratch accompanying it. There was something ominous about it, and for a moment we were all frozen with apprehension – then, before we could move, the most fearsome monster emerged from behind our Globe.

Every historic travellers' tale pales beside the reality of the thing we faced. Never would I have believed that such a creature could exist had I not seen it for myself. The first we saw of it was an enormous face, thrusting round the side of the Globe, hanging in the air far above us. It was a sight to make the bravest shudder.

It was black, too, so that in the darkness it was difficult to be certain of its outline; but it widened across the top, and above the head itself one seemed to catch a glimpse of two towering pointed ears. It looked down on us out of two vast, glowing eyes set somewhat aslant.

It paused for a moment, the great eyes blinked, and then it came closer. The legs which then came into view were like massive pillars, yet they moved with a dexterity and control that was amazing in anything so vast. Both legs and feet were covered with close set fibres that looked like strands of shining black metal. It bent its legs, lowering its head to look at us, and the fearful stench of its breath blew over us. The face was still more alarming at close quarters. It opened a cavern of a mouth; an enormous pink tongue flicked out and back. Above the mouth huge, pointed spines stood out sideways, trembling. The eyes which were fixed on us were cold, cruel, non-intelligent.

Until then we had been transfixed, but now panic took some of us. Those nearest to it fell back hurriedly, and at that one of the monstrous feet moved like lightning. A huge black paw with suddenly out-thrust claws smacked down. When it drew back, twenty of our men and women were no more than smears on the ground.

We were paralysed, all of us except Sunss. He, forgetting his instructions about personal safety, ran towards the creature. The great paw rose, hovered, and struck again. Eleven more fell at that second murderous blow.

Then I noticed Sunss again. He was standing right between the paws. His fire-rod was in his hands, and he was looking up at the monstrous head above him. As I watched, he lifted the weapon, and aimed. It seemed such folly against that huge thing, heroic folly. But Sunss was wiser than I. Suddenly the head jerked, a tremor shook the limbs, and without a sound the monster dropped where it stood.

And Sunss was under it. A very brave man. . . .

Then Iss took charge.

He decided that we must find a place of safety as soon as possible in case there were other such monsters lurking near. Once we had found that, we could start to remove our instruments and equipment from the Globe, and consider our next step. He decided to lead us forward down the broad way between two of the crevasses.

After travelling a considerable distance we reached the foot of a towering and completely perpendicular cliff with curiously regular rectangular formations on its face. At the base of it we found this cavern which seems to run a great distance both inwards and to both sides, and with a height that is oddly regular. Perhaps the man who spoke about a geometrical world was not so stupid as he seemed. . . .

Anyway, here we have a refuge from monsters such as that which Sunss killed. It is too narrow for those huge paws to reach, and even the fearful claws could only rake a little way inside.

Later. A terrible thing has happened! Iss and a party of twenty went exploring the cavern to see if they could find another way out other than on to the plain where our Globe lay.

Yes – lay! Past tense. That is our calamity.

After he had gone off, the rest of us waited, keeping watch. For some time nothing happened. Evidently and mercifully the monster had been alone. It lay in a great black mound where it had fallen, close to the Globe. Then a curious thing took place. More light suddenly poured over the plain. An enormous hooked object descended upon the slain monster, and dragged it away out of sight. Then there was a thunderous noise which shook everything about us, and the light dimmed again.

I do not pretend to explain these things: none of us can understand them. I simply do my best to keep a faithful record.

Another, much longer, period passed without any event. We were beginning to worry about what might have happened to Iss and his party for they had been a long time away, when almost the worst thing that could happen to us occurred without warning.

Again the plain became lighter. The ground beneath us set up a reverberating rumble and shook so violently to a series of shocks that we were hard put to keep on our feet. Peering out of the cavern I saw a sight that even now I can scarcely credit. Forms beside which our previous monster was insignificant: living, moving creatures reared up to three or four times the height of our vast Globe. I know this will not be believed – but it is the truth. Little wonder that the whole plain groaned and rumbled under the burden of four such. They bent over our Globe, they put their forelegs to it, and lifted it – yes, actually lifted that stupendous mass of metal from the ground. Then the shaking all about us became worse as they took its weight and tramped away on colossal feet.

The sight of that was too much for some of us. A hundred men ran out from our cavern, cursing, weeping, and brandishing their fire-rods. But it was too late, and the range was too great for them to do anything effective, besides, how could we hope to affect colossi such as these?

Now our Globe, with all its precious contents is lost. Our inheritance is gone. We have nothing now; nothing, but our own few trifling possessions, with which to start building our new world. . . .

It is bitter, bitter to have worked so hard and come so far, for this . . .

Nor was that the only calamity. Only a little later two of Iss's companions came back with a dreadful tale.

Behind our cavern they had discovered a warren of broad tunnels, foul with the smell of unknown creatures and their droppings. They had made their way down them with difficulty. Several times they had been beset by different varieties of six-legged creatures, and sometimes eight-legged ones, all of horrible appearance. Many of these were a great deal larger than themselves, armed with fearful jaws and claws, and filled with a vicious ferocity which made them attack on sight. Terrifying though they looked, it soon became clear, however, that they were only really dangerous when they made unexpected attacks for they were non-sentient and the fire-rods made short work of them once they had been seen.

After a number of such encounters Iss had succeeded in reaching open country beyond the tunnels without the loss of a man. It had been when they were on the way back to fetch us that catastrophe had overtaken them. They had been attacked by fierce grey creatures about half the size of our first monster, which they guessed to be the builders of the tunnels. It was a terrible fight in which almost all the party perished before the monsters were overcome. Iss himself had fallen, and of all his men only these two had been left in a fit condition to make the journey back to the rest of us.

This new, ghastly tragedy is starting to sap our spirits, and our courage. . . .

We have chosen Muin as our new leader. He has decided that we must go forward, through the tunnels. The plain behind us is quite barren, our Globe is gone, if we stay here we shall starve; so we must try to get through to the open country beyond, trusting that Iss's sacrifice has not been in vain, and that there are no more grey monsters to attack us. . . .

God grant that beyond the tunnels this nightmare world gives place to sanity. . . .

Is it so much that we ask – simply to live, to work, to build, in peace . . . ?

Graham looked in to see Sally and her father a couple of days later.

'Thought you might like an interim report on your "meteor",' he said to Mr Fontain.

'What was it, actually?' asked the older man.

'Oh, I don't say they've got that far. They've established that it was no meteor; but just what it really was still has them absolutely guessing. I'd got pretty curious by the time they decided to take it away, and after I'd talked big and waved my wartime status at them a bit, they consented to stretch a point and take me along, too. So you'd better grade this as confidential.

'When we went over the thing carefully at the research place it appeared to be simply a solid ball of some metal on which there's been no report issued as yet. But in one place there was a hole, quite smooth, about half an inch in diameter, which went straight in, roughly to the middle. Well, they scratched their heads about the best way to tackle it, and decided in the end to cut it in half and see what. So they rigged up an automatic sawing device in a pit and set it going, and we all retreated to a reasonable distance, just in case. Now they're all a bit more puzzled than they were before.'

'Why, what happened?' Sally asked.

'Well, nothing actually *happened*. When the saw ran free we switched off and went back, and there was the ball lying in neat halves. But they weren't solid halves as we had expected. There *was* a solid metal rind about six inches thick, but then there was an inch or so of soft, fine dust, which has insulating qualities that seem to be interesting them quite a bit. Then inside a thinner metal wall was an odd formation of cells; more like a section of honeycomb than anything, only made of some flexible, rubbery material, and every one empty. Next a belt about two inches wide, divided into metal compartments this time, all considerably larger than the cells in the outer part, and crammed with all sorts of things – packs of minute tubes, things that look like tiny seeds, different sorts of powders that have spilled about when the thing came apart, and which nobody's got around to examining properly yet, and finally a four-inch space in the middle separted into layers by dozens of paper-thin fins, and absolutely empty otherwise.

'So there is the secret weapon – and if you can make anything of that lot, I'm sure they'll be pleased to hear about it. Even the dust layer disappointed them by not being explosive. Now they're asking one another what the hell such a thing could be remotely expected to do.'

'That's disappointing. It seemed so like a meteor – until it started sizzling,' said Mr Fontain.

'One of them has suggested that in a way it may be. A sort of artificial meteor,' Graham said. 'That's a bit too fancy for the rest, though. They feel that if something could be sent across space at all, surely it would be something more intelligible.'

'It would be exciting if it were,' Sally said. 'I mean, it would be such a much more hopeful thing than just another secret weapon – a sort of sign that perhaps one day we shall be able to do it ourselves....

'Just think how wonderful it might be if we really could do that! Think of all the people who are sick to death of secret weapons, and wars, and cruelties setting out one day in a huge ship for a clean, new planet where we could start again. We'd be able to leave behind all the things that make this poor old world get boggier and boggier. All we'd want is a place where people could live, and work, and build, and be happy. If we could only start again somewhere else, what a lovely, lovely world we might –' She stopped suddenly at the sound of a frenzied yapping outside. She jumped up as it changed to a long-drawn howl.

'That's Mitty!' she said. 'What on earth –?'

The two men followed her out of the house.

'Mitty! Mitty!' she called, but there was no sign of the dog, nor sound from it now.

They made round to the left, where the sound had seemed to come from. Sally was the first to see the white patch lying in the grass beside the outhouse wall. She ran towards it, calling; but the patch did not move.

'Oh, poor Mitty!' she said. 'I believe she's dead!'

She went down on her knees beside the dog's limp body.

'She *is*!' she said. 'I wonder what –' She broke off abruptly, and stood up. 'Oh, something stung me! Oh, it *hurts*!' She clutched at her leg, tears of anguish suddenly coming into her eyes.

'What on earth –?' began her father, looking down at the dog. 'What are all those things – ants?'

Graham bent down to look.

'No, they're not ants. I don't know what they are.'

He picked one of the little creatures up and put it on the palm of his hand to look at it more closely.

'Never seen anything like that before,' he said.

Mr Fontain beside him, peered at it, too.

It was a queer-looking little thing, under a quarter of an inch long. Its body seemed to be an almost perfect hemisphere with the flat side below and the round top surface coloured pink, and as shiny as a ladybird's wing-cases. It was insect-like, except that it stood on only four short legs. There was no clearly defined head; just two eyes set in the edge of the shiny dome. As they watched, it reared up on two of its legs, showing a pale, flat underside, with a mouth set just below the eyes. In its forelegs it seemed to be holding a bit of grass or thin wire.

Graham felt a sudden, searing pain in his hand.

'Hell's bells!' he said, shaking it off. 'The little brute certainly can sting. I don't know what they are, but they're nasty things to have around. Got a spray handy?'

'There's one in the scullery,' Mr Fontain told him. He turned his attention to his daughter. 'Better?' he inquired.

'Hurts like hell,' Sally said, between her teeth.

'Just hang on a minute till we've dealt with this, then we'll have a look at it,' he told her.

Graham hurried back with the spray in his hand. He cast around and discovered several hundreds of the little pink objects crawling towards the wall of the outhouse. He pumped a cloud of insecticide over them and watched while they slowed, waved feeble legs, and then lay still. He sprayed the locality a little more, to make sure.

'That ought to fix 'em,' he said. 'Nasty, vicious little brutes. Never seen anything quite like them – I wonder what on earth they were?'

Survival

As the spaceport bus trundled unhurriedly over the mile or more of open field that separated the terminal buildings from the embarkation hoist, Mrs Feltham stared intently forward across the receding row of shoulders in front of her. The ship stood up on the plain like an isolated silver spire. Near its bow she could see the intense blue light which proclaimed it all but ready to take off. Among and around the great tailfins, dwarf vehicles and little dots of men moved in a fuss of final preparations. Mrs Feltham glared at the scene, at this moment loathing it and all the inventions of men, with a hard, hopeless hatred.

Presently she withdrew her gaze from the distance and focused it on the back of her son-in-law's head, a yard in front of her. She hated him, too.

She turned, darting a swift glance at the face of her daughter in the seat beside her. Alice looked pale; her lips were firmly set, her eyes fixed straight ahead.

Mrs Feltham hesitated. Her glance returned to the spaceship. She decided on one last effort. Under cover of the bus noise she said:

'Alice, darling, it's not too late, even now, you know.'

The girl did not look at her. There was no sign that she had heard, save that her lips compressed a little more firmly. Then they parted.

'Mother, please!' she said.

But Mrs Feltham, once started, had to go on.

'It's for your own sake, darling. All you have to do is to say you've changed your mind.'

The girl held a protesting silence.

'Nobody would blame you,' Mrs Feltham persisted. 'They'd not think a bit worse of you. After all, everybody knows that Mars is no place for –'

'Mother, please stop it,' interrupted the girl. The sharpness of her tone took Mrs Feltham aback for a moment.

She hesitated. But time was growing too short to allow herself the luxury of offended dignity. She went on:

'You're not used to the sort of life you'll have to live there, darling. Absolutely primitive. No kind of life for any woman. After all, dear, it is only a five-year appointment for David. I'm sure if he really loves you he'd rather know that you *are* safe here and waiting –'

The girl said, harshly:

'We've been over all this before, Mother. I tell you it's no good. I'm not a child. I've thought it out, and I've made up my mind.'

Mrs Feltham sat silent for some moments. The bus swayed on across the field, and the rocketship seemed to tower further into the sky.

'If you had a child of your own –' she said, half to herself. '– Well, I expect some day you will. Then you will begin to understand. . . .'

'I think it's you who don't understand,' Alice said. 'This is hard enough, anyway. You're only making it harder for me.'

'My darling, I love you. I gave birth to you. I've watched over you always and I *know* you. I *know* this can't be the kind of life for you. If you were a hard, hoydenish kind of girl, well, perhaps – but you aren't, darling. You know quite well you aren't.'

'Perhaps you don't know me quite as well as you imagine you do, Mother.'

Mrs Feltham shook her head. She kept her eyes averted, boring jealousy into the back of her son-in-law's head.

'He's taken you right away from me,' she said dully.

'That's not true, Mother. It's – well, I'm no longer a child. I'm a woman with a life of my own to live.'

' "Whither thou goest, I will go . . ." ' said Mrs Feltham reflectively. 'But that doesn't really hold now, you know. It was all right for a tribe of nomads, but nowadays the wives of soldiers, sailors, pilots, spacemen –'

'It's more than that, Mother. You don't understand. I must become adult and real to myself. . . .'

The bus rolled to a stop, puny and toylike beside the ship that seemed too large ever to lift. The passengers got out and stood staring upwards along the shining side. Mr Feltham put his arms round his daughter. Alice clung to him, tears in her eyes. In an unsteady voice he murmured:

'Good-bye, my dear. And all the luck there is.'

He released her, and shook hands with his son-in-law.

'Keep her safe, David. She's everything –'

'I know. I will. Don't you worry.'

Mrs Feltham kissed her daughter farewell, and forced herself to shake hands with her son-in-law.

A voice from the hoist called: 'All passengers aboard, please!'

The doors of the hoist closed. Mr Feltham avoided his wife's eyes. He put his arm round her waist, and led her back to the bus in silence.

As they made their way, in company with a dozen other vehicles, back to the shelter of the terminal, Mrs Feltham alternately dabbed her eyes with a wisp of white handkerchief and cast glances back at the spaceship standing tall, inert, and apparently deserted now. Her hand slid into her husband's.

'I can't believe it even now,' she said. 'It's so utterly unlike her. Would you ever have thought that our little Alice ... ? Oh, why did she have to marry him ... ?' Her voice trailed to a whimper.

Her husband pressed her fingers, without speaking.

'It wouldn't be so surprising with some girls,' she went on. 'But Alice was always so quiet. I used to worry because she was so quiet – I mean in case she might become one of those timid bores. Do you remember how the other children used to call her Mouse?

'And now this! Five years in that dreadful place! Oh, she'll never stand it, Henry. I know she won't, she's not the type. Why didn't you put your foot down, Henry? They'd have listened to you. You could have stopped it.'

Her husband sighed. 'There are times when one can give advice, Miriam, though it's scarcely ever popular, but what one must not do is to try to live other people's lives for them. Alice is a woman now, with her own rights. Who am I to say what's best for her?'

'But you could have stopped her going.'

'Perhaps – but I didn't care for the price.'

She was silent for some seconds, then her fingers tightened on his hand.

'Henry – Henry, I don't think we shall ever see them again. I feel it.'

'Come, come, dear. They'll be back safe and sound, you'll see.'

'You don't really believe that, Henry. You're just trying to cheer me up. Oh, why, why must she go to that horrible place? She's so young. She could have waited five years. Why is she so stubborn, so hard – not like my little Mouse at all?'

Her husband patted her hand reassuringly.

'You must try to stop thinking of her as a child, Miriam. She's not; she's a woman now and if all our women were mice, it would be a poor outlook for our survival. . . .'

The Navigating Officer of the s/r *Falcon* approached his captain.

'The deviation, sir.'

Captain Winters took the piece of paper held out to him.

'One point three six five degrees,' he read out. 'H'm. Not bad. Not at all bad, considering. South-east sector again. Why are nearly all deviations in the S.E. sector, I wonder, Mr Carter?'

'Maybe they'll find out when we've been at the game a bit longer, sir. Right now it's just one of those things.'

'Odd, all the same. Well, we'd better correct it before it gets any bigger.'

The Captain loosened the expanding book-rack in front of him and pulled out a set of tables. He consulted them and scribbled down the result.

'Check, Mr Carter.'

The navigator compared the figures with the table, and approved.

'Good. How's she lying?' asked the Captain.

'Almost broadside, with a very slow roll, sir.'

'You can handle it. I'll observe visually. Align her and stabilize. Ten seconds on starboard laterals at force two. She should take about thirty minutes, twenty seconds to swing over, but we'll watch that. Then neutralize with the port laterals at force two. Okay?'

'Very good, sir.' The Navigating Officer sat down in the control chair, and fastened the belt. He looked over the keys and switches carefully.

'I'd better warn 'em. May be a bit of a jolt,' said the Captain. He switched on the address system, and pulled the microphone bracket to him.

'Attention all! Attention all! We are about to correct course. There will be several impulses. None of them will be violent, but all fragile objects should be secured, and you are advised to seat yourselves and use the safety belts. The operation will take approximately half an hour and will start in five minutes from now. I shall inform you when it has been completed. That is all.' He switched off.

'Some fool always thinks the ship's been holed by a meteor if you don't spoon it out,' he added. 'Have that woman in hysterics, most likely. Doesn't do any good.' He pondered idly. 'I wonder what the devil she thinks she's doing out here, anyway. A quiet little thing like that; what she ought to be doing is sitting in some village back home, knitting.'

'She knits here,' observed the Navigating Officer.

'I know – and think what it implies! What's the idea of that kind going to Mars? She'll be as homesick as hell, and hate every foot of the place on sight. That husband of hers ought to have had more sense. Comes damn near cruelty to children.'

'It mightn't be his fault, sir. I mean, some of those quiet ones can be amazingly stubborn.'

The captain eyed his officer speculatively.

'Well, I'm not a man of wide experience, but I know what I'd say to my wife if she thought of coming along.'

'But you can't have a proper ding-dong with those quiet ones, sir. They kind of featherbed the whole thing, and then get their own way in the end.'

'I'll overlook the implication of the first part of that remark, Mr Carter, but out of this extensive knowledge of women can you suggest to me why the devil she is here if he didn't drag her along? It isn't as if Mars were domestically hazardous, like a convention.'

'Well, sir – she strikes me as the devoted type. Scared of her own shadow ordinarily, but with an awful amount of determination when the right string's pulled. It's sort of – well, you've heard of ewes facing lions in defence of their cubs, haven't you?'

'Assuming that you mean lambs,' said the Captain, 'the answers would be, A: I've always doubted it; and, B: she doesn't have any.'

'I was just trying to indicate the type, sir.'

The Captain scratched his cheek with his forefinger.

'You may be right, but I know if I were going to take a wife to Mars, which heaven forbid, I'd feel a tough, gun-toting Momma was less of a liability. What's his job there?'

'Taking charge of a mining company office, I think.'

'Office hours, huh? Well, maybe it'll work out some way, but I still say the poor little thing ought to be in her own kitchen. She'll spend half the time scared to death, and the rest of it pining for home comforts.' He glanced at the clock. 'They've had enough time to batten down the chamber-pots now. Let's get busy.'

He fastened his own safety-belt, swung the screen in front of him on its pivot, switching it on as he did so, and leaned back watching the panorama of stars move slowly across it.

'All set, Mr Carter?'

The Navigating Officer switched on a fuel line, and poised his right hand above a key.

'All set, sir.'

'Okay. Straighten her up.'

The Navigating Officer glued his attention to the pointers before him. He tapped the key beneath his fingers experimentally. Nothing happened. A slight double furrow appeared between his brows. He tapped again. Still there was no response.

'Get on with it, man,' said the Captain irritably.

The Navigating Officer decided to try twisting her the other way. He tapped one of the keys under his left hand. This time there was response without delay. The whole ship jumped violently sideways and trembled. A crash jangled back and forth through the metal members around them like a diminishing echo.

Only the safety belt kept the Navigating Officer in his seat. He stared stupidly at the gyrating pointers before him. On the screen the stars were streaking across like a shower of fireworks. The Captain watched the display in ominous silence for a moment, then he said coldly:

'Perhaps when you have had your fun, Mr Carter, you will kindly straighten her up.'

The navigator pulled himself together. He chose a key, and pressed it. Nothing happened. He tried another. Still the needles on the dials revolved smoothly. A slight sweat broke out on his forehead. He switched to another fuel line, and tried again.

The Captain lay back in his chair, watching the heavens stream across his screen.

'Well?' he demanded curtly.

'There's – no response, sir.'

Captain Winters unfastened his safety-belt and clacked across the floor on his magnetic soles. He jerked his head for the other to get out of his seat, and took his place. He checked the fuel line switches. He pressed a key. There was no impulse: the pointers continued to turn without a check. He tried other keys, fruitlessly. He looked up and met the navigator's eyes. After a long moment he moved

back to his own desk, and flipped a switch. A voice broke
into the room:

'– would I know? All I know is that the old can's just
bowling along head over elbow, and that ain't no kind of
way to run a bloody spaceship. If you ask me –'

'Jevons,' snapped the Captain.

The voice broke off abruptly.

'Yes, sir?' it said, in a different tone.

'The laterals aren't firing.'

'No, sir,' the voice agreed.

'Wake up, man. I mean they *won't* fire. They've packed
up.'

'What – all of 'em, sir?'

'The only ones that have responded are the port laterals
– and they shouldn't have kicked the way they did. Better
send someone outside to look at 'em. I didn't like that kick.'

'Very good, sir.'

The Captain flipped the communicator switch back, and
pulled over the announcement mike.

'Attention, please. You may release all safety-belts and
proceed as normal. Correction of course has been post-
poned. You will be warned before it is resumed. That is
all.'

Captain and navigator looked at one another again.
Their faces were grave, and their eyes troubled. ...

Captain Winters studied his audience. It comprised
everyone aboard the *Falcon*. Fourteen men and one woman.
Six of the men were his crew; the rest passengers. He
watched them as they found themselves places in the ship's
small living-room. He would have been happier if his cargo
had consisted of more freight and fewer passengers. Passengers, having nothing to occupy them, were always making mischief one way and another. Moreover, it was not a
quiet, subservient type of man who recommended himself
for a job as a miner, prospector, or general adventurer on
Mars.

The woman could have caused a great deal of trouble

aboard had she been so minded. Luckily she was diffident, self-effacing. But even though at times she was irritatingly without spirit, he thanked his luck that she had not turned out to be some incendiary blonde who would only add to his troubles.

All the same, he reminded himself, regarding her as she sat beside her husband, she could not be quite as meek as she looked. Carter must have been right when he spoke of a stiffening motive somewhere – without that she could never have started on the journey at all, and she would certainly not be coming through steadfast and uncomplaining so far. He glanced at the woman's husband. Queer creatures, women. Morgan was all right, but there was nothing about him, one would have said, to lead a woman on a trip like this. ...

He waited until they had finished shuffling around and fitting themselves in. Silence fell. He let his gaze dwell on each face in turn. His own expression was serious.

'Mrs Morgan and gentlemen,' he began. 'I have called you here together because it seemed best to me that each of you should have a clear understanding of our present position.

'It is this. Our lateral tubes have failed. They are, for reasons which we have not yet been able to ascertain, useless. In the case of the port laterals they are burnt out, and irreplaceable.

'In case some of you do not know what that implies, I should tell you that it is upon the laterals that the navigation of the ship depends. The main drive tubes give us the initial impetus for take-off. After that they are shut off, leaving us in free fall. Any deviations from the course plotted are corrected by suitable bursts from the laterals.

'But it is not only for steering that we use them. In landing, which is an infinitely more complex job than take-off, they are essential. We brake by reversing the ship and using the main drive to check our speed. But I think you can scarcely fail to realize that is an operation of the greatest delicacy to keep the huge mass of such a ship as this perfectly balanced upon the thrust of her drive as she descends. It is the laterals which make such balance possible. Without them it cannot be done.'

A dead silence held the room for some seconds. Then a voice asked, drawling:

'What you're saying, Captain, is, the way things are, we can neither steer nor land – is that it?'

Captain Winters looked at the speaker. He was a big man. Without exerting himself, and, apparently, without intention, he seemed to possess a natural domination over the rest.

'That is exactly what I mean,' he replied.

A tenseness came over the room. There was the sound of a quickly drawn breath here and there.

The man with the slow voice nodded, fatalistically. Someone else asked:

'Does that mean that we might crash on Mars?'

'No,' said the Captain. 'If we go on travelling as we are now, slightly off course, we shall miss Mars altogether.'

'And so go on out to play tag with the asteroids,' another voice suggested.

'That is what would happen if we did nothing about it. But there is a way we can stop that, if we can manage it.' The Captain paused, aware that he had their absorbed attention. He continued:

'You must all be well aware from the peculiar behaviour of space as seen from our ports that we are now tumbling along all as – er – head over heels. This is due to the explosion of the port laterals. It is a highly unorthodox method of travelling, but it does mean that by an impulse from our main tubes given at exactly the critical moment we should be able to alter our course approximately as we require.'

'And how much good is that going to do us if we can't land?' somebody wanted to know. The Captain ignored the interruption. He continued:

'I have been in touch by radio with both home and Mars, and have reported our state. I have also informed them that I intend to attempt the one possible course open to me. That is of using the main drive in an attempt to throw the ship into an orbit about Mars.

'If that is successful we shall avoid two dangers – that of shooting on towards the outer parts of the system, and of crashing on Mars. I think we have a good chance of bringing it off.'

When he stopped speaking he saw alarm in several faces, thoughtful concentration in others. He noticed Mrs Morgan holding tightly to her husband's hand, her face a little paler than usual. It was the man with the drawl who broke the silence.

'You *think* there is a good chance?' he repeated questioningly.

'I do. I also think it is the only chance. But I'm not going to try to fool you by pretending complete confidence. It's too serious for that.'

'And if we do get into this orbit?'

'They will try to keep a radar fix on us, and send help as soon as possible.'

'H'm,' said the questioner. 'And what do you personally think about that, Captain?'

'I – well, it isn't going to be easy. But we're all in this together, so I'll tell you just what they told me. At the very best we can't expect them to reach us for some months. The ship will have to come from Earth. The two planets are well past conjunction now. I'm afraid it's going to mean quite a wait.'

'Can we – hold out long enough, Captain?'

'According to my calculations we should be able to hold out for about seventeen or eighteen weeks.'

'And that will be long enough?'

'It'll have to be.'

He broke the thoughtful pause that followed by continuing in a brisker manner.

'This is not going to be comfortable, or pleasant. But, if we all play our parts, and keep strictly to the necessary measures, it can be done. Now, there are three essentials:

air to breathe – well, luckily we shan't have to worry about that. The regeneration plant and stock of spare cylinders, and cylinders in cargo will look after that for a long time. Water will be rationed. Two pints each every twenty-four hours, for *everything*. Luckily we shall be able to draw water from the fuel tanks, or it would be a great deal less than that. The thing that is going to be our most serious worry is food.'

He explained his proposals further, with patient clarity. At the end he added: 'And now I expect you have some questions?'

A small, wiry man with a weather-beaten face asked:

'Is there no hope at all of getting the lateral tubes to work again?'

Captain Winters shook his head.

'Negligible. The impellent section of a ship is not constructed to be accessible in space. We shall keep on trying, of course, but even if the others could be made to fire, we should still be unable to repair the port laterals.'

He did his best to answer the few more questions that followed in ways that held a balance between easy confidence and despondency. The prospect was by no means good. Before help could possibly reach them they were all going to need all the nerve and resolution they had – and out of sixteen persons some must be weaker than others.

His gaze rested again on Alice Morgan and her husband beside her. Her presence was certainly a possible source of trouble. When it came to the pinch the man would have more strain on account of her – and, most likely, fewer scruples.

Since the woman was here, she must share the consequences equally with the rest. There could be no privilege. In a sharp emergency one could afford a heroic gesture, but preferential treatment of any one person in the long ordeal which they must face would create an impossible situation. Make any allowances for her, and you would be called on to make allowances for others on health or other grounds – with heaven knew what complications to follow.

A fair chance with the rest was the best he could do for her – not, he felt, looking at her as she clutched her husband's hand and looked at him from wide eyes in a pale face, not a very good best.

He hoped she would not be the first to go under. It would be better for morale if she were not the very first....

She was not the first to go. For nearly three months nobody went.

The *Falcon*, by means of skilfully timed bursts on the main tubes, had succeeded in nudging herself into an orbital relationship with Mars. After that, there was little that the crew could do for her. At the distance of equilibrium she had become a very minor satellite, rolling and tumbling on her circular course, destined, so far as anyone could see, to continue this untidy progress until help reached them, or perhaps for ever....

Inboard, the complexity of her twisting somersaults was not perceptible unless one deliberately uncovered a port. If one did, the crazy cavortings of the universe outside produced such a sense of bewilderment that one gladly shut the cover again to preserve the illusion of stability within. Even Captain Winters and the Navigating Officer took their observations as swiftly as possible and were relieved when they had shut the whizzing constellations off the screen, and could take refuge in relativity.

For all her occupants the *Falcon* had become a small, independent world, very sharply finite in space, and scarcely less so in time.

It was, moreover, a world with a very low standard of living; a community with short tempers, weakening distempers, aching bellies, and ragged nerves. It was a group in which each man watched on a trigger of suspicion for a hairsbreadth difference in the next man's ration, and where the little he ate so avidly was not enough to quiet the rumblings of his stomach. He was ravenous when he went to sleep; more ravenous when he woke from dreams of food.

Men who had started from Earth full-bodied were now gaunt and lean, their faces had hardened from curved contours into angled planes and changed their healthy colours for a grey pallor in which their eyes glittered unnaturally. They had all grown weaker. The weakest lay on their couches torpidly. The more fortunate looked at them from time to time with a question in their eyes. It was not difficult to read the question: 'Why do we go on wasting good food on this guy? Looks like he's booked, anyway.' But as yet no one had taken up that booking.

The situation was worse than Captain Winters had foreseen. There had been bad stowage. The cans in several cases of meat had collapsed under the terrific pressure of other cans above them during take-off. The resulting mess was now describing an orbit of its own around the ship. He had had to throw it out secretly. If the men had known of it, they would have eaten it gladly, maggots and all. Another case shown on his inventory had disappeared. He still did not know how. The ship had been searched for it without trace. Much of the emergency stores consisted of dehydrated foods for which he dared not spare sufficient water, so that though edible they were painfully unattractive. They had been intended simply as a supplement in case the estimated time was overrun, and were not extensive. Little in the cargo was edible, and that mostly small cans of luxuries. As a result, he had had to reduce the rations expected to stretch meagrely over seventeen weeks. And even so, they would not last that long.

The first who did go owed it neither to sickness nor malnutrition, but to accident.

Jevons, the chief engineer, maintained that the only way to locate and correct the trouble with the laterals was to effect an entry into the propellent section of the ship. Owing to the tanks which backed up against the bulkhead separating the sections this could not be achieved from within the ship herself.

It had proved impossible with the tools available to cut a

slice out of the hull; the temperature of space and the conductivity of the hull caused all their heat to run away and dissipate itself without making the least impression on the tough skin. The one way he could see of getting in was to cut away round the burnt-out tubes of the port laterals. It was debatable whether this was worth while since the other laterals would still be unbalanced on the port side, but where he found opposition solidly against him was in the matter of using precious oxygen to operate his cutters. He had to accept that ban, but he refused to relinquish his plan altogether.

'Very well,' he said, grimly. 'We're like rats in a trap, but Bowman and I aim to do more than just keep the trap going, and we're going to try, even if we have to cut our way into the damned ship by hand.'

Captain Winters had okayed that; not that he believed that anything useful would come of it, but it would keep Jevons quiet, and do no one else any harm. So for weeks Jevons and Bowman had got into their spacesuits and worked their shifts. Oblivious after a time of the wheeling heavens about them, they kept doggedly on with their sawing and filing. Their progress, pitifully slow at best, had grown even slower as they became weaker.

Just what Bowman was attempting when he met his end still remained a mystery. He had not confided in Jevons. All that anyone knew about it was the sudden lurch of the ship and the clang of reverberations running up and down the hull. Possibly it was an accident. More likely he had become impatient and laid a small charge to blast an opening.

For the first time for weeks ports were uncovered and faces looked out giddily at the wheeling stars. Bowman came into sight. He was drifting inertly, a dozen yards or more outboard. His suit was deflated, and a large gash showed in the material of the left sleeve.

The consciousness of a corpse floating round and round you like a minor moon is no improver of already lowered morale. Push it away, and it still circles, though at a greater distance. Some day a proper ceremony for the situation would be invented – perhaps a small rocket would launch the poor remains upon their last, infinite voyage. Meanwhile, lacking a precedent, Captain Winters decided to pay the body the decent respect of having it brought inboard. The refrigeration plant had to be kept going to preserve the small remaining stocks of food, but several sections of it were empty....

A day and a night by the clock had passed since the provisional interment of Bowman when a modest knock came on the control-room door. The Captain laid blotting-paper carefully over his latest entry in the log, and closed the book.

'Come in,' he said.

The door opened just widely enough to admit Alice Morgan. She slipped in, and shut it behind her. He was somewhat surprised to see her. She had kept sedulously in the background, putting the few requests she had made through the intermediation of her husband. He noticed the changes in her. She was haggard now as they all were, and her eyes anxious. She was also nervous. The fingers of her thin hands sought one another and interlocked themselves for confidence. Clearly she was having to push herself to raise whatever was in her mind. He smiled in order to encourage her.

'Come and sit down, Mrs Morgan,' he invited, amiably.

She crossed the room with a slight clicking from her magnetic soles, and took the chair he indicated. She seated herself uneasily, and on the forward edge.

It had been sheer cruelty to bring her on this voyage, he reflected again. She had been at least a pretty little thing, now she was no longer that. Why couldn't that fool husband of hers have left her in her proper setting – a nice quiet suburb, a gentle routine, a life where she would be protected from exaction and alarm alike. It surprised him again that she had had the resolution and the stamina to survive conditions on the *Falcon* as long as this. Fate would probably have been kinder to her if it had disallowed that.

He spoke to her quietly, for she perched rather than sat, making him think of a bird ready to take off at any sudden movement.

'And what can I do for you, Mrs Morgan?'

Alice's fingers twined and intertwined. She watched them doing it. She looked up, opened her mouth to speak, closed it again.

'It isn't very easy,' she murmured apologetically.

Trying to help her, he said:

'No need to be nervous, Mrs Morgan. Just tell me what's on your mind. Has one of them been – bothering you?'

She shook her head.

'Oh, no, Captain Winters. It's nothing like that at all.'

'What is it, then?'

'It's – it's the rations, Captain. I'm not getting enough food.'

The kindly concern froze out of his face.

'None of us is,' he told her, shortly.

'I know,' she said, hurriedly. 'I know, but –'

'But what?' he inquired in a chill tone.

She drew a breath.

'There's the man who died yesterday. Bowman. I thought if I could have his rations –'

The sentence trailed away as she saw the expression on the Captain's face.

He was not acting. He was feeling just as shocked as he looked. Of all the impudent suggestions that ever had come his way, none had astounded him more. He gazed dumbfounded at the source of the outrageous proposition. Her eyes met his, but, oddly, with less timidity than before. There was no sign of shame in them.

'I've *got* to have more food,' she said, intensely.

Captain Winters' anger mounted.

'So you thought you'd just snatch a dead man's share as well as your own! I'd better not tell you in words just where I class that suggestion, young woman. But you can understand this: we share, and we share equally. What Bowman's death means to us is that we can keep on having the same ration for a little longer – that, and only that. And now I think you had better go.'

But Alice Morgan made no move to go. She sat there with her lips pressed together, her eyes a little narrowed, quite still save that her hands trembled. Even through his indignation the Captain felt surprise, as though he had watched a hearth cat suddenly become a hunter. She said stubbornly:

'I haven't asked for any privilege until now, Captain. I wouldn't ask you now if it weren't absolutely necessary. But that man's death gives us a margin now. And I *must* have more food.'

The Captain controlled himself with an effort.

'Bowman's death has *not* given us a margin, or a windfall – all it has done is to extend by a day or two the chance of our survival. Do you think that every one of us doesn't ache just as much as you do for more food? In all my considerable experience of effrontery –'

She raised her thin hand to stop him. The hardness of her eyes made him wonder why he had ever thought her timid.

'Captain. Look at me!' she said, in a harsh tone.

He looked. Presently his expression of anger faded into shocked astonishment. A faint tinge of pink stole into her pale cheeks.

'Yes,' she said. 'You see, you've *got* to give me more food. My baby *must* have the chance to live.'

The Captain continued to stare at her as if mesmerized. Presently he shut his eyes, and passed his hand over his brow.

'God in heaven. This is terrible,' he murmured.

Alice Morgan said seriously, as if she had already considered that very point:

'No. It isn't terrible – not if my baby lives.' He looked at her helplessly, without speaking. She went on:

'It wouldn't be robbing anyone, you see. Bowman doesn't need his rations any more – but my baby does. It's quite simple, really.' She looked questioningly at the Captain. He had no comment ready. She continued: 'So you couldn't call it unfair. After all, I'm two people now, really, aren't I? I *need* more food. If you don't let me have it you will be murdering my baby. So you *must* ... *must* ... My baby has *got* to live – he's got to....'

When she had gone Captain Winters mopped his forehead, unlocked his private drawer, and took out one of his carefully hoarded bottles of whisky. He had the self-restraint to take only a small pull on the drinking-tube and then put it back. It revived him a little, but his eyes were still shocked and worried.

Would it not have been kinder in the end to tell the woman that her baby had no chance at all of being born? That would have been honest; but he doubted whether the coiner of the phrase about honesty being the best policy had known a great deal about group-morale. Had he told her that, it would have been impossible to avoid telling her why, and once she knew why it would have been impossible for her not to confide it, if only to her husband. And then it would be too late.

The Captain opened the top drawer, and regarded the pistol within. There was always that. He was tempted to take hold of it now and use it. There wasn't much use in playing the silly game out. Sooner or later it would have to come to that, anyway.

He frowned at it, hesitating. Then he put out his right hand and gave the thing a flip with his finger, sending it floating to the back of the drawer, out of sight. He closed the drawer. Not yet....

But perhaps he had better begin to carry it soon. So far, his authority had held. There had been nothing worse than safety-valve grumbling. But a time would come when he was going to need the pistol either for them or for himself.

If they should begin to suspect that the encouraging bulletins that he pinned up on the board from time to time were fakes: if they should somehow find out that the rescue ship which they believed to be hurtling through space towards them had not, in fact, even yet been able to take off from Earth – that was when hell would start breaking loose.

It might be safer if there were to be an accident with the radio equipment before long. . . .

'Taken your time, haven't you?' Captain Winters asked. He spoke shortly because he was irritable, not because it mattered in the least how long anyone took over anything now.

The Navigating Officer made no reply. His boots clicked across the floor. A key and an identity bracelet drifted towards the Captain, an inch or so above the surface of his desk. He put out a hand to check them.

'I –' he began. Then he caught sight of the other's face. 'Good God, man, what's the matter with you?'

He felt some compunction. He wanted Bowman's identity bracelet for the record, but there had been no real need to send Carter for it. A man who had died Bowman's death would be a piteous sight. That was why they had left him still in his spacesuit instead of undressing him. All the same, he had thought that Carter was tougher stuff. He brought out a bottle. The last bottle.

'Better have a shot of this,' he said.

The navigator did, and put his head in his hands. The Captain carefully rescued the bottle from its mid-air drift, and put it away. Presently the Navigating Officer said, without looking up:

'I'm sorry, sir.'

'That's okay, Carter. Nasty job. Should have done it myself.'

The other shuddered slightly. A minute passed in silence while he got a grip on himself. Then he looked up and met the Captain's eyes.

'It – it wasn't just that, sir.'

The Captain looked puzzled.

'How do you mean?' he asked.

The officer's lips trembled. He did not form his words properly, and he stammered.

'Pull yourself together. What are you trying to say?' The Captain spoke sharply to stiffen him.

Carter jerked his head slightly. His lips stopped trembling.

'He – he –' he floundered; then he tried again, in a rush. 'He – hasn't any legs, sir.'

'Who? What *is* this? You mean Bowman hasn't any legs?'

'Y – yes, sir.'

'Nonsense, man. I was there when he was brought in. So were you. He had legs, all right.'

'Yes, sir. He did have legs then – but he hasn't now!'

The Captain sat very still. For some seconds there was no sound in the control-room but the clicking of the chronometer. Then he spoke with difficulty, getting no further than two words:

'You mean – ?'

'What else could it be, sir?'

'*God in heaven!*' gasped the Captain.

He sat staring with eyes that had taken on the horror that lay in the other man's. . . .

Two men moved silently, with socks over their magnetic soles. They stopped opposite the door of one of the refrigeration compartments. One of them produced a slender key. He slipped it into the lock, felt delicately with it among the wards for a moment, and then turned it with a click. As the door swung open a pistol fired twice from within the refrigerator. The man who was pulling the door sagged at the knees, and hung in mid-air.

The other man was still behind the half-opened door. He snatched a pistol from his pocket and slid it swiftly round the corner of the door, pointing into the refrigerator. He pulled the trigger twice.

A figure in a spacesuit launched itself out of the refrigerator, sailing uncannily across the room. The other man shot at it as it swept past him. The spacesuited figure collided with the opposite wall, recoiled slightly, and hung there. Before it could turn and use the pistol in its hand, the other man fired again. The figure jerked, and floated back against the wall. The man kept his pistol trained, but the spacesuit swayed there, flaccid and inert.

The door by which the men had entered opened with a sudden clang. The Navigating Officer on the threshold did not hesitate. He fired slightly after the other, but he kept on firing. . . .

When his pistol was empty the man in front of him swayed queerly, anchored by his boots; there was no other movement in him. The Navigating Officer put out a hand and steadied himself by the doorframe. Then, slowly and painfully, he made his way across to the figure in the spacesuit. There were gashes in the suit. He managed to unlock the helmet and pull it away.

The Captain's face looked somewhat greyer than undernourishment had made it. His eyes opened slowly. He said in a whisper:

'Your job now, Carter. Good luck!'

The Navigating Officer tried to answer, but there were no words, only a bubbling of blood in his throat. His hands relaxed. There was a dark stain still spreading on his uniform. Presently his body hung listlessly swaying beside his Captain's.

'I figured they were going to last a lot longer than this,' said the small man with the sandy moustache.

The man with the drawl looked at him steadily.

'Oh, you did, did you? And do you reckon your figuring's reliable?'

The smaller man shifted awkwardly. He ran the tip of his tongue along his lips.

'Well, there was Bowman. Then those four. Then the two that died. That's seven.'

'Sure. That's seven. Well?' inquired the big man softly. He was not as big as he had been, but he still had a large frame. Under his intent regard the emaciated small man seemed to shrivel a little more.

'Er – nothing. Maybe my figuring was kind of hopeful,' he said.

'Maybe. My advice to you is to quit figuring and keep on hoping. Huh?'

The small man wilted. 'Er – yes. I guess so.'

The big man looked round the living-room, counting heads.

'Okay. Let's start,' he said.

A silence fell on the rest. They gazed at him with uneasy fascination. They fidgeted. One or two nibbled at their finger nails. The big man leaned forward. He put a space-helmet, inverted, on the table. In his customary leisurely fashion he said :

'We shall draw for it. Each of us will take a paper and hold it up unopened until I give the word. *Un*opened. Got that?'

They nodded. Every eye was fixed intently upon his face.

'Good. Now one of those pieces of paper in the helmet is marked with a cross. Ray, I want you to count the pieces there and make sure that there are nine –'

'Eight!' said Alice Morgan's voice sharply.

All the heads turned towards her as if pulled by strings. The faces looked startled, as though the owners might have heard a turtle-dove roar. Alice sat embarrassed under the combined gaze, but she held herself steady and her mouth was set in a straight line. The man in charge of the proceedings studied her.

'Well, well,' he drawled. 'So you don't want to take a hand in our little game!'

'No,' said Alice.

'You've shared equally with us so far – but now we have reached this regrettable stage you don't want to?'

'No,' agreed Alice again.

He raised his eyebrows.

'You are appealing to our chivalry, perhaps?'

'No,' said Alice once more. 'I'm denying the equity of

what you call your game. The one who draws the cross dies – isn't that the plan?'

'*Pro bono publico*,' said the big man. 'Deplorable, of course, but unfortunately necessary.'

'But if *I* draw it, two must die. Do you call that equitable?' Alice asked.

The group looked taken aback. Alice waited.

The big man fumbled it. For once he was at a loss.

'Well,' said Alice, 'isn't that so?'

One of the others broke the silence to observe: 'The question of the exact stage when the personality, the soul of the individual, takes form is still highly debatable. Some have held that until there is separate existence –'

The drawling voice of the big man cut him short. 'I think we can leave that point to the theologians, Sam. This is more in the Wisdom of Solomon class. The point would seem to be that Mrs Morgan claims exemption on account of her condition.'

'My baby has a right to live,' Alice said doggedly.

'We all have a right to live. We all want to live,' someone put in.

'Why should you – ?' another began; but the drawling voice dominated again:

'Very well, gentlemen. Let us be formal. Let us be democratic. We will vote on it. The question is put: do you consider Mrs Morgan's claim to be valid – or should she take her chance with the rest of us? Those in –'

'Just a minute,' said Alice, in a firmer voice than any of them had heard her use. 'Before you start voting on that you'd better listen to me a bit.' She looked round, making sure she had the attention of all of them. She had; and their astonishment as well.

'Now the first thing is that I am a lot more important than any of you,' she told them simply. 'No, you needn't smile. I am – and I'll tell you why.

'Before the radio broke down –'

'Before the Captain wrecked it, you mean,' someone corrected her.

'Well, before it became useless,' she compromised. 'Captain Winters was in regular touch with home. He gave them news of us. The news that the Press wanted most was about me. Women, particularly women in unusual situations, are always news. He told me I was in the headlines: GIRL-WIFE IN DOOM ROCKET, WOMAN'S SPACEWRECK ORDEAL, that sort of thing. And if you haven't forgotten how newspapers look, you can imagine the leads, too: "Trapped in their living space tomb, a girl and fifteen men now wheel helplessly around the planet Mars. . . ."

'All of you are just men – hulks, like the ship, I am a woman, therefore my position is romantic, so I am young, glamorous, beautiful. . . .' Her thin face showed for a moment the trace of a wry smile. 'I am a heroine. . . .'

She paused, letting the idea sink in. Then she went on:

'I was a heroine even before Captain Winters told them that I was pregnant. But after that I became a phenomenon. There were demands for interviews, I wrote one, and Captain Winters transmitted it for me. There have been interviews with my parents and my friends, anyone who knew me. And now an enormous number of people know a great deal about me. They are intensely interested in me. They are even more interested in my baby – which is likely to be the first baby ever born in a spaceship. . . .

'Now do you begin to see? You have a fine tale ready. Bowman, my husband, Captain Winters, and the rest were heroically struggling to repair the port laterals. There was an explosion. It blew them all away out into space.

'You may get away with that. But if there is no trace of me and my baby – or of our bodies – *then* what are you going to say? How will you explain that?'

She looked round the faces again.

'Well, what *are* you going to say? That I, too, was outside repairing the port laterals? That I committed suicide by shooting myself out into space with a rocket?

'Just think it over. The whole world's press is wanting to know about me – with all the details. It'll have to be a mighty good story to stand up to that. And if it doesn't stand up – well, the rescue won't have done you much good.

'You'll not have a chance in hell. You'll hang, or you'll fry, every one of you – unless it happens they lynch you first. . . .'

There was silence in the room as she finished speaking. Most of the faces showed the astonishment of men ferociously attacked by a Pekinese, and at a loss for suitable comment.

The big man sat sunk in reflection for a minute or more. Then he looked up, rubbing the stubble on his sharpboned chin thoughtfully. He glanced round the others and then let his eyes rest on Alice. For a moment there was a twitch at the corner of his mouth.

'Madam,' he drawled, 'you are probably a great loss to the legal profession.' He turned away. 'We shall have to reconsider this matter before our next meeting. But, for the present, Ray, *eight* pieces of paper as the lady said. . . .'

'It's her!' said the Second, over the Skipper's shoulder.

The Skipper moved irritably. 'Of course it's her. What else'd you expect to find whirling through space like a sozzled owl?' He studied the screen for a moment. 'Not a sign. Every port covered.'

'Do you think there's a chance, Skipper?'

'What, after all this time! No, Tommy, not a ghost of it. We're – just the morticians, I guess.'

'How'll we get aboard her, Skip?'

The Skipper watched the gyrations of the *Falcon* with a calculating eye.

'Well, there aren't any rules, but I reckon if we can get a cable on her we *might* be able to play her gently, like a big fish. It'll be tricky, though.'

Tricky, it was. Five times the magnet projected from the rescue ship failed to make contact. The sixth attempt was better judged. When the magnet drifted close to the *Falcon* the current was switched on for a moment. It changed course, and floated nearer to the ship. When it was almost in contact the switch went over again. It darted forward, and glued itself limpet-like to the hull.

Then followed the long game of playing the *Falcon*; of keeping tension on the cable between the two ships, but not too much tension, and of holding the rescue ship from being herself thrown into a roll by the pull. Three times the cable parted, but at last, after weary hours of adroit manoeuvre by the rescue ship the derelict's motion had been reduced to a slow twist. There was still no trace of life aboard. The rescue ship closed a little.

The Captain, the Third Officer, and the doctor fastened on their spacesuits and went outboard. They made their way forward to the winch. The Captain looped a short length of line over the cable, and fastened both ends of it to his belt. He laid hold of the cable with both hands, and with a heave sent himself skimming into space. The others followed him along the guiding cable.

They gathered beside the *Falcon*'s entrance port. The Third Officer took a crank from his satchel. He inserted it in an opening, and began to turn until he was satisfied that the inner door of the airlock was closed. When it would turn no more, he withdrew it, and fitted it into the next opening; that should set the motors pumping air out of the lock – if there were air, and if there were still current to work the motors. The Captain held a microphone against the hull, and listened. He caught a humming.

'Okay. They're running,' he said.

He waited until the humming stopped.

'Right. Open her up,' he directed.

The Third Officer inserted his crank again, and wound it. The main port opened inwards, leaving a dark gap in the shining hull. The three looked at the opening sombrely for some seconds. With a grim quietness the Captain's voice said: 'Well. Here we go!'

They moved carefully and slowly into the blackness, listening.

The Third Officer's voice murmured:

'The silence that is in the starry sky,
　　The sleep that is among the lonely hills ...'

Presently the Captain's voice asked:
'How's the air, Doc?'
The doctor looked at his gauges.
'It's okay,' he said, in some surprise. 'Pressure's about six ounces down, that's all.' He began to unfasten his helmet. The others copied him. The Captain made a face as he took his off.
'The place stinks,' he said, uneasily. 'Let's – get on with it.'
He led the way towards the lounge. They entered it apprehensively.
The scene was uncanny and bewildering. Though the gyrations of the *Falcon* had been reduced, every loose object in her continued to circle until it met a solid obstruction and bounced off it upon a new course. The result was a medley of wayward items churning slowly hither and thither.
'Nobody here, anyway,' said the Captain, practically. 'Doc, do you think – ?'
He broke off at the sight of the doctor's strange expression. He followed the line of the other's gaze. The doctor was looking at the drifting flotsam of the place. Among the flow of books, cans, playing-cards, boots, and miscellaneous rubbish, his attention was riveted upon a bone. It was large and clean and had been cracked open.
The Captain nudged him. 'What's the matter, Doc?'
The doctor turned unseeing eyes upon him for a moment, and then looked back at the drifting bone.
'That' – he said in an unsteady voice – 'that, Skipper is a human femur.'
In the long moment that followed while they stared at the grisly relic the silence which had lain over the *Falcon* was broken. The sound of a voice rose, thin, uncertain, but perfectly clear. The three looked incredulously at one another as they listened:

> *'Rock-a-bye baby*
> *On the tree top*
> *When the wind blows*
> *The cradle will rock ...'*

Alice sat on the side of her bunk, swaying a little, and holding her baby to her. It smiled, and reached up one miniature hand to pat her cheek as she sang:

> *'... When the bough breaks*
> *The cradle will fall.*
> *Down will —'*

Her song cut off suddenly at the click of the opening door. For a moment she stared as blankly at the three figures in the opening as they at her. Her face was a mask with harsh lines drawn from the points where the skin was stretched tightly over the bones. Then a trace of expression came over it. Her eyes brightened. Her lips curved in a travesty of a smile.

She loosed her arms from about the baby, and it hung there in mid-air, chuckling a little to itself. She slid her right hand under the pillow of the bunk, and drew it out again, holding a pistol.

The black shape of the pistol looked enormous in her transparently thin hand as she pointed it at the men who stood transfixed in the doorway.

'Look, baby,' she said. 'Look there! Food! Lovely food. ...'

Pawley's Peepholes

WHEN I called round at Sally's I showed her the paragraph in the *Westwich Evening News*.

'What do you think of that?' I asked her.

She read it, standing, and with an impatient frown on her pretty face.

'I don't believe it,' she said, finally.

Sally's principles of belief and disbelief are a thing I've never got quite lined up. How a girl can dismiss a pack of solid evidence as though it were kettle steam, and then go and fall for some advertisement that's phoney from the first word as though it were holy writ, I just don't ... Oh, well, it keeps on happening, anyway.

This paragraph read:

MUSIC WITH A KICK

Patrons of the concert at the Adams Hall last night were astonished to see a pair of legs dangling knee-deep from the ceiling during one of the items. The whole audience saw them, and all reports agree that they were bare legs, with some kind of sandals on the feet. They remained visible for some three or four minutes, during which time they several times moved back and forth across the ceiling. Finally, after making a kicking movement, they disappeared upwards, and were seen no more. Examination of the roof shows no traces, and the owners of the Hall are at a loss to account for the phenomenon.

'It's just one more thing,' I said.

'What does it prove, anyway?' said Sally, apparently forgetful that she was not believing it.

'I don't know that – yet,' I admitted.

'Well, there you are, then,' she said.

Sometimes I get the feeling that Sally has no real respect for logic.

However, most people were thinking the way Sally was, more or less, because most people like things to stay nice and normal. But it had already begun to look to me as if there were things happening that ought to be added to-gether and make something.

The first man to bump up against it – the first I can find on record, that is – was one Constable Walsh. It may be that others before him saw things, and just put them down as a new kind of pink elephant; but Constable Walsh's idea of a top-notch celebration was a mug of strong tea with a lot of sugar, so when he came across a head sitting up on the pavement on what there was of its neck, he stopped to look at it pretty hard. The thing that really upset him, according to the report he turned in when he had run half a mile back to the station and stopped gibbering, was that it had looked back at him.

Well, it isn't good to find a head on a pavement at any time, and 2 a.m. does somehow make it worse, but as for the rest, well, you can get what looks like a reproachful glance from a cod on a slab if your mind happens to be on something else. Constable Walsh did not stop there, how-ever. *He* reported that the thing opened its mouth 'as if it was trying to say something'. If it did, he should not have mentioned it; it just naturally brought the pink elephants to mind. However, he stuck to it, so after they had examined him and taken disappointing sniffs at his breath, they sent him back with another man to show just where he had found the thing. Of course, there wasn't any head, nor blood, nor signs of cleaning up. And that's about all there was to the incident – save, doubtless, a few curt re-marks on a conduct-sheet to dog Constable Walsh's future career.

But the Constable hadn't a big lead. Two evenings later a block of flats was curdled by searing shrieks from a Mrs Rourke in No. 35, and simultaneously from a Miss Farrell who lived above her. When the neighbours arrived, Mrs Rourke was hysterical about a pair of legs that had been dangling from her bedroom ceiling, and Miss Farrell the same about an arm and shoulder that had stretched out from under her bed. But there was nothing to be seen on the ceiling, and nothing more than a discreditable amount of dust to be found under Miss Farrell's bed.

And there were a number of other incidents, too.

It was Jimmy Lindlen who works, if that isn't too strong a word for it, in the office next to mine who drew my attention to them in the first place. Jimmy collects facts. His definition of a fact is anything that gets printed in a newspaper – poor fellow. He doesn't mind a lot what subjects his facts cover as long as they look queer. I suspect that he once heard that the truth is never simple, and deduced from that that everything that's not simple must be true.

I was used to him coming into my room, full of inspiration, and didn't take much account of it, so when he brought in his first batch of cuttings about Constable Walsh and the rest I didn't ignite much.

But a few days later he was back with some more. I was a bit surprised by his playing the same kind of phenomena twice running, so I gave it a little more attention than usual.

'You see. Arms, heads, legs, torsos, all over the place. It's an epidemic. There's something behind it. *Something's happening!*' he said, as near as one can vocalize italics.

When I had read a few of them I had to admit that this time he had got hold of something where the vein of queerness was pretty constant.

A bus driver had seen the upper half of a body set up vertically in the road before him – but a bit too late. When he stopped and climbed out, sweating, to examine the mess, there was nothing there. A woman hanging out of a window, watching the street, saw another head below her doing the same, but this one was projecting out of the solid brickwork. Then there was a pair of arms that had risen out of the floor of a butcher's shop and seemed to grope for something; after a minute or two they had withdrawn into the solid cement without trace – unless one were to count some detriment to the butcher's trade. There was the man on a building job who had become aware of a strangely dressed figure standing close to him, but supported by empty air – after which he had to be helped down and sent home. Another figure was noticed between the rails in the path of a heavy goods train, but was found to have vanished without trace when the train had passed.

While I skimmed through these and some others, Jimmy stood waiting, like a soda siphon. I didn't have to say more than, 'Huh!'

'You see,' he said. 'Something *is* happening.'

'Supposing it is,' I conceded cautiously, 'then what is it?'

'The manifestation zone is limited,' Jimmy told me impressively, and produced a town plan. 'If you look where I've marked the incidents you'll see that they're grouped. Somewhere in that circle is "the focus of disturbance".' This time he managed to vocalize the inverted commas, and waited for me to register amazement.

'So?' I said. 'Disturbance of just what?'

He dodged that one.

'I've a pretty good idea now of the cause,' he told me weightily.

That was normal, though it might be a different idea an hour later.

'I'll buy it,' I offered.

'Teleportation!' he announced. 'That's what it is. Bound to come sooner or later. Now someone's on to it.'

'H'm,' I said.

'But it *must* be.' He leaned forward earnestly. 'How else'd you account for it?'

'Well, if there could be teleportation, or teleportage, or whatever it is, surely there would have to be a transmitter and some sort of reassembly station,' I pointed out. 'You couldn't expect a person or object to be kind of broadcast and then come together again in any old place.'

'But you don't *know* that,' he said. 'Besides, that's part of what I was meaning by "focus". The transmitter is somewhere else, but focused on that area.'

'If it is,' I said, 'he seems to have got his levels and positions all to hell. I wonder just what happens to a fellow who gets himself reassembled half in and half out of a brick wall?'

It's details like that that get Jimmy impatient.

'Obviously its early stages. Experimental,' he said.

It still seemed to me uncomfortable for the subject, early stages or not, but I didn't press it.

That evening was the first time I mentioned it to Sally, and, on the whole, it was a mistake. After making it quite clear that she didn't believe it, she went on to say that if it was true it was probably just another invention.

'What do you mean, "just another invention"? Why, it'd be revolutionary!' I told her.

'The wrong kind of revolution, the way we'd use it.'

'Meaning?' I asked.

Sally was in one of her withering moods. She turned on her disillusioned voice:

'We've got two ways of using inventions,' she said. 'One is to kill more people more easily: the other is to enable quick-turnover spivs to make easy money out of suckers. Maybe there are a few exceptions like X-rays, but not many. Inventions! What we do with the product of genius is first of all ram it down to the lowest common denominator and then multiply it by the vulgarest possible fraction. What a century! What a world! When I think what other centuries are going to say about ours it makes me go hot all over.'

'I shouldn't worry. You won't be hearing them,' I said.

The withering eye was on me.

'I should have known. That is a remark well up to the Twentieth-Century standard.'

'You're a funny girl,' I told her. 'I mean, the way you think may be crazy, but you do do it, in your own way. Now most girl's futures are all cloud-cuckoo beyond next season's hat or next year's baby. Outside of that it might be going to snow split atoms for all they care – they've got a comforting feeling deep down that nothing's ever changed much, or ever will.'

'A lot you know about what most girls think,' said Sally.

'That's what I was meaning. How could I?' I said.

She seemed to have set her mind so firmly against the whole business that I dropped it for the evening.

A couple of days later Jimmy looked into my room again.

'He's laid off,' he said.

'Who's laid off what?'

'This teleporting fellow. Not a report later than Tuesday. Maybe he knows somebody's on to him.'

'Meaning you?' I asked.

'Maybe.'

'Well, are you?'

He frowned. 'I've started. I took the bearings on the map of all the incidents, and the fix came on All Saints' Church. I had a look all over the place, but I didn't find anything. Still, I must be close – why else'd he stop?'

I couldn't tell him that. Nor could anyone else. But that very evening there was a paragraph about an arm and a leg that some woman had watched travel along her kitchen wall. I showed it to Sally.

'I expect it will turn out to be some new kind of advertisement,' she said.

'A kind of secret advertising?' I suggested. Then, seeing the withering look working up again: 'How about going to a picture?' I suggested.

It was overcast when we went in; when we came out it was raining hard. Seeing that there was less than a mile to her place, and all the taxis in the town were apparently busy, we decided to walk it. Sally pulled on the hood of her mackintosh, put her arm through mine, and we set out through the rain. For a bit we didn't talk, then:

'Darling,' I said, 'I know that I can be regarded as a frivolous person with low ethical standards, but has it ever occurred to you what a field there is there for reform?'

'Yes,' she said, decisively, but not in the right tone.

'What I mean is,' I told her patiently, 'if you happened to be looking for a good work to devote your life to, what

could be better than a reclamation job on such a character.
The scope is tremendous, just –'

'Is this a proposal of some kind?' Sally inquired.

'*Some* kind! I'd have you know – Good God!' I broke
off.

We were in Tyler Street. A short street, rainswept now,
and empty, except for ourselves. What stopped me was the
sudden appearance of some kind of vehicle, further along.
I couldn't make it out very clearly on account of the rain,
but I had the impression of a small, low-built lorry with
several figures in light clothes on it driving across Tyler
Street quite quickly, and vanishing. That wouldn't have
been so bad if there were any street crossing Tyler Street,
but there isn't; it had just come out of one side and gone
into the other.

'Did you see what I saw?' I asked.

'But how on earth – ?' she began.

We walked a little further until we came to the place
where the thing had crossed, and looked at the solid brick
wall on one side and the housefronts on the other.

'You must have been mistaken,' said Sally.

'Well, for – *I* must have been mistaken!'

'But it just couldn't have happened, could it?'

'Now, listen, darling –' I began.

But at that moment a girl stepped out from the solid
brick about ten feet ahead of us. We stopped, and gaped
at her.

I don't know whether her hair would be her own, art
and science together can do so much for a girl, but the way
she was wearing it, it was like a great golden chrysanthe-
mum a good foot and a half across, and with a red flower
set in it a little left of centre. It looked sort of top-heavy.
She was wearing some kind of brief pink tunic, silk perhaps, and more appropriate to one of those elderly gentleman floor-shows than Tyler Street on a filthy wet night.
What made it a real shocker was the things that had been
achieved by embroidery. I never would have believed that

any girl could – oh, well, anyway, there she stood, and there we stood. . . .

When I say 'she stood', she certainly did, but somehow she did it about six inches above ground level. She looked at us both, then she stared back at Sally just as hard as Sally was staring at her. It must have been some seconds before any of us moved. The girl opened her mouth as if she were speaking, but no sound came. Then she shook her head, made a forget-it gesture, and turned and walked back into the wall.

Sally didn't move. With the rain shining on her mackintosh she looked like a black statue. When she turned so that I could see her face under the hood it had an expression I had never seen there before. I put my arm round her, and found that she was trembling.

'I'm scared, Jerry,' she said.

'No need for that, Sal. There's bound to be a simple explanation of some kind,' I said, falsely.

'But it's more than that, Jerry. Didn't you see her face? She was exactly like me!'

'She was pretty much like –' I conceded.

'Jerry, she was *exactly* like – I'm – I'm scared.'

'Must have been some trick of the light. Anyway, she's gone now,' I said.

All the same, Sally was right. That girl was the image of herself. I've wondered about that quite a bit since . . .

Jimmy brought a copy of the morning paper into my room next day. It carried a brief, facetious leader on the number of local citizens who had been seeing things lately.

'They're beginning to take notice, at last,' he proclaimed.

'How's your own line going?' I asked.

He frowned. 'I'm afraid it can't be quite the way I thought. I reckon it *is* still in the experimental stage, all right, but the transmitter may not be in these parts at all. It could be that this is just the area he has trained it on for tests.'

'But why here?'

'How would I know? It has to be somewhere – and the transmitter itself could be anywhere.' He paused, struck by a portentous thought. 'It might be really serious. Suppose the Russians had a transmitter which could project people – or bombs – here by teleportation. . . ?'

'Why here?' I said again. 'I should have thought that Harwell or a Royal Arsenal –'

'Experimental, so far,' he reminded me.

'Oh,' I said, abashed. I went on to tell him what Sally and I had seen the previous night. 'She sort of didn't look much like the way I think of Russians,' I added.

Jimmy shook his head. 'Might be camouflage. After all, behind that curtain they have to get their idea of the way our girls look mostly from magazines and picture papers,' he pointed out.

The next day, after about seventy-five per cent of its readers had written in to tell about the funny things they had been seeing, the *News* dropped the facetious angle. In two days more, the thing had become factional, dividing sharply into what you might call the Classical and Modern camps. In the latter, schismatic groups argued the claims of teleportage against three-dimensional projection, or some theory of spontaneous molecular assembly: in the former, opinions could be sorted as beliefs in a ghostly invasion, a suddenly acquired visibility of habitually wandering spirits, or the imminence of Judgement Day. In the heat of debate it was rapidly becoming difficult to tell who had seen how much of what, and who was enthusiastically bent on improving his case at some expense of fact.

On Saturday Sally and I met for lunch. Afterwards, we started off in the car for a little place in the hills which seemed to me an ideal spot for a proposal. But at the main crossing in the High Street the man in front jumped on his brakes. So did I, and the man behind me. The one behind him didn't quite. There was an interesting crunch of metal going on on the other side of the crossing, too. I stood up to see what it was all about, and then pulled Sally up beside me.

'Here we go again,' I said. 'Look!'

Slap in the middle of the crossing was – well, you could scarcely call it a vehicle – it was more like a flat trolley or platform, about a foot off the ground. And when I say off the ground, I mean just that. No wheels, or legs. It kind of hung there, from nothing. Standing on it, dressed in coloured things like long shirts or smocks, were half a dozen men looking interestedly around them. Along the edge of the platform was lettered: PAWLEY'S PEEP-HOLES. One of the men was pointing out All Saints' Church to another; the rest were paying more attention to the cars and the people. The policeman on duty was hanging a goggling face over the edge of his traffic-control box. Then he pulled himself together. He shouted, he blew his whistle, then he shouted again. The men on the platform took no notice at all. The policeman got out of his box and went across the road looking like a volcano that had seen a nice place to erupt.

'Hey!' he shouted to them.

It didn't worry them, but when he got within a yard or two of them they noticed him, and they nudged one another, and grinned. The policeman's face was purplish, he spoke to them luridly, but they just went on watching him with amused interest. He reached a truncheon out of his back pocket, and went closer. He grabbed at a fellow in a yellow shirt – and his arm went right through him.

The policeman stepped back. You could see his nostrils sort of spread, the way a horse's do. Then he took a firmer hold of his truncheon and made a fine circular sweep at the lot of them. They kept on grinning back at him as the stick went through them.

I take off my hat to that policeman. He didn't run. He stared at them for a moment with a very queer expression on his face, then he turned, and walked deliberately back to his box; just as deliberately he signalled the north-south traffic across. The man ahead of me was ready for it. He drove right at, and through, the platform. It began to move, but I'd have nicked it myself, had it been nickable. Sally, looking back, said that it slid away on a curve and disappeared through the front of the Penny Savings Bank.

When we got to the spot I'd had in mind the weather had come over bad to make the place look dreary and unpropitious, so we drove about a bit, and then back to a nice quiet roadside restaurant just outside Westwich. I was getting the conversation round to the mood where I wanted it when who should come across to our table but Jimmy.

'Fancy meeting you two!' he said. 'Did you hear what happened at the Crossing this afternoon, Jerry?'

'We were there,' I told him.

'You know, Jerry, this is something bigger than we thought – a whole lot bigger. That platform thing. These people are away ahead of us technically. Do you know what I reckon they are?'

'Martians?' I suggested.

He stared at me, taken aback. 'Now, how on earth did *you* guess that?' he said, amazedly.

'I sort of saw it had to come,' I admitted. 'But,' I added, 'I do have a kind of feeling that Martians wouldn't be labelled "Pawley's Peepholes".'

'Oh, were they? Nobody told me that,' said Jimmy.

He went away sadly, but even by breaking in at all he had wrecked the mood I'd been building up.

On Monday morning our typist, Anna, arrived even more scatterated than commonly.

'The most terrible thing happened to me,' she told us as soon as she was inside the door. 'Oh, dear. And did I blush all over!'

'*All* over?' inquired Jimmy interestedly.

She scorned him.

'There I was in my bath, and when I happened to look up there was a man in a green shirt, standing watching me. Of course, I screamed, at once.'

'Of course,' agreed Jimmy. 'Very proper. And what happened then, or shouldn't we –'

'He just stood there,' said Anna. 'Then he sniggered, and walked away *through the wall*. Was I mortified!'

'Very mortifying thing, a snigger,' Jimmy agreed.

Anna explained that it was not entirely the snigger that had mortified her. 'What I mean is,' she said, 'things like that oughtn't to be allowed. If a man is going to be able to walk through a girl's bathroom wall, where is he going to stop?'

Which seemed a pretty fair question.

The boss arrived just then. I followed him into his room. He wasn't looking happy.

'What the hell's going on in this damned town, Jerry?' he demanded. 'Wife comes home yesterday. Finds two incredible girls in the sitting-room. Thinks it's something to do with me. First bust-up in twenty years. In the middle of it girls vanish,' he said succinctly.

One couldn't do more than make a few sympathetic sounds.

That evening when I went to see Sally I found her sitting on the steps of the house, in the drizzle.

'What on earth –?' I began.

She gave me a bleak look.

'Two of them came into my room. A man and a girl. They wouldn't go. They just laughed at me. Then they started to behave just as though I weren't there. It got – well, I just couldn't stay, Jerry.'

She went on looking miserable, and then suddenly burst into tears.

From then on it was stepped up. There was a brisk, if one-sided, engagement in the High Street next morning. Miss Dotherby, who comes of one of Westwich's most respected families, was outraged in every lifelong principle by the appearance of four mop-headed girls who stood giggling on the corner of Northgate. Once she had retracted her eyes and got her breath back, she knew her duty. She gripped her umbrella as if it had been her grand-father's sword, and advanced. She sailed through them, smiting right and left – and when she turned round they were laughing at her. She swiped wildly through them again, and they kept on laughing. Then she started bab-bling, so someone called an ambulance to take her away.

By the end of the day the town was full of mothers crying shame and men looking staggered, and the Town Clerk and the police were snowed under with demands for some-body to do something about it.

The trouble seemed to come thickest in the district that Jimmy had originally marked out. You *could* meet them elsewhere, but in that area you couldn't help encountering gangs of them, the men in coloured shirts, the girls with their amazing hair-do's and even more amazing decora-tions on their shirts, sauntering arm-in-arm out of walls, and wandering indifferently through cars and people alike. They'd pause anywhere to point things out to one another and go off into helpless roars of silent laughter. What tickled them most was when people got angry with them. They'd make signs and faces at the stuffier sort until they got them tearing mad – and the madder, the funnier. They ambled as the spirit took them, through shops and banks, and offices, and homes, without a care for the raging occu-pants. Everybody started putting up 'Keep Out' signs; that amused them a lot, too.

It didn't seem as if you could be free of them anywhere in the central area, though they appeared to be operating on levels that weren't always the same as ours. In some places they did have the look of walking on the ground or floor, but elsewhere they'd be inches above it, and then in some places you would encounter them moving along as though they were wading through the solid surface. It was very soon clear that they could no more hear us than we could hear them, so that there was no use appealing to them or threatening them in that way, and none of the notices that people put up seemed to do anything but whet their curiosity.

After three days of it there was chaos. In the worst affected parts there just wasn't any privacy any more. At the most intimate moments they were liable to wander through, visibly sniggering or guffawing. It was all very well for the police to announce that there was no danger, that the visitants appeared unable actually to *do* anything, so the best way was to ignore them. There are times and places when giggling bunches of youth and maidens demand more ignore-power than the average person has got. It could send even a placid fellow like me wild at times, while the women's leagues of this-and-that, and the watch-committee minded were living in a constant state of blown tops.

The news had begun to get about, and that didn't help, either. News collectors of all kinds came streaming in. They overflowed the place. The streets were snaked with leads to movie cameras, television cameras, and microphones, while the press-photographers were having the snappy-picture time of their lives, and, being solid, they were almost as much of a nuisance as the visitants themselves.

But we hadn't reached the peak of it yet. Jimmy and I happened to be present at the inception of the next stage. We were on our way to lunch, doing our best to ignore visitants, as instructed, by walking through them. Jimmy was subdued. He had had to give up theories because the facts had largely submerged him. Just short of the café we noticed that there was some commotion further up the High Street, and seemingly it was coming our way, so we waited for it. After a bit it emerged through a tangle of halted cars further down, and approached at a rate of some six or seven miles an hour. Essentially it was a platform like the one that Sally and I had seen at the crossroads the previous Saturday, but this was a de luxe model. There were sides to it, glistening with new paint, red, yellow, and blue, enclosing seats set four abreast. Most of the passengers were young, though there was a sprinkling of middle-aged men and women dressed in a soberer version of the same fashions. Behind the first platform followed half a dozen others. We read the lettering on their sides and backs as they went by:

> *Pawley's Peepholes on the Past — Greatest Invention of the age*
> *History Without Tears — for £1*
> *See How Great Great Grandma Lived*
> *Ye Quainte Olde 20th Century Expresse*
> *See Living History in Comfort — Quaint Dresses, Old Customs*
> *Educational! Learn Primitive Folkways — Living Conditions*
> *Visit Romantic 20th Century — Safety Guaranteed*
> *Know Your History — Get Culture — £1 Trip*
> *Big Money Prize if you Identify Own Granddad/Ma*

Most of the people on the vehicles were turning their heads this way and that in gog-eyed wonder interspersed with spasms of giggles. Some of the young men waved their arms at us and produced silent witticisms which sent their companions into inaudible shrieks of laughter. Others leant back comfortably, bit into large, yellow fruits, and munched. They cast occasional glances at the scene, but reserved most of their attention for the ladies whose waists they clasped. On the back of the next-to-last car we read:

> *Was Great Great Grandma as Good as she Made Out?*
> *See the Things Your Family History Never Told You*

and on the final one:

> *Spot the Famous before they got Careful — The Real Inside Dope may win you a Big Prize!*

As the procesion moved away, it left the rest of us looking at one another kind of stunned. Nobody seemed to have much left to say just then.

The show must have been something in the nature of a grand premiere, I fancy, for after that you were liable anywhere in the town to come across a platform labelled something like:

History is Culture – Broaden Your Mind Today for only £1!

or:

Know the Answers About Your Ancestors

with full, good-time loads aboard, but I never heard of another regular procession.

In the Council Offices they were tearing what was left of their hair, and putting up notices left, right, and centre about what was not allowed to the 'tourists' – and giving them more good laughs – but all the while the thing got more embarrassing. Those 'tourists' who were on foot took to coming close up and peering into your face, and comparing it with some book or piece of paper they were carrying – after which they looked disappointed and annoyed with you, and moved on to someone else. I came to the conclusion there was no prize at all for finding me.

Well, work has to go on: we couldn't think of any way of dealing with it, so we had to put up with it. Quite a number of families moved out of the town for privacy and to stop their daughters from catching the new ideas about dress, and so on, but most of us just had to keep along as best we could. Pretty nearly everyone one met those days looked either dazed or scowling – except, of course, the 'tourists'.

I called for Sally one evening about a fortnight after the platform procession. When we came out of the house there was a ding-dong going on further down the road. A couple of girls with heads that looked like globes of gilded basketwork were scratching the daylights out of one another. One of the fellows standing by was looking proud of himself, the rest of the party was whooping things on. We went the other way.

'It just isn't like our town any more,' said Sally. 'Even our homes aren't ours any more. Why can't they all go away and leave us in peace? Oh, damn them, all of them! I hate them!'

But just outside the park we came upon one little chrysanthemum-head sitting on apparently nothing at all, and crying her heart out. Sally softened a little.

'Perhaps they are human, some of them. But what right have they to turn our town into a horrible fun-fair?'

We found a bench and sat on it, looking at the sunset. I wanted to get her away out of the place.

'It'd be grand away in the hills now,' I said.

'It'd be lovely to be there, Jerry,' she sighed.

I took her hand, and she didn't pull it away.

'Sally, darling –' I began.

And then, before I could get any further, two tourists, a man and a girl, had to come along and anchor themselves in front of us. That time I was angry. You might see the platforms almost anywhere, but you did reckon to be free of the walking tourists in the park where there was nothing to interest them, anyway – or should not have been. These two, however, had found something. It was Sally, and they stood staring at her, unabashed. She took her hand out of mine. They conferred. The man opened a folder he was carrying, and took a piece of paper out of it. They looked at the paper, then at Sally, then back to the paper. It was too much to ignore. I got up and walked through them to see what the paper was. There I had a surprise. It was a piece of the *Westwich Evening News*, obviously taken from a very ancient copy indeed. It was badly browned and tattered, and to keep it from falling to bits entirely it had been mounted inside some thin, transparent plastic. I wish I had noticed the date, but naturally enough I looked where they were looking – and Sally's face looked back at me from a smiling photograph. She had her arms spread

wide, and a baby in the crook of each. I had just time to see
the headline: 'Twins for Town Councillor's Wife', when
they folded up the paper, and made off along the path,
running. I reckoned they would be hot on the trail of one
of their damned prizes – and I hoped it would turn round
and bite them.

I went back and sat down again beside Sally. That picture certainly had spoilt things – 'Councillor's Wife'!
Naturally she wanted to know what I'd seen on the paper,
and I had to sharpen up a few lies to cut my way out of
that one.

We sat on awhile, feeling gloomy, saying nothing.

A platform went by, labelled:

*Trouble free Culture – Get Educated in Modern Com-
fort*

We watched it glide away through the railings and into
the traffic.

'Maybe it's time we moved,' I suggested.

'Yes,' agreed Sally, dully.

We walked back towards her place, me still wishing that
I had been able to see the date on that paper.

'You wouldn't,' I asked her casually, 'you wouldn't happen to know any Councillors?'

She looked surprised.

'Well – there's Mr Falmer,' she said, rather doubtfully.

'He'd be a – a youngish man?' I inquired, off-handedly.

'Why, no. He's ever so old – as a matter of fact, it's really
his wife I know.'

'Ah!' I said. 'You don't know any of the younger ones?'

'I'm afraid not. Why?'

I put over a line about a situation like this needing
young men of ideas.

'Young men of ideas don't have to be councillors,' she
remarked, looking at me.

Maybe, as I said, she doesn't go much on logic, but she

has her own ways of making a fellow feel better. I'd have
felt better still if I had had some ideas, though.

The next day found public indignation right up the
scale again. It seems there had been an evening service
going on in All Saints' Church. The vicar had ascended his
pupit and was just drawing breath for a brief sermon when
a platform labelled:

> Was Gt Gt Granddad one of the Boys? – Our £1 Trip
> may Show you

floated in through the north wall and slid to a stop in front
of the lectern. The vicar stared at it for some seconds in
silence, then he crashed his fist down on his reading
desk.

'This,' he boomed. 'This is *intolerable*! We shall wait
until this *object* is removed.'

He remained motionless, glaring at it. The congregation
glared with him.

The tourists on the platform had an air of waiting for
the show to begin. When nothing happened they started
passing round bottles and fruit to while away the time. The
vicar maintained his stony glare. When still nothing happened the tourists began to get bored. The young men
tickled the girls, and the girls giggled them on. Several of
them began to urge the man at the front end of their craft.
After a bit he nodded, and the platform slid away through
the south wall.

It was the first point our side had ever scored. The vicar
mopped his brow, cleared his throat, and then extempor-
ized the address of his life, on the subject of 'The Cities of
the Plain'.

But no matter how influential the tops that were blow-
ing, there was still nothing getting done about it. There
were schemes, of course. Jimmy had one of them: it concerned either ultra-high or infra-low frequencies that were

going to shudder the projections of the tourists to bits.
Perhaps something along those lines might have been
worked out sometime, but it was a quicker kind of cure
that we were needing; and it is damned difficult to know
what you can do about something which is virtually no
more than a three-dimensional movie portrait unless you
can think up some way of fouling its transmission. All its
functions are going on not where you see it, but in some
unknown place where the origin is – so how do you get at
it? What you are actually seeing doesn't feel, doesn't eat,
doesn't breathe, doesn't sleep ... It was while I was considering what it actually does do that I had my idea. It
struck me all of a heap – so simple. I grabbed my hat and
took off for the Town Hall.

By this time the daily processions of sizzling citizens,
threateners, and cranks had made them pretty cautious
about callers there, but I worked through at last to a man
who got interested, though doubtful.

'No one's going to like that much,' he said.

'No one's meant to like it. But it couldn't be much worse
than this – and it's likely to do local trade a bit of good,
too,' I pointed out.

He brightened a bit at that. I pressed on:

'After all, the Mayor has his restaurants, and the pubs'll
be all for it, too.'

'You've got a point there,' he admitted. 'Very well, we'll
put it to them. Come along.'

For the whole of three days we worked hard on it. On
the fourth we went into action. Soon after daylight there
were gangs out on all the roads fixing barriers at the muni-
cipal limits, and when they'd done that they put up big
white boards lettered in red:

WESTWICH
THE CITY THAT LOOKS AHEAD
COME AND SEE
IT'S BEYOND THE MINUTE — NEWER THAN TOMORROW
SEE
THE WONDER CITY OF THE AGE
TOLL (Non-Residents) 2/6

The same morning the television permission was revoked, and the national papers carried large display advertisements:

COLOSSAL! — UNIQUE! — EDUCATIONAL!
WESTWICH
presents the only authentic
FUTURAMATIC SPECTACLE

WANT TO KNOW:

What Your Great Great Granddaughter will Wear?
How Your Great Great Grandson will Look?
Next Century's Styles?
How Customs will Change?

COME TO WESTWICH AND SEE FOR YOURSELF
THE OFFER OF THE AGES
THE FUTURE for 2/6

We reckoned that with the publicity there had been already there'd be no need for more detail than that — though we ran some more specialized advertisements in the picture dailies:

WESTWICH
GIRLS! GIRLS!! GIRLS!!!
THE SHAPES TO COME
SAUCY FASHIONS — CUTE WAYS
ASTONISHING — AUTHENTIC — UNCENSORED
GLAMOUR GALORE FOR 2/6

and so on. We bought enough space to get it mentioned in the news columns in order to help those who like to think they are doing things for sociological, psychological, and other intellectual reasons.

And they came.

There had been quite a few looking in to see the sights before, but now they learnt that it was something worth charging money for the figures jumped right up – and the more they went up, the gloomier the Council Treasurer got because we hadn't made it five shillings, or even ten.

After a couple of days we had to take over all vacant lots, and some fields further out, for car parks, and people were parking far enough out to need a special bus service to bring them in. The streets became so full of crowds stooging around greeting any of Pawley's platforms or tourists with whistles, jeers, and catcalls, that local citizens simply stayed indoors and did their smouldering there.

The Treasurer began to worry now over whether we'd be liable for Entertainment Tax. The list of protests to the Mayor grew longer each day, but he was so busy arranging special convoys of food and beer for his restaurants that he had little time to worry about them. Nevertheless, after a few days of it I started to wonder whether Pawley wasn't going to see us out, after all. The tourists didn't care for it much, one could see, and it must have interfered a lot with their prize-hunts, but it hadn't cured them of wandering about all over the place, and now we had the addition of thousands of trippers whooping it up with pandemonium for most of the night. Tempers all round were getting short enough for real trouble to break out.

Then, on the sixth night, when several of us were just beginning to wonder whether it might not be wiser to clear out of Westwich for a bit, the first crack showed – a man at the Town Hall rang me up to say he had seen several platforms with empty seats on them.

The next night I went down to one of their regular routes to see for myself. I found a large, well-lubricated

crowd already there, exchanging cracks and jostling and
shoving, but we hadn't long to wait. A platform slid out on
a slant through the front of the Coronation Café, and the
label on it read:

CHARM & ROMANCE OF 20TH CENTURY – 15/-

and there were half a dozen empty seats, at that.

The arrival of the platform brought a well-supported
Bronx cheer, and a shrilling of whistles. The driver remained indifferent as he steered straight through the
crowds. His passengers looked less certain of themselves.
Some of them did their best to play up; they giggled, made
motions of returning slap for slap and grimace for grimace
with the crowd to start with. Possibly it was as well that the
tourist girls couldn't hear the things the crowd was shout-
ing to them, but some of the gestures were clear enough. It
couldn't have been a lot of fun gliding straight into the
men who were making them. By the time the platform was
clear of the crowd and disappearing through the front of
the Bon Marché pretty well all the tourists had given up
pretending that it was; some of them were looking a little
sick. By the expression on several of the faces I reckoned
that Pawley might be going to have a tough time explaining the culture aspect of it to a deputation somewhere.

The next night there were more empty seats than full
ones, and someone reported that the price had come down
to 10s.

The night after that they did not show up at all, and we
all had a busy time with the job of returning the half-
crowns, and refusing claims for wasted petrol.

And the next night they didn't come, either; or the one
after that; so then all we had to do was to pitch into the job
of cleaning up Westwich, and the affair was practically
over – apart from the longer term business of living down
the reputation the place had been getting lately.

At least, we say it's over. Jimmy, however, maintains that that is probably only the way it looks from here. According to him, all they had to do was to modify out the visibility factor that was causing the trouble, so it's possible that they are still touring around here – and other places.

Well, I suppose he could be right. Perhaps that fellow Pawley, whoever he is, or will be, has a chain of his fun-fairs operating all round the world and all through history at this very moment. But we don't know – and, as long as he keeps them out of sight, I don't know that we care a lot, either.

Pawley has been dealt with as far as we are concerned. He was a case for desperate measures; even the vicar of All Saints' appreciated that; and undoubtedly he had a point to make when he began his address of thanksgiving with: 'Paradoxical, my friends, paradoxical can be the workings of vulgarity...'

Once it was settled I was able to make time to go round and see Sally again. I found her looking brighter than she'd been for weeks, and lovelier on account of it. She seemed pleased to see me, too.

'Hullo, Jerry,' she said. 'I've just been reading in the paper how you organized the plan for getting rid of them. I think it was just wonderful of you.'

A little time ago I'd probably have taken that for a cue, but it was no trigger now. I sort of kept on seeing her with her arms full of twins, and wondering in a dead-inside way how they got there.

'There wasn't a lot to it, darling,' I told her modestly. 'Anyone else might have hit on the idea.'

'That's as maybe – but a whole lot of people don't think so. And I'll tell you another thing I heard today. They're going to ask you to stand for the Council, Jerry.'

'Me on the Council. That'd be a big laugh –' I began. Then I stopped suddenly. 'If – I mean, would that mean I'd be called "Councillor"?' I asked her.

'Why – well, yes, I suppose so,' she said, looking puzzled. Things shimmered a bit.

'Er – Sally, darling – er, sweetheart, there's – er – something I've been trying to get round to saying to you for quite a time . . .' I began.

Opposite Number

SEEING the couple when I did was simply a matter of chance. Probably I should have run across them just a little later, anyway, but the results could have been quite different. It simply happened that I turned into the cross-corridor when they were up the other end of it, with their backs towards me, and I noticed them peering up and down the far main-passage in the manner of people making sure that the coast was clear. Jean I recognized at once; even the distant glimpse of her profile was enough. Of the man, with his back towards me, I registered only that there was something familiar about him.

But for the furtive, scouting look about them I doubt whether I should have paid much attention – at least, I should not have followed them – but once I had noticed that, it occurred to me that there was only one place they could have come from, and that was old Whetstone's room – it is still known as 'old Whetstone's room' although he died more than two years ago.

There wasn't any reason why Jean shouldn't go there if she wanted to. After all, since Whetstone was her father, all the stuff in the room is, legally speaking, hers – although in point of fact it just stays there under dustsheets because nobody has liked to start taking it to pieces. The old man was always greatly respected for his work – his official work in the labs up above, and although he was undoubtedly a bit – well, let's say obsessed, by his own project, and in spite of the fact that the project never did, nor ever seemed likely to do, what he wanted it to; yet, somehow, his prestige still protects the room and the apparatus. It is a kind of temporary memorial to him .

Besides, there is an idea among the several of us who helped him at different times that he really was on to something. There were some results, of a kind, enough, anyway, to suggest that if the old mule hadn't been so stubborn on his own theory he might have got somewhere by following them up. So this feeling, that some day someone with the time and inclination might find something there, has helped in keeping the room and the stuff just as he left it.

But I couldn't imagine any reason why Jean should want to be furtive about visiting the room – except, of course, that whoever her companion was, he wasn't her husband ...

I shall have to admit that when I turned off my intended way and followed them, it was out of sheer snooping curiosity. After all, it was Jean, not anybody else, and I couldn't imagine her having the kind of hole and corner affair that had to be conducted in a dusty workroom among sheet-shrouded apparatus; so why ... ?

When I looked round the corner they were well along the passage; not exactly furtive now, but still circumspect. I noticed him catch her hand, and press it encouragingly. I let them get round the next corner, and followed.

When I reached the door they were half-way across the quadrangle in the direction of the canteen; not furtive at all now, but looking about them at all the people in sight as though they might be searching for someone. I was still too far off to identify the man. They went into the canteen, and I followed.

They hadn't sat down at a table; they were standing a little way up the hall, with their backs to me, and from the way they were turning their heads there could be no doubt that they were searching. One or two people waved to them, and they waved back, but they didn't go to join them.

I began to feel a little foolish – and a trifle mean, too. Indeed, their business was none of mine, and there was nothing whatever clandestine about them now. I had just made up my mind to go back out when I caught my first good look at the man's face, in one of the wall-mirrors. There was something quite startlingly familiar about it, yet I failed to place it immediately: in fact, several seconds must have elapsed before I realized that it was the face I was accustomed to see every morning while I shaved.

The likeness was so exact that I sat down on the nearest chair, with an odd weakness in my knees, and feeling, for some reason I didn't understand, a little scared.

He was still looking over the other people. If he had seen me through the looking-glass he'd not been interested. They both walked slowly on up the room, searching it as they went. Finally, they left by the door at the other end. I slipped back by the door behind me, and worked round the outside of the building. They had come to a stop on the gravel spread, a few yards from the door, and were deep in discussion.

I was tempted to go up to them, but – well, it was some time since Jean and I had been on chatting terms: and there is something rather fatuous about the idea of going up to a perfect stranger simply to announce: 'I say, you look just like me, you know!' So I waited.

Presently they came to a decision, and turned along the path that leads to the main gate. Jean was pointing things out, and seemed amused by them, though I couldn't see why they should amuse her. She moved closer to him, and linked her arm in his as they walked along.

I must say I considered that unwise. The Pleybell Research Institute holds together one of those intraregarding, not to say ingrowing, communities where nothing is missed. The unemployed wives can follow scents that would baffle a bloodhound, and the turn of an eye, let alone a hand on the arm, is enough to start people building law courts in the air. The gesture, though possibly innocent, became almost flamboyant bravado in our milieu. I was not the only one to observe it. Indeed, people seemed to be in a rather observing mood that afternoon: several of them gave me an intense and rather puzzled look as we met.

Outside the gates the pair turned left, and I let them get a little further ahead – not that it greatly mattered, for even if Jean should look back and notice me, what more natural than that I should be found on a part of my regular homeward route? They had just turned the second corner to the right, which is that of the road in which my house stands, when there came a thudding of feet behind me, and a voice gasping: 'Mr Ruddle! Mr Ruddle, sir!' I turned to find one of the lab messengers. Through gasps he said:

'The Director saw you leaving, sir. He sent me to remind you that he must have your figures for the final co-ordination by five. He thought you might have forgotten it, sir.'

Which was what I had done. I looked at my watch, and saw that it was getting on for four-thirty already. That drove Jean and her friend out of my mind, and I hurried back towards the Institute.

There were only a couple of minor calculations to finish off, and I had the results in the Director's office by four fifty-five. He looked at me rather hard.

'I am sorry to intrude business upon your – ah – domestic arrangements, Ruddle, but it is quite necessary that all these findings should be assembled tonight,' he said, rather coldly, I thought.

I apologized for leaving it until the last minute. He received that somewhat coldly, too, considering that I was the right side of the last minute. It was not until I was outside his room that a possible explanation occurred to me. Even I had been surprised by the extraordinary likeness of Jean's companion to myself: it was scarcely a matter where I could make a mistake as to which was which, but others might . . . I recalled the arm-in-arm progress in full public view. . . .

The best thing to do seemed to be to get home as quickly as possible, hoping to put my word in before gossip said hers. . . .

There was only another twenty yards before I should reach my house, when I encountered Jean and her companion turning out of my own gateway, and we came face to face. Jean was looking flushed and embarrassed, and he was looking embarrassed and angry. Their expressions changed with astonishing speed as they recognized me.

'Oh, there you are! Thank goodness,' said Jean. 'Where on earth have you been?'

It was not the kind of opening I was prepared for. After all, it was nearly three years since we had exchanged anything more than a necessary politeness. While I was trying to collect myself I took refuge in a touch of dignity.

'I don't think I quite understand,' I said, and looked from her to her companion. 'Perhaps you will introduce me to your friend –?' I suggested.

'Oh, don't be so stiff and silly, Peter,' she told me impatiently.

But the man was looking at me closely. There was a rather curious expression on his face: I did not greatly wonder at it; very likely the expression on my own was no less curious. For the similarity – no, it was more than that – the duplication, was uncanny. The clothes were different, certainly. I had none like those he was wearing, but apart from that . . . I suddenly caught sight of his wrist-watch: it, and the metal bracelet that held it were the exact double of mine. I felt my own wrist to make sure that it hadn't somehow got transferred. My own was still there, all right. He said:

'I'm afraid this is a bit complicated. And we've both pulled a most frightful gaff in your house. Both feet, right up to the neck. I'm terribly sorry. We just didn't know.'

'*Oh!* That *woman*!' said Jean, furiously. 'Oh, I could strangle her, cheerfully.'

With a feeling of drowning slowly, I gasped.

'What woman?' I inquired.

'The one in your house. That dreadful Tenter woman.'

I stared at them.

'Look here!' I said. 'This is going a bit far. My wife is –'

'She *is*? She said she was, but I couldn't believe it. Oh, Peter, not really! You couldn't marry *her*! Oh, you *couldn't*!'

I looked at her hard – clearly there was something much more than ordinarily wrong somewhere. I don't say that half the people you meet may not be *thinking* like that

about other people's wives; but it is a thing that doesn't get
said, not in the second person, at any rate. One can only
meet it with anger – or compassion.

'I'm afraid you aren't well,' I suggested. 'Suppose you
come indoors and lie down for a little while I ring up for a
taxi. I'm sure . . .'

Jean stared at me.

'Ha! Ha!' she said, in a decisively mirthless way.

'I'm sorry to say that is just where we put the feet in,' her
companion explained. 'You see, we very much wanted to
get hold of you, and there was nobody at home, so we
thought we'd just sit and wait there until you came in. But
then it wasn't you who came in, it was Miss Tenter. We
hadn't expected her at all, and then she wouldn't believe
that I wasn't you, and she behaved atrociously – I'm sorry
to say it, but it *was* atrociously – to Jean, and – oh, well, it
all became very unpleasant and difficult. . . .' He kind of
ebbed away, in confusion.

There certainly was something up the pole about this.

'Why on earth do you say "Miss Tenter"?' I said. 'Jean,
at any rate, knows perfectly well that she's been Mrs Peter
Ruddle for more than two years now.'

'Oh *dear!*' said Jean. 'It is so confusing. But I never,
never could have imagined that you'd marry *her*.'

It wasn't easy to keep tolerantly in mind that she must
be a bit off her rocker. Her *manner* was as normal as could
be.

'Indeed!' I said coldly. 'And who, may I ask, did you
think I would marry?'

'Why, me, of course,' said Jean.

'Look here –' began her companion, in a rather desperate
way, but I cut him off.

'You pretty firmly shut the door on any chance of that
when you took up with Freddie Tallboy,' I reminded her –
and not without a touch of bitterness: the skin on the
old wound was still a little more sensitive than I had
thought.

'Freddie Tallboy?' she repeated. 'Who's he?'

That was too much for my patience.

'Mrs Tallboy,' I said, 'I don't pretend to understand the reason for this fooling – but I've had enough of it.'

'But I'm not Mrs Tallboy,' she said. 'I'm Mrs Peter Ruddle.'

'I suppose you find that amusing,' I told her, bitterly, 'but to me it isn't very funny,' I added. And it was not: there had been a time when what I hoped for above all else was to hear Jean call herself Mrs Peter Ruddle. I looked at her steadily.

'Jean,' I said. 'This is not your kind of joke – it's a cruel kind.'

She looked as steadily back at me for some seconds. Then I saw her eyes change; they glistened a little.

'Oh!' she said, as if she had seen something there. 'Oh, this is dreadful! ... Oh, dear! ... I – Oh, Peter, help me,' she said – but the appeal was to the other man, not to me. I turned to him, too.

'Look here,' I said. 'I don't know who you are, or what's going on, but –'

'Oh,' he said, as if suddenly enlightened. 'No, of course you don't. I'm Peter Ruddle.'

There was a longish pause. I decided I had had enough of being made to look a fool, and started to turn away. He said:

'Isn't there somewhere we can go and talk? You see, we're both of us Peter Ruddle, that's what's making it all so difficult.'

'I look on "difficult" as an understatement,' I said, coldly, and started to walk off.

'But you don't *see*,' said his voice behind me. 'It's old Whetstone's machine, man. It *works*!'

My own house was evidently barred to us, and the only nearby place that I could think of at the moment was the upstairs room of the Jubilee Café. Most of the people who worked at the Institute would be knocking off about now, and still trickling out for an hour to come. I had no desire to confirm the impression of my private affairs that had already reached the Director, so I went ahead to the café, found there was no one in the upstairs room, and beckoned through the window to them. The girl who brought us tea was not a bright type. If she noticed our likeness at all, it made no perceptible impression on her. When she had left, Jean poured out, and we started to get down to things.

'You'll remember,' said my double, leaning forward earnestly, 'you'll remember old Whetstone's concept of time? He used to give that rough analogy about the sea freezing. The present was represented by the leading edge of the ice, gradually building up and advancing. Behind it was the solid ice that represented the past: in front, the still fluid water represented the future. You could tell that a given number of the moving molecules which represented the future would become frozen in a given space of time, but you couldn't predict which, nor in what relationship they would be to one another.

'About the solid stuff behind, the past, he thought you could probably do nothing; but he reckoned that somehow or other you ought to be able to find a way of pushing out a little ahead of the main freezing line, which is the present. If you could do that, you would be creating little advanced bridgeheads of frozen – that is to say, factualized – matter. This *must*, in due course, be overtaken by, and thus become part of, the advancing present. In other words, by going a little ahead you would create a bit of a future which would *have* to come true. You couldn't choose which molecules you would bind together, but those that you found would be solidified by your finding them, and therefore become inevitable.'

'Yes, I remember that well,' I told him. 'It was cock-eyed.'

'Certainly it was cock-eyed,' he agreed promptly. 'Everyone who ever tried to give him a hand came to that conclusion sooner or later, and cleared out. But he wouldn't see it. Obstinate as a mule over that, he was.' He glanced at Jean.

'It's all right. I know,' she said, sadly. He went on:

'He would keep on trying to make that machine of his support his theory – which, of course, it couldn't possibly do with a theory that was all up the pole. And because of that he wouldn't follow up the leads that the thing *did* give. Nothing would loosen him up on that theory, with the result that he overworked and worried himself by trying to pin down the impossible.

'And so he died – sooner than he need have done – and his stuff just stayed there, with no one quite liking to disturb it.

'Now, shortly after Jean and I got married –'

I felt the fog beginning to come down on me again.

'But Jean didn't marry you. She married Freddie,' I objected.

'Wait a minute. I'm just coming to that. As I said, not long after we were married I had an idea, quite a different idea about this time business. Jean agreed that I should use her father's apparatus – as much of it as could be useful – to see if I could work the idea out, if possible. To some extent I have succeeded, and this is the result.' He paused.

'I'm in just about as thick a fog as I was before,' I told him.

'Well, here's the basis – mind you, I don't claim that it may not be misconceived in some ways, but the *empirical* result is that I'm talking to you now.

'Now, time is something similar to a quantum-radiation. The atoms of time are not dissimilar from radio-active atoms – that is to say, they are in a continual state of disintegration, or fission, and they throw off quanta. There must, presumably, be a half-life, but, so far, I've not been able to determine it. Obviously it has to be something very, very much smaller than a second, so let's just call it an "instant" for illustration.

'So every "instant" an atom of time splits. The two halves then continue upon different paths and encounter different influences as they diverge – but they don't diverge as constant units; each of them is splitting every instant, too. The pattern of it is the radiating ribs of a fan; and along each of the ribs, more fans; and along the ribs of those, still more fans; and so, *ad infinitum*.

'So, here we have Peter Ruddle. An instant later, that atom of time in which he exists is split, and so there are two Peter Ruddles, slightly diverging. Both those time-atoms split, and there are four Peter Ruddles. A third instant, and there are eight, then sixteen, then thirty-two. Very shortly there are thousands of Peter Ruddles. And because the diversion must actually occur many, many times in a second, there is an infinite number of Peter Ruddles, all originally similar, but all different by force of circumstances, and all inhabiting different worlds – imperceptibly different, or widely different; that depends chiefly on the distance from the original point of fission. And, of course, there is also an infinite number of worlds in which Peter Ruddle never managed to get born at all....'

He paused a little to let me stop whizzing, and get the hang of it. When I thought I had, several points for argument immediately presented themselves. I shelved them for the moment, however, and let him continue:

'Well, then, the problem ceased to be that of travelling in time, as old Whetstone had supposed it to be. You obviously can't put split atoms together again to reconstruct a past: nor can you observe the result of fission among atoms that have not yet split – at least, I think not, though it would appear that multiple futures must be latent in the present.

'So the place of that problem was taken by another – was it possible to move from one's own branch of descent to one of the, so to speak, cognate branches? Well, I went into that – and here we are to show that, within certain limits, one can ...'

He paused again for me to take it in.

'Yes,' I admitted, at length. 'I see it in plan, all right. But what I'm finding it really hard to feel is that we – you and I – are both equally – er – valid. I have to accept the theory, at least in the rough, since you are here, but I still feel that

I am the real Peter Ruddle, and that you must be the Peter Ruddle I might have been. I suppose that's a natural subjective view.'

Jean looked up and joined in for the first time.

'That's not how I see it, at all. We are the *real* Peter and Jean. You are what might have happened to Peter. . . .' She sat looking at me for a long moment, then: 'Oh, my dear! Why, oh why, did you do it? And you aren't happy with her, either. I can see that.'

'This –' began the other Peter. Then he broke off as the door opened. Somebody looked in. A woman's voice said: 'Oh, I'm sorry!' and the door shut again. It was hidden from me where I sat. I looked inquiringly at Jean.

'Mrs Terry,' she told me.

The other Peter started again: 'Obviously we're all equally real: it's just that you and I normally exist on, well, different ribs of the fan.' He went on expanding that a bit, then he said: 'Although I've done it, I've only a very crude notion of how I've done it. So I had this idea: you know how one's mind tends to work in a groove – well, it occurred to me that if I could start one of my "doubles" working on this thing, too, it might lead to a better understanding of it. Obviously our minds must be like enough to be interested in the same kinds of things, but since part of our experience has been different they aren't likely to run in exactly the same grooves of thought – that's obvious, really, because if our lines of thought were exactly similar you would have made the same discoveries as I have, and you'd have made them at the same time.'

Certainly his tracks of thought were very similar. I have never had a swifter, clearer understanding of what another person was attempting to convey. It was due to more than the mere words. I asked:

'When do you reckon, in our case, that this fission took place?'

'I've been wondering about that,' he told me. He held out his left hand. 'It must have been less than five years ago. We've both got the same watch, you see.'

I thought. 'Well, it must be more than three years ago, because that's when Freddie Tallboy first showed up here; and, judging by Jean's question, he doesn't seem to have shown up at all on your level.'

'Never heard of him,' he agreed, shaking his head.

'You're lucky,' I told him, with a glance at Jean.

We thought again.

'It must have been before your father died, too, because Tallboy was here by then,' I said to Jean.

But my double shook his head. 'The old man's death isn't a constant. It could have occurred earlier or later in different streams.'

That point had not occurred to me. I tried again:

'There was a row,' I said, looking at Jean.

'A row?' inquired Jean.

'You can't have forgotten that,' I said, incredulously. 'That was the night that finished things between us. After I said I wasn't going to help your father any more.'

Her eyes opened widely.

'*Finished* things!' she repeated. 'That was the night we got engaged.'

'Of course it was, darling,' my double supported her.

I shook my head. 'It was the night I went and got dead drunk because the world didn't have any bottom any more,' I said.

'Now we're getting warm,' observed the other Peter, leaning forward, with the light of the chase in his eye.

I did not share his enthusiasm. I was remembering one of the more painful occasions in my life.

'I told you I'd had enough of helping your father because he would cling pig-headedly to a demonstrably absurd theory,' I reminded her.

'And I said you must at least pretend to believe in it because he was getting to be an old man, and another disappointment might do him harm, and the doctor was worried about him anyway.'

I shook my head, decisively.

'I remember exactly what you said, Jean. You said: "So

you're just as callous as the rest of them; you're just going to walk out on a poor old man and leave him in the lurch." Those were your exact words.' They were both staring at me. 'We went right on from there,' I recalled, 'until I said obstinacy seemed to run in your family, and you said that you were glad to have discovered in time the sort of selfishness and callousness there was in mine.'

'Oh, no, Peter, never –' Jean began.

My double broke in excitedly:

'That must have been it – that was the moment! *I* never said anything about obstinacy in Jean's family. I said I'd give it another trial and do my best to be patient with him.'

We sat silent for a bit. Then Jean said, in a shaky voice:

'Just that! And so you went and married *her* instead of me!' There were almost tears in her eyes. 'Oh, how dreadful! Oh, Peter, my dear!'

'You were engaged to Tallboy before I proposed to her,' I said. 'At least, I suppose I mean not you, of course. The other Jean.'

She stretched out her left hand and took her husband's.

'Oh, dear!' she said again, in a half-frightened voice. 'Oh, think of that poor, poor other me. ...' She paused a moment. 'Perhaps we oughtn't to have come at all. It was all right to begin with,' she added. 'And, you see, we thought that if we went to our house – your house, on this level, I mean – we thought we'd find you and the other me there, and that'd be all right. I ought to have known sooner. The moment I saw those curtains *she's* put in the windows I had a feeling something was wrong. I'm sure I wouldn't have chosen them – and I don't think the other me would, either. And the furniture – that wasn't a bit like me. And then that *woman* ... ! And this has all happened wrong, just because ... Oh, this is dreadful, Peter, dreadful ... !'

She pulled a handkerchief out of her bag, dabbed at her eyes, and blew her nose; then she leant earnestly towards me again, her eyes still swimming a little.

'You *can't*, Peter. . . . It wasn't meant to be this way. . . . It's all *wrong*. . . . That other me, the other Jean – where is she?'

'She's still here,' I told her. 'She lives a little outside, along the Reading road.'

'You must go to her, Peter.'

'Now, look here –' I began, with some bitterness.

'But she loves you, Peter, and she needs you. She's me, and I know how she must feel. . . . Don't you see that I *know*?'

I looked back at her, and shook my head.

'What you *don't* seem to know,' I told her, 'is how it feels to have the knife turned. She is married to someone else, I am married to someone else, and there's an end to it.'

'Oh, no – *no*!' she said. Her hand sought her husband's again. 'No. You can't do that to her, or to yourself. It's –' She broke off and turned in distress to the other Peter. 'Oh, darling, if only we could make him understand somehow what it means. He doesn't – he can't understand, how should he?'

The other Peter's eyes rested on mine.

'I think he does – well enough,' he said.

I got up.

'I hope you'll excuse me now,' I said to them. 'I've had about as much of this as I can stand.'

Jean got up quickly, too. Contritely she said:

'I'm sorry, Peter. I don't want to hurt you. I only want you to be happy – you, and the other me. I . . . I . . .' she choked a little. The other Peter put in quickly:

'Look, if you can spare half an hour or so, do come over to old Whetstone's room. It'll be much easier there to give you a rough idea of the adaptations his stuff needs. That's what I really came for, after all.'

'What did you come for?' I asked Jean.

She had her back towards me now, and did not turn.

'Curiosity,' she said, in an unsteady voice.

I hesitated, but he was right about the similarity of

our minds – what had caught his interest caught mine, too.

'All right,' I agreed, more than half reluctantly.

The street was almost empty when we came out into the dusk, and turned towards the Institute. The grounds beyond the gates were quite deserted: the building itself showed a few lighted windows where there were some people still at work. We walked along, with Jean silent, and Peter talking about time quantum-radiation, and explaining how the scope appeared to have quite natural limits at present – how it was possible, for instance, to move on to another rib of the fan only if there happened to be the space for you to do so.

One could, for instance, move only to a line of existence where old Whetstone's room was arranged in such a way that there was a clear area ready to receive what he called the transfer-chamber. If there were something else occupying that space it would be destroyed, so there must always be a preliminary practical test to ensure that it would return intact. That established quite a narrow limit: go too far round the fan, so to speak, and you would hit a time-sequence in which the room did not exist at all because the Institute had never been built. The consequences to a transfer-chamber trying to occupy an already occupied space, or making its début in the new time-sequence in mid air, would be quite disastrous.

When we reached the room everything looked as usual except for the transfer-chamber itself, standing in the middle of the sheeted apparatus. It looked rather like a sentry-box with a door added.

We cleared the covers off some of the rest of the stuff, and the other Peter started explaining to me what he had done in the way of altering circuits and introducing new stages. Jean dusted off a chair and sat on it, smoking a cigarette patiently. We should have got along more quickly had we been able to refer to the old man's notes and diagrams, but unfortunately the steel filing-cabinet which held them was locked. Nevertheless, he was able to give me the general theory and a fair working idea of how to set about making the necessary changes.

After a time Jean looked pointedly at her watch, and got up.

'Sorry to interrupt,' she said, 'but we really must get back. I told the girl we'd not be later than seven – and it's half past already.'

'What girl?' inquired my double, absently.

'That baby-sitter girl, of course,' she told him.

Somehow that brought me up more sharply than anything yet.

'You – you've got a baby?' I asked, stupidly.

Jean looked at me. 'Yes,' she said, gently. 'And she's a lovely little baby, isn't she, Peter?'

'Definitely quite the best baby known to us,' agreed Peter.

I stood there, blankly.

'Oh, don't look like that, my dear,' Jean said.

She came closer. She put her right hand on the left side of my face, and pressed my other cheek against hers.

'Go to her, Peter. Go to her. She wants you,' she whispered close to my ear.

The other Peter opened the door of the transfer-chamber, and they got in. It was a close fit for two. Then he got out again, and indicated a piece of the floor.

'When you've got it working, come and find us,' he said. 'We'll keep that area clear for you.'

'Bring her with you,' said Jean.

Then he got back, and pulled the door to. The last thing I saw as it closed was Jean's face, with tears in her eyes. ...

While I was still looking at it the transfer-chamber vanished: it did not fade, or dim, it went in a split second. It might never have been, but for four flattened cigarette-ends by the chair where Jean had sat. ...

I was in no mood to go home. I hung about the room, going over the apparatus and memorizing what the other Peter had told me, trying to lose myself in the technicalities

of it. The attention with which I went over the principles
was rather grimly forced; I felt I should have had more of
a chance to become absorbed if I had been able to get hold
of the locked-up notes and diagrams.

After an hour or so I gave it up. I walked back home
from the Institute, but I arrived with something more than
a disinclination to go into the house. Instead, I got out the
car. And then, somehow, I was driving out along the Reading road. . . .

Jean looked startled when she answered the doorbell.

'Oh!' she said, and went a little pale, and then a little
flushed. In a carefully calm voice she said: 'Freddie is
working over in Number Four Lab.'

'I don't want Freddie,' I told her. 'I wanted to talk to
you – about your father's stuff in the room over there.'

She hesitated, and then opened the door wider.

'All right,' she said, in a non-committal voice. 'You'd
better come inside.'

It was the first time I had set foot in her house. I followed her to a large, comfortable sitting-room which
looked out on the back-garden. The interview began with
as much awkwardness as anything I've known. All the time
I had to keep on reminding myself that she was another
Jean from the one of the afternoon. This Jean was a person
I had not spoken to for over three years except when some
Institute function forced us to recognize one another's
existence. The more I looked at her, the more incredibly
crass that barrier became.

I stumbled along, explaining that I had a new theory I
would like to work on. I said that her father, in spite of his
lack of success, had done a lot of groundwork which should
not be wasted, and which I was sure he would not want
wasted. . . .

Jean listened as though she were extremely interested in
the pattern of the rug before the fire. After a while, however, she looked up and met my eyes. I lost the thread of
what I had been saying, and floundered about after it. I
grasped wildly at a few phrases and laboured on with a

curious feeling that I was talking a language I did not know. After a long time I reached the end, not knowing whether I had been coherent at all.

She went on looking at me for a moment, but not quite so distantly as before, then she said:

'Yes, I think so, Peter. I know you fell out with him, like all the others, but the apparatus will have to be used by someone sooner or later, or dismantled – and I think he'd sooner it was you than any of the rest. You'd probably like me to give a written consent?'

'It might be as well,' I agreed. 'Some of the stuff there cost a lot of money.'

She nodded, and crossed to a small bureau. Presently she came back holding a piece of paper.

'Jean –' I began.

She stood, holding the paper out towards me.

'What, Peter . . .?'

'Jean –' I began once more. But then the wretched impossibility of the whole situation came home to me again.

She was watching me. I pulled myself together.

'It's – it's just that I can't get at his notes. They're locked up,' I said, in a rush.

'Oh,' she said, 'oh, yes,' as if she were somewhere a long way off. Then, in a different voice, she added:

'Would you know the key if you saw it? There's a box of his keys upstairs.'

I was pretty sure I should. I'd seen it often enough when I had been working with old Whetstone.

We went upstairs. One of the rooms was unfurnished, a lumber-room, with a lot of old junk and half a dozen trunks in it. The box of keys were in the second trunk she tried. There were two of them that might fit, so I pocketed both, and we went downstairs again.

We were half-way down the stairs when the front door opened, and her husband came in. . . .

Well, there it is. . . .

Twenty or thirty people, including the Director, saw us

crossing the Institute grounds arm in arm. My wife, discovered me entertaining my ex-fiancée in my own house, during her absence. Mrs Terry intruded upon us in the upstairs room of the Jubilee Café. Other people saw us in other places – and nearly everybody, it turns out, has had long-standing suspicions. Finally, her husband surprised his wife descending from the bedroom storey of his house with her ex-fiancé. . . .

So . . .

And the nature of any evidence that I could produce to the contrary would, I think, sound somewhat unconvincing in court.

Besides, and rather importantly, we have both decided that nothing could be further from our wishes than to defend . . .

Pillar to Post

Forcett Mental Clinic,
Delano, Conn.
28 Feb.

To
Messrs Thompson, Handett & Thompson
Attorneys-at-Law
512 Gable Street
Philadelphia, Pa.
Gentlemen,

In response to your request we have conducted a thorough examination of our patient, Stephen Dallboy, and have taken steps which establish his identity beyond legal question. Attested documents in support of this are enclosed, and dispose entirely of his claim to the Terence Molton property.

At the same time we admit ourselves surprised. The condition of the patient has altered quite radically since our last examination when he was indubitably feeble-minded. Indeed, but for this obsession that he is Terence Molton, which he maintains with complete consistency, we should now classify him as normal. In view of the obsession and the remarkable assertions with which he supports it we feel that he should remain here under observation for a time which may give us the opportunity of dispelling the whole fantasy system – and at the same time of clearing up several points which we find puzzling.

In order that you may more clearly understand the situation we are enclosing a copy of a statement written by the patient which we beg you to study before reading our concluding remarks.

STATEMENT – *by* Terence Molton

I know this is difficult to believe. In fact, when the thing first happened I didn't believe it myself. I reckoned it was just a stage, maybe, in the deteriorating process. I've had dope enough long enough to play hell with my nervous system – yet the funny thing was how real it seemed right away. Still, I thought that's likely the way of it; I reckon everything would seem real to De Quincey when he was under, and to Coleridge, too.

A damsel with a dulcimer
In a vision once I saw . . .

Vision is a poor word – all quality and no quantity. How strong was that vision? Could he put out his hand and touch that damsel? He heard her sing, but did she speak to him? And did he find himself a new man, free from pain? I guess even honeydew and the milk of Paradise are relative. There'll be fellows who are yearning for a kind of celestial Hollywood, but, for me, just having no pain and being complete was paradise right then.

It was just over four years since that cannonshell had got me – four years, nine operations, and more to come, for, with all their carving, they'd not stopped the trouble yet. And what good was that to me? Interesting for the doctors, no doubt, but it had brought me to being just a hulk in a chair, with the only one half of one leg under the rug. And they said: 'Go easy on the dope!' I should laugh. If they'd given me anything else to keep the pain away, maybe I would. But if they'd stopped letting me have the dope then I'd have killed myself. They knew that.

I don't blame Sally for calling it off. Some of them thought I felt sore about that, but I didn't – not after the first. The sample I'd offered her was a healthy young man – what was delivered from hospital was pretty different from the sample. Poor Sally. It nearly broke her up. I reckon she'd have tried it out of mistaken loyalty if I'd pressed her. But I was thanking God I hadn't – at least I hadn't that on my conscience. They tell me her husband's a good guy, and the baby's cute. That's the way it should be.

All the same, when every woman you see is kind to you – in much the same way as she would be to a sick dog. . . . Oh, well, there was always the dope.

And then, when I wasn't expecting anything at all except rotting slowly, there was this . . . this . . . *vision*.

I'd had a bad day. My right leg was hurting a lot, and my left foot. But as most of the right leg was taken off and thrown to the sharks four years ago, and the left foot had to go, too, a little later, there wasn't a lot to be done about it. I'd been keeping the dope down because I still sometimes got an idea that I'd be acquiring virtue by holding off when I wanted it – I wasn't, of course; I was acquiring nothing but bad temper, and radiating it, too, but you get brought up with these ideas, and they keep on cropping up again. Ten o'clock was to be my limit, I'd decided, and I kept to it. For the last quarter hour I watched the big hand snailing, then I watched the second-hand crawling, then I reached for the bottle.

Maybe I took a little more than usual, but the moment I had taken it I was telling myself what a damn fool I had been to wait. I'd gained nothing. It was just a variation of those limit-setting games kids invent for themselves. For all the difference it made to anyone else I might as well be doped up to the eyes all the time. Wonderful, it was. Blissful. I lay back, feeling as if I'd never rested like that before. The pain faded out, and all feeling with it. I seemed to float smoothly and gently up and away. I was disembodied, boundless, and filled with a surging lightness. The day must have made me pretty tired, I guess, because I could feel myself falling asleep before I'd properly got round to enjoying it. . . .

When I opened my eyes, there, in front of me, was the vision of the damsel. She hadn't a dulcimer, and she certainly did not look Abyssinian, but she was singing, very quietly. It was an odd song, and for all I knew it might have been about Mount Abora, for I couldn't understand a word of it.

We were in a room – well, yes, it was a room, though it was rather like being inside a bubble. It was all cool green, with a pearly iridescence, and the walls curving up so that you couldn't tell where they became ceiling. There were two arched openings in the sides. Through them were tree tops, and a patch of blue sky. Close to one of them the girl was fiddling with something I couldn't see. She glanced towards me, and saw that my eyes were open. She turned, and said something that sounded like a question, but it meant absolutely nothing to me. I just looked back at her. She was worth looking at. A tall, beautifully proportioned figure, with brown hair caught back by a ribbon. The material of her dress was diaphanous, yet there was a vast amount of it, arranged in multitudes of cunning folds. It made me think of the pre-Raphaelites' versions of the classical, and it must have been cobweb-light, for as she moved it swirled and hesitated in mid air. The result was rather like that frozen-high-wind effect so popular in later Greek sculpture.

When I did not reply, she frowned a little and repeated her question – or so it seemed. I did not pay a lot of attention to the words. As a matter of fact I was thinking: 'Well, that's that. I've had it', and deciding that I was now in some kind of ante-room to heaven, or – well, anyway, an ante-room. I wasn't scared; not even greatly surprised. I remember feeling, 'Good, that's a nasty experience finished with', and wondering a little that the prelude to eternity should so favour certain Victorian schools of painting.

When I still did not answer, her dark eyes widened a little. There was a look of wonder in them, perhaps a slight tinge of alarm, as she came towards me. Slowly she said:

'You – are – not – Hymorell?'

Her English had a strange accent, and anyway I did not know what hymorell meant. I might be, or I might not. She went on:

'Not – Hymorell? Some – other – person?'

It sounded as if Hymorell should be a name.

'I'm Terry,' I told her. 'Terry Molton.'

There was a block of the green stuff near me. It looked hard, but she sat down on it, and stared at me. Her expression was half disbelief, mixed with surprise.

By this time I was beginning to discover myself. I was lying on a long couch with some kind of coverlet over me. Experimentally I moved what ought to be my right leg – and the coverlet moved, too, right down to the foot. There wasn't any pain, either. I sat up suddenly, and excitedly, feeling my legs, both of them. Then I did a thing I'd not let myself do in years – I burst into tears. . . .

I can't remember what we spoke of first. I suppose I was just too excited and bewildered to take it in. I do recall learning her name, and thinking it rather a mouthful – Clytassamine. I have a recollection of her speaking in her uncertain, foreign English, and of wondering how it came about that there could be a language problem at the gates of Paradise, but I was more concerned with myself. I threw back the coverlet, and found that I was naked beneath it. That didn't worry me, nor apparently her. I sat staring at the legs. They weren't mine. Now I came to look at it, the hand with which I felt them was not mine, either – but I could wriggle the toes and bend the fingers. I swung the legs over the side of the couch, and then I stood on them – for the first time in more than four years, I *stood*. . . .

I am not going into a lot of detail. I have a nasty feeling that what I might say would be about as informative as a Trobriand Islander's first impressions of New York. I just had to take most things on trust, the way he would.

There was a dressing machine. Clytassamine operated it someway, and the product came out of a slot in the wall. There was a whale of a lot of it, and not a seam to be seen. Pretty filmy and sissy, it seemed to me, but it satisfied her, so I let her help me put it on. When I was fixed she led the way out of the room. We emerged into a great hall built of the same green composition. I reckoned that if Manhattan were to sink into the Hudson, Grand Central Station might look a bit the way this place did.

There was a number of people about, none of them hurrying. All their clothes were of the filmy stuff, and all voluminous, but as far as colour and design went, it was apparently each to his own taste. To my unaccustomed eye all this swirling of draperies suggested a stately and somewhat decadent ballet. Our slippers were silent on the floor. There was scarcely a sound other than the hum of quiet voices which rose and dispersed in the huge place without echo. To a stranger this deadening of sound felt oppressive.

Clytassamine led the way to a row of double seats set against a wall, and pointed to the end one. I sat in it, and she beside me. It rose a little, perhaps four inches, from the floor, and began to drift across the room. In the middle we turned and slid silently towards a great arch at the far end. Once outside we rose a little more until we had an elevation of about one yard above ground level. From the shallow platform to which the chair was attached a curved windscreen rose to cover us, and while I was still puzzling how such a thing could be contrived we speeded up to some twenty-five miles an hour, and swept out smoothly across park-like country, navigating a course between occasional trees and clumps of bushes. I supposed that she was controlling the contraption in some way, though I could not see how. I had to admit right off that in everything except speed it was a sweeter flying machine than any other I've known – more in the magic-carpet class.

It was a strange journey. Something over an hour, I imagine, and in all that time we never crossed nor even saw a road, though twice I noticed footpaths which looked little used. We sped through country which seemed to be an unending eighteenth-century park with never a cultivated field or garden. To help the illusion there were occasional herds of deer-like creatures which paid us no attention. The only signs of human existence were a few large buildings to be seen above the trees, but none of them on our course. Threading our way across the landscape was an eerie sensation. It took me a while to get used to it. Every time I saw a wood ahead I tried to pull back on a non-existent stick and hop over it, but apparently the contrivance didn't work that way, for we always went round.

After half an hour or so I began to catch glimpses of a building on a hill ahead of us. I'm no architect, and I can't describe it, but it was like nothing I had ever seen or imagined because every building I knew was based on some geometrical figure: this looked more as if it had grown. The walls were pearly, and without window openings. Bushes grew close up against it, and some were even sprouting on top of it. The only reason I was sure it was a building was because it couldn't be anything natural. I began to keep on looking for it as we got nearer, and with each new glimpse I was more astonished. I could see now that what I had thought to be small bushes were full-grown trees, even those on top of it. The thing was unbelievably immense. Then, in the midst of my amazement, I remembered myself, and smiled – the dope dream was running true to form:

> *It was a miracle of rare device,*
> *A sunny pleasure-dome with caves of ice.*

But when we did get there it wasn't that. It rose before us like an artificial mountain. We swept into it through an entrance sixty yards wide, and several hundred feet high to emerge into a central hall of staggering size. There was no suggestion whatever of 'pleasure-dome', though something of the 'caves of ice' feeling came from the translucency of the pearly walls. More slowly, and seeming to drift like a feather in a draught, we floated across the place. There were a few men and women walking in a leisurely fashion, and a few chairs gliding as our own did. Beyond the great hall we passed through passages and lesser halls until we came to one where a dozen or so men and women were gathered and apparently awaiting us. There the chair stopped. It lowered the few inches to the floor, we got out, whereupon, by some mysterious agency it lifted just clear, and drifted away to the wall. Clytassamine spoke to the group of people and indicated me. They nodded gravely in my direction. It seemed the polite thing to do to nod back. Then, with her as interpreter, a kind of catechism began.

I think it was during that questioning that I really began to feel that there was something seriously wrong with my dream. They wanted to know my name, where I came from, what I did, when I did it, and a great deal more, and the answers I gave caused them pauses from time to time to confer. It was all very logical and detailed – that was what was wrong. Dreams – my dreams, at any rate – have a more cinematic quality. They do not proceed in smooth sequence, but jump rather suddenly from one scene to another as though a not quite sane director somewhere were ordering 'Take!' and 'Cut!' when he felt like it. But this was not at all that way. I was acutely aware of what was going on, both physically and mentally. . . .

Progress was slow on account of Clytassamine's indifferent English, but we made enough of it to produce longer and more involved conferences. At last she said:

'They – wish – you – learn – language. More – easy – to speak.'

'That's going to take a long time,' I said, for no word that any of them had yet spoken had the least familiar relation for me.

'No. Few – thlana.'

I looked blank.

'Quarter – day,' she explained.

She gave me some food first – a box of things which looked like candies and tasted good, but not sweet.

'Now – sleep,' said Clytassamine, pointing to a cold, unfriendly looking block.

I got on it, and found that it was neither chill nor hard. I lay wondering if this was the end of it and I would wake up to find myself back in my own bed with the old pain where my legs ought to be. But I didn't wonder long – maybe there was something in the food.

When I woke up I was still there. Hanging over me was a kind of canopy of rose-coloured metal which had not been there before. It was – but I am going to give up attempting to describe things. Frankly, I could understand about one per cent of what I saw, so what is the use? There was too much basic unfamiliarity. What would an ancient Egyptian know of a telephone by looking at it? What would a Roman or a Greek make of a jet plane, or of

radio? Or, coming right down to the simple things, if you
saw a slab of chocolate for the first time you might think
it was for mending shoes, lighting the fire, or building
houses – about the last thing you'd think was that that
hard brown rectangle was meant for eating – and when
you did find it out, you'd most likely try eating soap, too,
because the texture was similar and the colour was more
attractive. That's the way it was with me. You grow up
with your network of thinking patterns on an acquired
foundation. You look at a machine, almost subconsciously
you say to yourself 'Ah, that works by steam, or oil, or electricity' and you go on from there. But nearly all of what
I was seeing now was fundamentally foreign to me. I'd no
place to start, and, not understanding what might bite me
or burn me any minute, I was scared of it – just like a child
or a backward aboriginal. Naturally I floundered around
with wild guesses, but mostly they had to remain just that.
I guessed now, for instance, that the canopy was a part of a
hypnotic teaching machine such as I'd heard of people
trying to develop. I guessed that because I found I could
now understand what the people were saying – some of it
– but of the how or the why, I knew nothing. In some way
I had acquired an understanding of the language they
spoke, but the concepts that were behind it did not necessarily follow. . . . I knew just what I could translate. The
word *thlana* that Clytassamine had used I now knew for a
measure of time – one hour and twelve minutes, making
twenty *thlana* to the day – and *dool* was electricity, but
laythal meant nothing to me. I had to work it out that it
was some form of power unknown to me, so that I had no
equivalent to translate it to.

This certainly had the effect of enhancing the dream-like
quality. The utter blankness of certain words, which kept
on cropping up like the dumb notes on a bar-room piano,
began to get me more bewildered than before. After a bit,
my distress must have begun to show pretty plainly because they laid off questioning, and told Clytassamine to
take me away and look after me. My mind was whirling so

much with the attempts to understand that the relief was
almost physical as I sat down beside her again, and I sighed
in relaxation when the seat floated us back once more into
the open air.

Before I understood anything about this world I was
immensely impressed by Clytassamine's power of mental
adjustment. It seemed to me that it must be a frightening
thing to find that one whom you have known intimately
has suddenly become a perfect stranger – with, maybe, unpredictable reactions. Yet she showed no alarm, and only
occasionally made the slip of calling me Hymorell.

I understood why somebody recovering consciousness
usually demands first of all 'Where am I?' I wanted to
know that very much; without some relation to my circumstances I didn't seem to be able to get my thinking started
properly. There was no fixed point to begin from. When
we were back in the green room again I began to ask questions. She looked at me doubtfully.

'You should rest. Simply relax and don't worry. We will
look after you. If I were to try to explain I would only
bewilder you more.'

'You couldn't,' I told her. 'Nothing could. I've got to the
stage where I can't pretend this is a dream any longer. I've
got to get some kind of orientation, or go crazy.'

She looked at me closely again, and then nodded.

'Very well. But where am I to begin? What is most
urgent?'

'I want to know where I am, who I am, and how it
happened.'

'As to who you are, you know that. You told me you are
Terry Molton.'

'But this' – I slapped my left thigh – 'this isn't Terry
Molton.'

'Temporarily it is,' she said. 'It was Hymorell's body,
but now everything that makes it individual – mentality,
personality, character – are yours: therefore it is Terry's
body.'

'And Hymorell?' I asked.

'He has transferred to what was your body.'

'Then he's made a remarkably bad deal,' I told her. I thought for a moment, then:

'That doesn't make sense,' I said. 'Disposition isn't constant. I know that. I'm not the same as I was before I was shot up, for instance. Physical differences make mental differences. Personality largely depends on the equilibrium of the glands. Injuries, and dope, changed mine to some extent – if they'd done it more I'd have quite a different personality.'

'Who told you that?' she asked.

'It's a matter of scientific knowledge – and common sense,' I told her.

'And your scientists postulate no constant? Surely there must be some constant factor to be affected by changes? And if there is that factor, may it not be a cause rather than simply an effect?'

'As I understand it, it's simply a matter of balance – an affair of forces held in equilibrium.'

'Then you *don't* understand it,' she told me.

'Oh,' I said.

I decided to drop that angle for the moment.

'What is this place?' I asked.

'The building is called Cathalu,' she said.

'No. I mean where is it? Is it on Earth? It looks like Earth, all right – but nowhere that I ever heard of.'

'Of course it's Earth – where else would it be? But it's in a different salany,' she said.

I looked back at her, up against one of those dumb words once more. Salany meant just nothing to me.

'Do you mean it's in a different –?' I began, and then I stopped, baffled. There didn't seem to be a word in her language for 'time' – at least not in the sense I was wanting it.

'I told you it would be bewildering,' she said. 'You think differently. In terms of old thinking – as near as I can understand it – you came from one end of the human race, now you are at the other.'

'But I don't,' I protested. 'There were some twenty million years of human evolution before me.'

'Oh, that!' she said, airily dismissing those twenty million years with a wave of her hand.

'Well, at least,' I went on, rather desperately, 'you can tell me how I got here.'

'Roughly, yes. It is an experiment of Hymorell's. He has been trying for a long time' – (and in this straightforward, day to day, sense. I noticed, there *did* seem to be a word for time) – 'but now he has made a new approach – a successful one at last. Several times before he has almost done it, but the transfer did not hold. His most successful attempts until now were about three generations ago. He –'

'I beg your pardon?' I said.

She looked questioningly.

'I thought you said he tried three generations ago?'

'So I did,' she agreed.

I got up from the block I'd been sitting on, and looked out of the arched windows. It was a peaceful, sunny, normal-looking day out there.

'Maybe you were right. I'd better rest,' I said.

'That's sensible,' she agreed. 'Don't bother your head about the hows and whys. After all, you won't be here long.'

'You mean, I'll be going back – to be as I was?'

She nodded.

I could feel my body under the unfamiliar robe. It was a good body, strong, well kept, lithe, whole – and there was no pain in it any place. . . .

'No,' I said. 'I don't know where I am, or what I am now, but one thing I do know – and that is that I'm not going back to the hell where I was.'

She just looked at me a little sadly, and shook her head slowly.

The next day, after we had fed on more of the candies that were not candies, and drunk an elusively flavoured milky stuff, she led the way into the hall, and towards the chairs. I stopped.

'Can't we walk?' I said. 'It's a long time since I walked.'

'Why, yes, of course,' she agreed, and we turned towards the doorway.

Several people spoke to her, and one or two of them to me. There was curiosity in their eyes, but their manners were kindly, as though to set a stranger at ease. It was evident that they knew I was not Hymorell, yet apparently I was not sensational. Outside, we walked across rough grass and found a path leading through a spinney. It was quiet, peaceful, Arcadianly beautiful. To me, now feeling the very ground beneath my feet as something precious, everything had the freshness of spring. The blood livened in my veins in a way that I had forgotten.

'Wherever it is, it's lovely,' I said.

'Yes, it is lovely,' she agreed.

We walked on in silence for a while, then my curiosity came back.

'What did you mean by "the other end of the race"?' I asked her.

'Just that. We think we are coming to the end, finishing. We are practically sure of it – though there is always chance.'

I looked at her.

'I have never seen anyone more healthy, or more beautiful,' I said.

She smiled.

'It's a nice body,' she agreed. 'My best, I think.'

For the moment I ignored that baffling addition.

'Then what is happening – it is infertility?' I asked.

'No. There are not a great many children, but that is more a result than a cause. It is that something in us is failing to reproduce – the thing that makes us human instead of just animal – we call it malukos.'

The word gave me an impression akin to a spirit or a soul, yet not quite either.

'Then the children – ?'

'They nearly all of them lack that. They are – feeble-minded,' she said. 'If things go on this way they will all be like that one day – and then it will be over.'

I pondered that, feeling that I was back in the dream again.

'How long has this been happening?' I asked.

'I don't know. One doesn't think of the salany arith-metically – though there is the perimetrical approach.'

I let her have best over that.

'Surely there are records?' I said.

'Oh, yes. That is how Hymorell and I learned your language. But there are very big gaps. Fives times at least the race all but destroyed itself. There are thousands of years missing from the records at different salany.'

'And how long is it going to be before it is all finished?' I asked.

'We don't know that, either. Our task is to prolong it because there is always chance. It *may* happen that the intelligence factors will become strong again.'

'How do you mean, "prolong it"? Prolong your own lives?'

'Yes, we transfer. When a body begins to fail, or when it is fifty years old or so, and getting past its best, we choose one of the feeble-minded, and transfer to that. This,' she added, holding up her perfect hand, and studying it, 'is my fourteenth body. It's a very nice one.'

I agreed. 'But do you mean you can go on and on trans-ferring?' I asked.

'Oh, yes – as long as there are bodies to transfer to.'

'But – but that's immortality.'

'No,' she said, scornfully, 'nothing like it. It is just pro-longation. Some day, sooner or later, there'll be an accident – that's mathematically inevitable. It might have been a hundred years ago, or it might be tomorrow –'

'Or a thousand years hence?' I suggested.

'Exactly, but one day it will come.'

'Oh,' I said. That seemed pretty near immortality to me. I did not for a moment doubt that she was telling me the truth. By this time I was prepared for any fantastic thing. All the same, I revolted against it. I had an instinctive sense of disapproval – prejudice, of course, the same prejudice which made me disapprove of the soft, flowing garments and the soft, easy manner of life: there is a hangover of the old Puritan censor in all of us. I couldn't help feeling that the process she spoke of was allied to cannibalism – in some symbolic fashion. She must have read my expression, for she said, explaining, not excusing:

'This body wasn't any good to the girl who had it. I don't suppose she was really even conscious of it. It was being wasted. I shall look after it. I shall have children. Some of them may be normal human children, then when they grow old they will be able to transfer. The urge to survival still exists, you see – something may happen, someone may make a discovery to save us even now.'

'And the girl who had this body? What happened to her?'

'Well, there wasn't very much there beyond a few instincts. What there was changed places with me.'

'Into a body aged fifty? – Losing thirty years of life?'

'Can you call it loss when she was incapable of using it?'

I did not reply to that, for a thought had struck me like a sudden illumination.

'So that's what Hymorell was working on! He was trying to extend this transference – to operate it at, well, long range. That's it, isn't it? That's why I'm here?'

She looked at me steadily.

'Yes,' she said. 'He's been successful at last. It is a real transference this time.'

I thought it over. I was strangely unsurprised. I suppose I had been working up to the realization before it actually came. But there was a lot I wanted to know about the why and how as it affected me. I asked her for more details.

'Hymorell wanted to get as far as possible,' she told me. 'The limit was the point where he could be sure of assembling the parts to make an instrument that would get him back here. If he went too far, certain essential metals would not be known, instruments would be inaccurate, electric power unavailable. In that case it might take him years to build the instrument, if he could do it at all. The knowledge of nuclear fission was the line he decided to draw. Further away than that, he thought, might be dangerous. Then he had to find a contact. It had to be a subject where the integration was not good – where there was a lesion weakening the attachment of the personality to the physical shape. When we perform the operation we can prepare the subject, so it is easy, but he had to find one already in a suitable state. Unfortunately, those he could find were nearly all on the point of death, but he found you at last, and then he had to study the strength of your tie. He was puzzled because it fluctuated a great deal.'

'That would be the dope?' I suggested.

'Possibly. Anyway, he worked out a rhythmic incidence of lesion, and then tried. This is the result.'

'I see,' I said, and thought awhile. 'How long did he reckon it was going to take him to build the instrument for his return?'

'He couldn't tell that. It depends on his facilities for assembling materials.'

'Then it's going to take him quite a while, I'd say. A legless cripple wasn't a convenient subject to choose, from that point of view.'

'But he'll do it,' she said.

'Not if I can help it,' I told her.

She shook her head. 'Once you have transferred you never can have the perfect integration you had with your own original body. If at no other time, he will put on more power and get at you when you're sleeping.'

'We'll see about that,' I said.

Afterwards I saw the instrument that he had used for the transfer. It was not large. In appearance it was little more than a liquid-filled lens mounted upon a box the size of a portable typewriter from which there protruded two polished, metal handles. But within the box there was such an intricacy of wiring, tubes, and strange whizzits as to fill me with great satisfaction. No one, I reckoned, was going to knock a thing like that together in a few days, or even a few weeks.

The days drifted the life by with them. That placidity which was their chief characteristic was, at first, restful; after that there came periods when I wanted to go wild and break up something just for the diversion. Clytassamine took me here and there in the great green building. There were concerts at which I understood not a thing. I sat there, bored and musing to myself, while around me the audience went into an intellectual trance, finding something in the strange scales and queerer harmonies that was utterly beyond my perception. And there was one hall where colours played on a large fluorescent screen. They seemed to be projected from the spectators themselves in some incomprehensible way. Everybody but me enjoyed it, you could feel that, and now and then, for no reason that I could perceive, they would all sigh or laugh together. Nevertheless, I thought some of the effects very pretty, and said so; by the way it was received it was the wrong thing to say. Only in the performances of three-dimensionally projected plays was I occasionally able to follow the action for a while, and when I thought I could, it usually shook me badly. Clytassamine became short with my comments. 'How can you expect to feel when you measure civilized behaviour by primitive taboos?' she asked curtly.

She took me to a museum. It was not like any I had thought of, being mostly a collection of instruments projecting sound or images, or both, according to selection. I saw some horrible things. We went back, back, and still further back. I wanted to see or hear something of my own time, but: 'There's only sound,' she said. 'No images from so far away.' 'All right,' I told her. 'Some music.' She worked at the keyboard of the machine. Into that great hall a familiar sound stole softly and mournfully. As I listened to it I had a sense of emptiness and vast desolation. Memories flooded back as if the old world – not, oddly enough, that which I had left, but that in which I was a child – were suddenly round me. A wave of sentimentality, of overwhelming self-pity and nostalgia, for all the hopes and joys and childhood that had vanished, utterly engulfed me, and the tears streamed down my face. I did not go to that museum again. And the music which conjured a whole world up from the aged dust? – No, it was not a Beethoven symphony, nor a Mozart concerto: it was, I confess, 'The Old Folks at Home'. ...

'Do you never work? Does nobody work?' I asked Clytassamine.

'Oh, yes – if he wants to,' she said.

'But what about the unpleasant things – the things that must be done?'

'What things?' she asked, puzzled.

'Well, growing food, providing power, disposing of waste, all that kind of thing.'

She looked surprised.

'Why, naturally, the machines do all that. You wouldn't expect men to do those things. Good heavens, what have we got brains for?'

'But who looks after the machines – keeps them in order?'

'Themselves, of course. A mechanism that couldn't maintain itself wouldn't be a machine, it would be just a form of tool, wouldn't it?'

'Oh,' I said. And I suppose that was so, though the thought was new to me.

'Do you mean to say,' I went on, 'that for your fourteen generations – some four hundred years or so – you've done nothing but this?'

'Well, I've had quite a lot of babies – and three of them were quite normal. And I've worked on eugenic research from time to time – almost everybody does that when he thinks he's got a new lead, but it never *does* lead anywhere.'

'But how can you stand it – just going on and on?'

'It is not easy sometimes – and some of us do give up, but that is a crime, because there is always chance. And it's not quite so monotonous as you think. Each transfer makes a difference. You feel as if the world had become a different place then. The spirit rises in you like sap in spring. ... And those glands you think so much of are not entirely without effect, because you are never quite the same person with quite the same tastes. Even in one body tastes can change quite a lot in one lifetime, and they inevitably differ slightly between bodies. But you are the same person, you have your memory, yet you are young again, you're hopeful, the world looks brighter, you think you'll be wiser this time. ... And then you fall in love again, just as sweetly and foolishly as before. It's wonderful – like a re-birth. You can only know just how wonderful if you have been fifty, and then become twenty.'

'I can guess,' I said. 'I was something worse than fifty before this happened. But love! ... For four years I haven't dared to think of love. ...'

'You dare now,' she said. 'Daren't you ... ?'

There was so much I wanted to know.

'What happened to *my* world?' I asked her. 'It seemed pretty well headed for disaster, as I saw it. I suppose it nearly wiped itself out in some vast global war?'

'Oh dear, no. It just died – the same way as all the early civilizations. Nothing spectacular.'

I thought of my world, its intricacies and complexities. The mastery of distance and speed; the progress of science.

' "Just died"!' I repeated. 'That's not good enough. It can't have "just died" like that. There must have been something that broke it up.'

'Oh, no. It died of Government – paternalism. The passion for order is a manifestation of the deep desire for security. The desire is natural – but the attainment is fatal. There was the means to produce a static world, and a static world was achieved. When the need for a new adaptation arose it found itself enmeshed in order. Unable to adapt, it inertly died of discouragement – it had happened to many primitive peoples before.'

She had no reason to lie, but it was hard to believe.

'We hoped for so much. Everything was opening before us. We were learning. We were going to reach out to other planets and beyond. . . .' I said.

'Ingenious you certainly were – like monkeys. But you neglected your philosophers – to your own ruin. Each new discovery was a toy. You never considered its true worth. You just pushed it into your system – a system already suffering from hardening of the arteries. And you were a greedy people. You took each discovery as if it were a bright new garment, but when you put it on you wore it over your old, verminous rags. You had grave need of disinfectants.'

'That's rather hard on us – and sweeping. We had very complex problems.'

'Mostly concerned with preservation of forms and habits. It never seems to have occurred to you that in Nature life is growth, and preservation is an accident. . . . What is preserved in the rocks or in ice is only the image of life, but you were always regarding local taboos as eternal verities, and attempting to preserve them.'

My mind switched suddenly to my present situation.

'But suppose I were to go back and tell them what is going to happen. It would alter things. Doesn't that show I'm not going back?' I said.

She smiled. 'You think they would listen to you while they neglect philosophers, Terry?'

'Anyway,' I said, 'it doesn't arise. I don't intend to go back. I don't like your world. I think it is decadent, and in many ways immoral, but at least I am a whole human being here.'

She smiled again. 'So young, Terry. So sure of right and wrong. It's rather sweet.'

'It's not sweet at all,' I said brusquely. 'There have to be standards – without standards where are you?'

'Well, where are you? Where's a tree, or a flower, or a butterfly.'

'We're more than plants or animals.'

'But not godlike in our judgements. What do you do about opposing standards? – Go gloriously to war?'

I dropped that.

'Did we get to other planets?' I asked.

'No, but the next civilization did. They found Mars too old for us, and Venus too young. You had a dream of men spreading out over the universe; I'm afraid that never happened, though it was tried again later. They bred men specially for it as they bred them for all kinds of things. In fact they produced some very strange men and women, highly specialized. They were even more zealous for order than your people – they would not admit chance, which is a great foolishness. When their end came it was disastrous. ... None of the specialized types could survive. The population dwindled down to a few hundred thousand who had enough adaptability left to start over again.'

'So you have come to distrust order – and standards?'

'We have ceased to think of society as a structural engineering problem, or of individuals as components for assembly into some arbitrary pattern.'

'And you just sit and wait supinely for the end?'

'Oh dear, no. We preserve ourselves as materials for chance to work on. Life was an accident in the beginning, survival has often been an accident. Perhaps there'll be no more accidents – on the other hand, there may be.'

'That sounds very near defeatism.'

'In the end, defeat, and the cold, must come. First to the system, then the galaxy, then the universe, and the rest will be silence. Not to admit that is a foolish vanity.' She paused. 'Yet one grows flowers because they are lovely – not because one wishes them to live for ever.'

I did not like that world. It was foreign in its very thought-streams. The strain to understand was constant and wearisome – it was also unprofitable. All the comfort and ease I had there were centred in Clytassamine. For her I pulled down the barriers I had so bitterly erected around myself in the last few years, and I fell the more deeply in love on account of them.

Thus there was a second reason not to let things happen tamely as Hymorell had envisaged. Even Clytassamine could not make the place heaven, but I had got out of hell, and intended to stay out. It was on account of that that I spent unnumbered hours poring over the transference machine, learning all I could of it. My progress was slow, but some idea of the way it operated did begin at last to come to me.

But I could not settle. The feeling of transience would not leave me, and the days began to pass in long nagging uncertainty. There was no way of telling whether Hymorell would be successful in getting all the parts he needed. I had a haunting, mind's eye picture of him in my wheel-chair working away all the time on the contrivance which would condemn me to suffering in that broken body again. As the weeks went by the strain began to affect me, and I grew nervy. I began to reach the point where I was afraid to go to sleep lest the next time I woke I should find myself back in that chair.

Clytassamine, too, began to look worried. I wished I could be quite sure what she was worried about. Her emotions must have been confused. She undoubtedly had some affection for me – with a slightly maternal flavour to it, and an air of responsibility. Her genuine sympathy over my distress at the idea of going back was cut across by her feeling for Hymorell who must now be suffering what I had. There was also the point that my mental strain wasn't doing my temporary mortal tenement any good, either.

And then, when six uneventful months had begun to give me hope, it happened. It did so without sign or warning. I went to sleep in the room of the great green building: I woke back home – with a raging pain in my missing leg.

All was just as it had been – so much so that I reached right away for the dope bottle.

When I grew calmer I found that there was something there which had not been before. It was on the table beside me, looking like a radio-set partially assembled. I certainly had not built it. But for that, the whole thing might have been a dream.

I leant back in my chair, considering that mass of wiring very carefully. Then I started to examine it closely, touching nothing. It was, of course, crude in construction compared with the transference machine I had studied in the place that Clytassamine had called Cathalu, but I began to see similarities and noticed adaptations. I was still looking at it when I fell asleep. By the hours I slept I reckoned that Hymorell must have been driving my body at considerable pressure.

When I awoke, I began to think hard. My spell of soundness and health had left me with one firm decision – I would not remain as I was now. There were two ways out. The first had always been there for the taking – and still was. But now, there was the transference instrument. I did not understand a lot about it. I doubted whether I could succesfully re-tune it if I tried – and I did not wish to try. For one thing, little as I liked that other world, Clytassamine would be there to help me; for another, what I had learned made me think that I might easily land in circumstances even less desirable. So I left it on Hymorell's setting.

The chief difficulty I foresaw was that the machine must remain. He had had to leave it, but never guessed, I suppose, that I should be able to use it. And if I were to use it, I should have to leave it there for him to use again. My object must be to stop him doing that. It would be risky to set the machine to destroy itself. The process is to some extent hypnotic, and by no means instantaneous. Something very queer indeed would be likely to happen if it were destroyed while the transmission was in progress. Besides, he would be able to build another. As long as he existed he would be able to build another. . . . That made the answer fairly obvious. . . .

When I had made my plan I tried the instrument several times, but he was well integrated and aware of himself. I saw that I should have to catch him asleep, as he had caught me, so I went on trying at intervals of four hours.

I don't know whether he outguessed me or whether he was just lucky. I had got hold of the poison a year before, to keep by me in case things got too bad. My first idea was to swallow it in a capsule which would take some little time to dissolve. But then I got to thinking what would happen if something should go wrong and I could not make the transfer in time, so I scared myself off that scheme. Instead, I poured the poison into the dope bottle. The crystals were white, just like the dope itself, only a little larger.

Once I got a response from the instrument it was easier than I had expected. I took hold of the two handles, and concentrated all my attention on the lens. I felt giddy, the room swayed and blurred, when it cleared I was back in that green room, with Clytassamine beside me. I reached my hands towards her, and then stopped, for I could hear her quietly crying. I had never known her to do that before.

'What is it, Clya? What is the matter?' I asked.

For a moment she went absolutely quiet. Then she said, incredulously:

'It's – it's not Terry?'

'But it is. I told you I was not going to be sent back there,' I assured her.

She drew in her breath. Then she started to cry again, but differently. I put my arm round her. After a while I asked:

'Clya, what is it? What's all this about?'

She sniffled. 'It's Hymorell. Your world's done something dreadful to him. When he came back he was harsh and bitter. He kept on talking of pain and suffering, and he was – cruel.'

It did not greatly surprise me. They knew little or nothing of illness or physical discomfort. If a body became in the least defective, they transferred. They had never had to learn the hard way.

'Why didn't it do that to you, too?' she asked.

'I think it did at first,' I admitted. 'But one has to learn that that doesn't help much.'

'I was afraid of him. He was cruel,' she repeated.

I kept myself awake for forty-eight hours, to make sure. I knew that one of the first things he would need when he woke was the dope, but there was no sense in taking chances. Then I let myself sleep.

When I opened my eyes, I was back here. It was no slow awakening. I knew in a flash that he had somehow suspected that dope, and avoided it. The instrument was beside me, and I saw a thin curl of smoke rising from it as though a cigarette had been left burning. I began to reach towards it, but then caution checked me. I caught the leads, and pulled them out. In among the wiring I found a small can with a glowing fuse attached. I flung the thing hastily through the window. He too, however, had had to allow a safety margin: it was half an hour before it went off.

I looked at the dope. I was needing it badly, but I didn't dare to touch it. I trundled my chair over to the cupboard where the spare supply was kept. But when I took out the bottle, I hesitated. It *looked* like the real stuff, and intact – but, then, of course, it was essential that it should. Deliberately I threw it into the fireplace, smashing the bottle, and wheeled my chair to the telephone. The doctor was pretty short with me, but he came, bringing the stuff with him, thank God.

Various plans occurred to me. A poisoned needle, for instance, set strategically in the arm of the chair. Or some infection which would take a few days to develop – but that was too risky on account of possible delays. And over the former I was up against a problem which also balked several other ideas. The disabled have so little privacy. It is difficult enough to get the deadlier poisons, anyway:

when it has to be done by finding a third party ready to flout the law, it becomes virtually impossible. And if someone did do it for me he would later appear as an accessory to suicide. The same objection applied to my laying hands on a few sticks of dynamite. But I could buy a time switch without many questions – and I did.

It was, I thought, a neat arrangement. My old service pistol was trained on the exact position my head would occupy when I was at the instrument. Only if you were searching for it would you notice the muzzle looking out from the book-shelves. It was fixed to fire when the two handles of the instrument were grasped – but not until the time-switch had gone in. Thus I could set the switch and operate the instrument. Two hours later, for safe margin, the switch would go over, and the thing become lethal. If I tried and failed to make contact, I had only to set the switch again.

I waited three days, reckoning that Hymorell would be as chary of sleep as I had been, and uncertain whether his little grenade had been successful. Then I tried, successfully. – But three days later I was back again in my chair.

Hymorell, damn him, was too cautious. He must have spotted the extra lead to the switch right away. It had been snipped off. . . . But I found his little surprise-packet, too – I would have melted the instrument, and most likely myself, too, if I had touched it before disconnecting. (The switch was thermostatic this time, set to cut in as the room cooled down – very neat.) The pistol and the time-switch had vanished, and I set about looking for them everywhere within range of my chair. I didn't find the pistol, but the switch was in the cupboard under the stairs. It was arranged to set off a percussion cap which would ignite a grey powder obviously taken from the pistol cartridges. There was paper and oily rag close by.

Once I had made sure there were no other booby traps around, I settled down to work out another little reception device of my own. There used to be a type of mine that the

Germans used which didn't go up until the seventh truck had passed over it. The idea had points. I spent a couple of days fixing that, and then turned to the transference instrument again.

I was getting sick of the game, but it seemed to be a duel which could only end with one of us outsmarting the other. But while I was keeping awake for a couple of days and trying to look ahead to what he might have laid for me if my present little gimmick failed to catch him, I had an idea. I took it to Clytassamine.

'Look here,' I said. 'Suppose I were to transfer to one of the feeble-minded the way you people do. Then when he operates again, it will be the half-wit who will take my place in the chair. We'll both be here and the whole thing will be solved.'

She shook her head. 'You need some sleep, Terry. You're getting fuddled. It's your *mind* he's working the exchange with. It wouldn't make any difference what kind of body you were using.'

She was right, of course. I was fuddled. On the third day I just had to sleep, come hell or high water. I slept for about fourteen of their hours – and woke up in the same place.

That was great. I couldn't believe he'd let that length of time pass without making an attempt if he were in a state to do so. There was justification for believing that my little gadget had brought it off this time, and at last I began to feel easier.

As the days went on, I began to grow sure. After the first half dozen times my dread of sleep diminished. At last I began to feel like a citizen of this other world, and to look for my place in it. With unlimited time ahead of me I didn't intend to spend it hanging around the way the rest of them did.

'Maybe there *is* only chance now,' I said to Clytassamine, 'but did you never hear of making chances?'

She smiled, but, it seemed to me, a little wearily.

'Yes,' she admitted, 'I know. I felt like that for my first

two generations. You are so young, Terry.' She sat looking
at me wistfully, and a little sadly.

Why the change should suddenly have come over me
then, I can't say. Maybe it wasn't that sudden, and had been
working up awhile, but as I looked back at her I found
myself seeing her quite differently, and a cold feeling came
over me. For the first time I saw beyond her perfect form
and young loveliness. Inside, she was old – old and wearied
– old, too, far beyond my reach. She thought of me as a
child, and had been treating me as one. The vigour of my
true youth had amused her – perhaps she had found that
it revived her own for a while. Now she was tired of it –
and of me. I saw that in the moment I fell out of love with
her, in that moment when her charm turned to experienced
sophistication, and every gesture showed as something
practised and known. I knew that the freshness I saw
was nothing but a sham. I must have stared at her quite a
while.

'You don't want me any more,' I told her. 'I've ceased to
be amusing. You want Hymorell.'

'Yes, Terry,' she said, quietly.

For the next day or two I pondered over what to do. I
had never liked that world. It was effete and decaying. And
now what pleasantness there had been had vanished. I felt
imprisoned, stifled, appalled at the prospect of spending
several lifetimes in it. Now that a return to my former
torments seemed improbable, the prospect here looked, in
another way, little, if any better. For the first time I began
to wonder whether finiteness wasn't one of life's more important qualities. I quailed miserably at the prospect of an
existence that was almost eternal. . . .

But my worry was not necessary. I am in no danger of
indefinite existence. I went to sleep despondent in the great
green building, and when I woke I was in this place.

How Hymorell can have done it I don't altogether understand. I guess he was equally tired of the game we'd
been playing. I think he must have constructed a transference instrument of the ordinary type they use in that world

of his. Then he must have used it in conjunction with the other to effect a kind of triangular transference – possibly in two stages. Assuming that the other part of it worked as well as mine, Hymorell returned to his own body, and a feeble-minded patient from this institution was transferred to my chair. It succeeded in its purpose of separating me from the transfer instrument.

When I realized what had happened I wrote at once under the name I have here inquiring about Terry Molton whom I claimed as an acquaintance. I learned that he was dead. He had apparently electrocuted himself with some experimental radio apparatus. The resulting fuse had started a fire in the room, but it had been discovered and put out before it could spread further. The time of its discovery was some three hours after I had woken to find myself in this place.

My position here is difficult. If I pretend to be Stephen Dallboy I am a moron committed for care; if I claim to be Terry Molton I am thought to have hallucinations. I see little chance that I shall be able to reclaim my rightful property, but I think I shall be able to show myself sufficiently normal to be released.

On balance that would not be too bad. I do at least have all the parts of a passable body now. And I reckon I ought to be able to use them profitably here in the kind of world where I do understand something of what's going on. So I gain more than I lose.

Nevertheless, I *am* Terry Molton.

... It is, as you will realize, a well-integrated hallucination, but if there is nothing more serious we shall undoubtedly release the patient experimentally in due course.

However, we do feel that we should acquaint you with one or two discrepant points. One is that, although the two men appear never to have met, Stephen Dallboy is informed in remarkably intimate detail of Terence Molton's affairs. Another is that when confronted for test purposes with two friends of Molton's he immediately addressed them by name and seemed to know all about them – to their great astonishment, for they protest that in no way whatever — save, perhaps, in manner of speech — does he in the least resemble Terence Molton.

You will find herewith full legal proof that the patient is indeed Stephen Dallboy. Should there be any further developments we will keep you advised.

Yours truly,
Jesse K. Johnson
(Medical Director)

Dumb Martian

WHEN Duncan Weaver bought Lellie for – no, there could be trouble putting it that way – when Duncan Weaver paid Lellie's parents one thousand pounds in compensation for the loss of her services, he had a figure of six, or, if absolutely necessary, seven hundred in mind.

Everybody in Port Clarke that he had asked about it assured him that that would be a fair price. But when he got up country it hadn't turned out quite as simple as the Port Clarkers seemed to think. The first three Martian families he had tackled hadn't shown any disposition to sell their daughters at all; the next wanted £1,500, and wouldn't budge; Lellie's parents had started at £1,500, too, but they came down to £1,000 when he'd made it plain that he wasn't going to stand for extortion. And when, on the way back to Port Clarke with her, he came to work it out, he found himself not so badly pleased with the deal after all. Over the five-year term of his appointment it could only cost him £200 a year at the worst – that is to say if he were not able to sell her for £400, maybe £500 when he got back. Looked at that way, it wasn't really at all unreasonable.

In town once more, he went to explain the situation and get things all set with the Company's Agent.

'Look,' he said, 'you know the way I'm fixed with this five-year contract as Way-load Station Superintendent on Jupiter IV/II? Well, the ship that takes me there will be travelling light to pick up cargo. So how about a second passage on her?' He had already taken the precautionary step of finding out that the Company was accustomed to grant an extra passage in such circumstances, though not of right.

The Company's Agent was not surprised. After consulting some lists, he said that he saw no objection to an extra passenger. He explained that the Company was also prepared in such cases to supply the extra ration of food for one person at the nominal charge of £200 per annum, payable by deduction from salary.

'What! A thousand pounds!' Duncan exclaimed.

'Well worth it,' said the Agent. 'It *is* nominal for the rations, because it's worth the Company's while to lay out the rest for something that helps to keep an employee from going nuts. That's pretty easy to do when you're fixed alone on a way-load station, they tell me – and I believe them. A thousand's not high if it helps you to avoid a crack-up.'

Duncan argued it a bit, on principle, but the Agent had the thing cut and dried. It meant that Lellie's price went up to £2,000 – £400 a year. Still, with his own salary at £5,000 a year, tax free, unspendable during his term on Jupiter IV/II, and piling up nicely, it wouldn't come to such a big slice. So he agreed.

'Fine,' said the Agent. 'I'll fix it, then. All you'll need is an embarkation permit for her, and they'll grant that automatically on production of your marriage certificate.'

Duncan stared.

'Marriage certificate! What, me! Me marry a Mart!'

The Agent shook his head reprovingly.

'No embarkation permit without it. Anti-slavery regulation. They'd likely think you meant to sell her – might even think you'd bought her.'

'What, me!' Duncan said again, indignantly.

'Even you,' said the Agent. 'A marriage licence will only cost you another ten pounds – unless you've got a wife back home, in which case it'll likely cost you a bit more later on.'

Duncan shook his head.

'I've no wife,' he assured him.

'Uh-huh,' said the Agent, neither believing, nor disbelieving. 'Then what's the difference?'

Duncan came back a couple of days later, with the certificate and the permit. The Agent looked them over.

'That's okay,' he agreed. 'I'll confirm the booking. My fee will be one hundred pounds.'

'Your fee! What the –?'

'Call it safeguarding your investment,' said the Agent.

The man who had issued the embarkation permit had required one hundred pounds, too. Duncan did not mention that now, but he said, with bitterness:

'One dumb Mart's costing me plenty.'

'Dumb?' said the Agent, looking at him.

'Speechless plus. These hick Mart s don't know they're born.'

'H'm,' said the Agent. 'Never lived here, have you?'

'No,' Duncan admitted. 'But I've laid-over here a few times.'

The Agent nodded.

'They act dumb, and the way their faces are makes them look dumb,' he said, 'but they were a mighty clever people, once.'

'Once, could be a long time ago.'

'Long before we got here they'd given up bothering to think a lot. Their planet was dying, and they were kind of content to die with it.'

'Well, I call that dumb. Aren't all planets dying, anyway?'

'Ever seen an old man just sitting in the sun, taking it easy? It doesn't have to mean he's senile. It may do, but very likely he can snap out of it and put his mind to work again if it gets really necessary. But mostly he finds it not worth the bother. Less trouble just to let things happen.'

'Well, this one's only about twenty – say ten and a half of your Martian years – and she certainly lets 'em happen. And I'd say it's a kind of acid test for dumbness when a girl doesn't know what goes on at her own wedding ceremony.'

And then, on top of that, it turned out to be necessary to lay out yet another hundred pounds on clothing and other things for her, bringing the whole investment up to £2,310. It was a sum which might possibly have been justified on a really *smart* girl, but Lellie ... But there it was. Once you made the first payment, you either lost on it, or were stuck for the rest. And, anyway, on a lonely way-load station even she would be company – of a sort. . . .

The First Officer called Duncan into the navigating room to take a look at his future home.

'There it is,' he said, waving his hand at a watch-screen.

Duncan looked at the jagged-surfaced crescent. There was no scale to it: it could have been the size of Luna, or of a basket-ball. Either size, it was still just a lump of rock, turning slowly over.

'How big?' he asked.

'Around forty miles mean diameter.'

'What'd that be in gravity?'

'Haven't worked it out. Call it slight, and reckon there isn't any, and you'll be near enough.'

'Uh-huh,' said Duncan.

On the way back to the mess-room he paused to put his head into the cabin. Lellie was lying on her bunk, with the spring-cover fastened over her to give some illusion of weight. At the sight of him she raised herself on one elbow.

She was small – not much over five feet. Her face and hands were delicate; they had a fragility which was not simply a matter of poor bone-structure. To an Earthman her eyes looked unnaturally round, seeming to give her permanently an expression of innocence surprised. The lobes of her ears hung unusually low out of a mass of brown hair that glinted with red among its waves. The paleness of her skin was emphasized by the colour on her cheeks and the vivid red on her lips.

'Hey,' said Duncan. 'You can start to get busy packing up the stuff now.'

'Packing up?' she repeated doubtfully, in a curiously resonant voice.

'Sure. Pack,' Duncan told her. He demonstrated by opening a box, cramming some clothes into it, and waving a hand to include the rest. Her expression did not change, but the idea got across.

'We are come?' she asked.

'We are nearly come. So get busy on this lot,' he informed her.

'Yith – okay,' she said, and began to unhook the cover.

Duncan shut the door, and gave a shove which sent him floating down the passage leading to the general mess and living-room.

Inside the cabin, Lellie pushed away the cover. She reached down cautiously for a pair of metallic soles, and attached them to her slippers by their clips. Still cautiously holding on to the bunk, she swung her feet over the side and lowered them until the magnetic soles clicked into contact with the floor. She stood up, more confidently. The brown overall suit she wore revealed proportions that might be admired among Martians, but by Earth standards they were not classic – it is said to be the consequence of the thinner air of Mars that has in the course of time produced a greater lung capacity, with consequent modification. Still ill at ease with her condition of weightlessness, she slid her feet to keep contact as she crossed the room. For some moments she paused in front of a wall mirror, contemplating her reflection. Then she turned away and set about the packing.

'– one hell of a place to take a woman to,' Wishart, the ship's cook, was saying as Duncan came in.

Duncan did not care a lot for Wishart – chiefly on account of the fact that when it had occurred to him that it was highly desirable for Lellie to have some lessons in weightless cooking, Wishart had refused to give the tuition for less than £50, and thus increased the investment cost to £2,360. Nevertheless, it was not his way to pretend to have misheard.

'One hell of a place to be given a job,' he said, grimly.

No one replied to that. They knew how men came to be offered way-load jobs.

It was not necessary, as the Company frequently pointed out, for superannuation at the age of forty to come as a hardship to anyone: salaries were good, and they could cite plenty of cases where men had founded brilliant subsequent careers on the savings of their space-service days. That was all right for the men who had saved, and had not

been obsessively interested in the fact that one four-legged
animal can run faster than another. But this was not even
an enterprising way to have lost one's money, so when it
came to Duncan's time to leave crew work they made him
no more than the routine offer.

He had never been to Jupiter IV/II, but he knew just
what it would be like – something that was second moon to
Callisto; itself fourth moon, in order of discovery, to
Jupiter; would inevitably be one of the grimmer kinds of
cosmic pebble. They offered no alternative, so he signed up
at the usual terms: £5,000 a year for five years, all found,
plus five months waiting time on half-pay before he could
get there, plus six months afterwards, also on half-pay,
during 'readjustment to gravity'.

Well – it meant the next six years taken care of; five of
them without expenses, and a nice little sum at the end.

The splinter in the mouthful was: could you get through
five years of isolation without cracking up? Even when the
psychologist had okayed you, you couldn't be sure. Some
could: others went to pieces in a few months, and had to
be taken off, gibbering. If you got through two years, they
said, you'd be okay for five. But the only way to find out
about the two was to try . . .

'What about my putting in the waiting time on Mars? I
could live cheaper there,' Duncan suggested.

They had consulted planetary tables and sailing
schedules, and discovered that it would come cheaper for
them, too. They had declined to split the difference on the
saving thus made, but they had booked him a passage for
the following week, and arranged for him to draw, on
credit, from the Company's agent there.

The Martian colony in and around Port Clarke is rich in
ex-spacemen who find it more comfortable to spend their
rearguard years in the lesser gravity, broader morality, and
greater economy obtaining there. They are great advisers.
Duncan listened, but discarded most of it. Such methods of
occupying oneself to preserve sanity as learning the Bible
or the works of Shakespeare by heart, or copying out three

pages of the Encyclopaedia every day, or building model spaceships in bottles, struck him not only as tedious, but probably of doubtful efficacy, as well. The only one which he had felt to show sound practical advantages was that which had led him to picking Lellie to share his exile, and he still fancied it was a sound one, in spite of its letting him in for £2,360.

He was well enough aware of the general opinion about it to refrain from adding a sharp retort to Wishart. Instead, he conceded:

'Maybe it'd not do to take a *real* woman to a place like that. But a Mart's kind of different. . . .'

'Even a Mart –' Wishart began, but he was cut short by finding himself drift slowly across the room as the arrester tubes began to fire.

Conversation ceased as everybody turned-to on the job of securing all loose objects.

Jupiter IV/II was, by definition, a sub-moon, and probably a captured asteroid. The surface was not cratered, like Luna's: it was simply a waste of jagged, riven rocks. The satellite as a whole had the form of an irregular ovoid; it was a bleak, cheerless lump of stone splintered off some vanished planet, with nothing whatever to commend it but its situation.

There have to be way-load stations. It would be hopelessly uneconomic to build big ships capable of landing on the major planets. A few of the older and smaller ships were indeed built on Earth, and so had to be launched from there, but the very first large, moon-assembled ship established a new practice. Ships became truly *space*ships and were no longer built to stand the strains of high gravitational pull. They began to make their voyages, carrying fuel, stores, freight, and changes of personnel, exclusively between satellites. Newer types do not put in even at Luna, but use the artificial satellite, Pseudos, exclusively as their Earth terminus.

Freight between the way-loads and their primaries is customarily consigned in powered cylinders known as crates; passengers are ferried back and forth in small rocket-ships. Stations such as Pseudos, or Deimos, the main way-load for Mars, handle enough work to keep a crew busy, but in the outlying, little-developed posts one man who is part-handler, part-watchman is enough. Ships visited them infrequently. On Jupiter IV/II one might, according to Duncan's information, expect an average of one every eight or nine months (Earth).

The ship continued to slow, coming in on a spiral, adjusting her speed to that of the satellite. The gyros started up to give stability. The small, jagged world grew until it overflowed the watch-screens. The ship was manoeuvred into a close orbit. Miles of featureless, formidable rocks slid monotonously beneath her.

The station site came sliding on to the screen from the left; a roughly levelled area of a few acres; the first and only sign of order in the stony chaos. At the far end was a pair of hemispherical huts, one much larger than the other. At the near end, a few cylindrical crates were lined up beside a launching ramp hewn from the rock. Down each side of the area stood rows of canvas bins, some stuffed full of a conical shape; others slack, empty or half-empty. A huge parabolic mirror was perched on a crag behind the station, looking like a monstrous, formalized flower. In the whole scene there was only one sign of movement – a small, space-suited figure prancing madly about on a metal apron in front of the larger dome, waving its arms in a wild welcome.

Duncan left the screen, and went to the cabin. He found Lellie fighting off a large case which, under the influence of deceleration, seemed determined to pin her against the wall. He shoved the case aside, and pulled her out.

'We're there,' he told her. 'Put on your space-suit.'

Her round eyes ceased to pay attention to the case, and turned towards him. There was no telling from them how she felt, what she thought. She said, simply:

'Thpace-thuit. Yith – okay.'

Standing in the airlock of the dome, the outgoing Superintendent paid more attention to Lellie than to the pressure-dial. He knew from experience exactly how long equalizing took, and opened his face-plate without even a glance at the pointer.

'Wish I'd had the sense to bring one,' he observed. 'Could have been mighty useful on the chores, too.'

He opened the inner door, and led through.

'Here it is – and welcome to it,' he said.

The main living-room was oddly shaped by reason of the dome's architecture, but it was spacious. It was also exceedingly, sordidly untidy.

'Meant to clean it up – never got around to it, some way,' he added. He looked at Lellie. There was no visible sign of what she thought of the place. 'Never can tell with Marts,' he said uneasily. 'They kind of non-register.'

Duncan agreed: 'I've figured this one looked astonished at being born, and never got over it.'

The other man went on looking at Lellie. His eyes strayed from her to a gallery of pinned-up terrestrial beauties, and back again.

'Sort of funny shape Marts are,' he said, musingly.

'This one's reckoned a good enough looker where she comes from,' Duncan told him, a trifle shortly.

'Sure. No offence, Bud. I guess they'll all seem a funny shape to me after this spell.' He changed the subject. 'I'd better show you the ropes around here.'

Duncan signed to Lellie to open her faceplate so that she could hear him, and then told her to get out of her suit.

The dome was the usual type: double-floored, double-walled, with an insulated and evacuated space between the two; constructed as a unit, and held down by metal bars let into the rock. In the living-quarters there were three more sizable rooms, able to cope with increased personnel if trade should expand.

'The rest,' the outgoing man explained, 'is the regular station stores, mostly food, air cylinders, spares of one kind and another, and water – you'll need to watch her on water; most women seem to think it grows naturally in pipes.'

Duncan shook his head.

'Not Marts. Living in deserts gives 'em a natural respect for water.'

The other picked up a clip of store-sheets.

'We'll check and sign these later. It's a nice soft job here. Only freight now is rare metalliferous earth. Callisto's not been opened up a lot yet. Handling's easy. They tell you when a crate's on the way: you switch on the radio beacon to bring it in. On dispatch you can't go wrong if you follow the tables.' He looked around the room. 'All home comforts. You read? Plenty of books.' He waved a hand at the packed rows which covered half the inner partition wall. Duncan said he'd never been much of a reader. 'Well, it helps,' said the other. 'Find pretty well anything that's known in that lot. Records there. Fond of music?'

Duncan said he liked a good tune.

'H'm. Better try the other stuff. Tunes get to squirrelling inside your head. Play chess?' He pointed to a board, with men pegged into it.

Duncan shook his head.

'Pity. There's a fellow over on Callisto plays a pretty hot game. He'll be disappointed not to finish this one. Still, if I was fixed up the way you are, maybe I'd not have been interested in chess.' His eyes strayed to Lellie again. 'What do you reckon she's going to do here, over and above cooking and amusing you?' he asked.

It was not a question that had occurred to Duncan, but he shrugged.

'Oh, she'll be okay, I guess. There's a natural dumbness about Marts – they'll sit for hours on end, doing damn all. It's a gift they got.'

'Well, it should come in handy here,' said the other.

The regular ship's-call work went on. Cases were unloaded, the metalliferous earths hosed from the bins into the holds. A small ferry-rocket came up from Callisto carry-

ing a couple of time-expired prospectors, and left again
with their two replacements. The ship's engineers checked
over the station's machinery, made renewals, topped up the
water tanks, charged the spent air cylinders, tested, tink-
ered, and tested again before giving their final okay.

Duncan stood outside on the metal apron where not long
ago his predecessor had performed his fantastic dance of
welcome, to watch the ship take off. She rose straight up,
with her jets pushing her gently. The curve of her hull
became an elongated crescent shining against the black
sky. The main driving jets started to gush white flame
edged with pink. Quickly she picked up speed. Before long
she had dwindled to a speck which sank behind the ragged
skyline.

Quite suddenly Duncan felt as if he, too, had dwindled.
He had become a speck upon a barren mass of rock which
was itself a speck in the immensity. The indifferent sky
about him had no scale. It was an utterly black void
wherein his mother-sun and a myriad more suns flared per-
petually, without reason or purpose.

The rocks of the satellite itself, rising up in their harsh
crests and ridges, were without scale, too. He could not
tell which were near or far away; he could not, in the
jumble of hard-lit planes and inky shadows, even make out
their true form. There was nothing like them to be seen on
Earth, or on Mars. Their unweathered edges were sharp as
blades: they had been just as sharp as that for millions
upon millions of years, and would be for as long as the
satellite should last.

The unchanging millions of years seemed to stretch out
before and behind him. It was not only himself, it was all
life that was a speck, a briefly transitory accident, utterly
unimportant to the universe. It was a queer little mote
dancing for its chance moment in the light of the eternal
suns. Reality was just globes of fire and balls of stone rolling on, senselessly rolling along through emptiness,
through time unimaginable, for ever, and ever, and
ever. . . .

Within his heated suit, Duncan shivered a little. Never before had he been so alone; never so much aware of the vast, callous, futile loneliness of space. Looking out into the blackness, with light that had left a star a million years ago shining into his eyes, he wondered.

'*Why?*' he asked himself. 'What the heck's it all about, anyway?'

The sound of his own unanswerable question broke up the mood. He shook his head to clear it of speculative nonsense. He turned his back on the universe, reducing it again to its proper status as a background for life in general and human life in particular, and stepped into the airlock.

The job was, as his predecessor had told him, soft. Duncan made his radio contacts with Callisto at prearranged times. Usually it was little more than a formal check on one another's continued existence, with perhaps an exchange of comment on the radio news. Only occasionally did they announce a dispatch and tell him when to switch on his beacon. Then, in due course, the cylinder-crate would make its appearance, and float slowly down. It was quite a simple matter to couple it up to a bin to transfer the load.

The satellite's day was too short for convenience, and its night, lit by Callisto, and sometimes by Jupiter as well, almost as bright; so they disregarded it, and lived by the calendar-clock which kept Earth time on the Greenwich Meridian setting. At first much of the time had been occupied in disposing of the freight that the ship had left. Some of it into the main dome – necessities for themselves, and other items that would store better where there was warmth and air. Some into the small, airless, unheated dome. The greater part to be stowed and padded carefully into cylinders and launched off to the Callisto base. But once that work had been cleared, the job was certainly soft, too soft. . . .

Duncan drew up a programme. At regular intervals he would inspect this and that, he would waft himself up to the crag and check on the sun-motor there, et cetera. But keeping to an unnecessary programme requires resolution. Sun-motors, for instance, are very necessarily built to run for long spells without attention. The only action one could take if it should stop would be to call on Callisto for a ferry-rocket to come and take them off until a ship should call to repair it. A breakdown there, the Company had explained very clearly, was the only thing that would justify him in leaving his station, with the stores of precious earth, unmanned (and it was also conveyed that to contrive a breakdown for the sake of a change was unlikely to prove worth while). One way and another, the programme did not last long.

There were times when Duncan found himself wondering whether the bringing of Lellie had been such a good idea after all. On the purely practical side, he'd not have cooked as well as she did, and probably have pigged it quite as badly as his precessor had, but if she had not been there, the necessity of looking after himself would have given him some occupation. And even from the angle of company – well, she was that, of a sort, but she was alien, queer; kind of like a half-robot, and dumb at that; certainly no fun. There were, indeed, times – increasingly frequent times, when the very look of her irritated him intensely; so did the way she moved, *and* her gestures, *and* her silly pidgin-talk when she talked, *and* her self-contained silence when she didn't, *and* her withdrawness, *and* all her differentness, *and* the fact that he would have been £2,360 better off without her. ... Nor did she make a serious attempt to remedy her shortcomings, even where she had the means. Her face, for instance. You'd think any girl would try to make her best of that – but did she, hell! There was that left eyebrow again: made her look like a sozzled clown, but a lot she cared. ...

'For heaven's sake,' he told her once more, 'put the cock-eyed thing straight. Don't you know how to fix 'em *yet*? And you've got your colour on wrong, too. Look at that picture – now look at yourself in the mirror: a great daub of red all in the wrong place. And your hair, too: getting all like seaweed again. You've got the things to wave it, then for crysake wave it again, and stop looking like a bloody mermaid. I know you can't help being a damn Mart, but you can at least *try* to look like a real woman.'

Lellie looked at the coloured picture, and then compared her reflection with it, critically.

'Yith – okay,' she said, with an equable detachment.

Duncan snorted.

'And that's another thing. Bloody baby-talk! It's not "yith", it's "yes". Y-E-S, yes. So say "yes".'

'Yith,' said Lellie, obligingly.

'Oh, for – Can't you *hear* the difference? S-s-s, not th-th-th. Ye-sss.'

'Yith,' she said.

'No. Put your tongue further back like this –'

The lesson went on for some time. Finally he grew angry.

'Just making a monkey out of me, huh! You'd better be careful, my girl. Now, say "yes".'

She hesitated, looking at his wrathful face.

'Go on, say it.'

'Y-yeth,' she said, nervously.

His hand slapped across her face harder than he had intended. The jolt broke her magnetic contact with the floor, and sent her sailing across the room in a spin of arms and legs. She struck the opposite wall, and rebounded to float helplessly, out of reach of any hold. He strode after her, turned her right way up, and set her on her feet. His left hand clutched her overall in a bunch, just below her throat, his right was raised.

'Again!' he told her.

Her eyes looked helplessly this way and that. He shook her. She tried. At the sixth attempt she managed: 'Yeths.'

He accepted that for the time being.

'You *can* do it, you see – when you try. What you need, my girl, is a bit of firm handling.'

He let her go. She tottered across the room, holding her hands to her bruised face.

A number of times while the weeks drew out so slowly

into months Duncan found himself wondering whether he was going to get through. He spun out what work there was as much as he could, but it left still too much time hanging heavy on his hands.

A middle-aged man who has read nothing longer than an occasional magazine article does not take to books. He tired very quickly, as his predecessor had prophesied, of the popular records, and could make nothing of the others. He taught himself the moves in chess from a book, and instructed Lellie in them, intending after a little practice with her to challenge the man on Callisto. Lellie, however, managed to win with such consistency that he had to decide that he had not the right kind of mind for the game. Instead, he taught her a kind of double solitaire, but that didn't last long, either; the cards seemed always to run for Lellie.

Occasionally there was some news and entertainment to be had from the radio, but with Earth somewhere round the other side of the sun just then, Mars screened off half the time by Callisto, and the rotation of the satellite itself, reception was either impossible, or badly broken up.

So mostly he sat and fretted, hating the satellite, angry with himself, and irritated by Lellie.

Just the phlegmatic way she went on with her tasks irritated him. It seemed an injustice that she could take it all better than he could simply *because* she was a dumb Mart. When his ill-temper became vocal, the look of her as she listened exasperated him still more.

'For crysake,' he told her one time, 'can't you make that silly face of yours *mean* something? Can't you laugh, or cry, or get mad, or something? It's enough to drive a guy nuts going on looking at a face that's fixed permanent like it was a doll just heard its first dirty story. I know you can't help being dumb, but for heaven's sake crack it up a bit, get some expression into it.'

She went on looking at him without a shadow of a change.

'Go on, you heard me! Smile, damn you – Smile!'

Her mouth twitched very slightly.

'Call that a smile! Now, there's a smile!' He pointed to a pin-up with her head split pretty much in half by a smile like a piano keyboard. 'Like that! Like this!' He grinned widely.

'No,' she said. 'My face can't wriggle like Earth faces.'

'Wriggle!' he said, incensed. 'Wriggle, you call it!' He freed himself from the chair's spring-cover, and came towards her. She backed away until she fetched up against the wall. 'I'll make yours wriggle, my girl. Go on, now – smile!' He lifted his hand.

Lellie put her hands up to her face.

'No!' she protested. 'No – no – no!'

It was on the very day that Duncan marked off the eighth completed month that Callisto relayed news of a ship on the way. A couple of days later he was able to make contact with her himself, and confirm her arrival in about a week. He felt as if he had been given several stiff drinks. There were the preparations to make, stores to check, deficiencies to note, a string of nil-nil-nil entries to be made in the log to bring it up to date. He bustled around as he got on with it. He even hummed to himself as he worked, and ceased to be annoyed with Lellie. The effect upon her of the news was imperceptible – but then, what would you expect . . . ?

Sharp on her estimated time the ship hung above them, growing slowly larger as her upper jets pressed her down. The moment she was berthed Duncan went aboard, with the feeling that everything in sight was an old friend. The Captain received him warmly, and brought out the drinks. It was all routine – even Duncan's babbling and slightly inebriated manner was the regular thing in the circumstances. The only departure from pattern came when the Captain introduced a man beside him, and explained him.

'We've brought a surprise for you, Superintendent. This is Doctor Whint. He'll be sharing your exile for a bit.'

Duncan shook hands. 'Doctor . . . ?' he said, surprisedly.

'Not medicine – science,' Alan Whint told him. 'The

Company's pushed me out here to do a geological survey — if geo isn't the wrong word to use. About a year. Hope you don't mind.'

Duncan said conventionally that he'd be glad of the company, and left it at that for the moment. Later, he took him over to the dome. Alan Whint was surprised to find Lellie there; clearly nobody had told him about her. He interrupted Duncan's explanations to say:

'Won't you introduce me to your wife?'

Duncan did so, without grace. He resented the reproving tone in the man's voice; nor did he care for the way he greeted Lellie just as if she were an Earth woman. He was also aware that he had noticed the bruise on her cheek that the colour did not altogether cover. In his mind he classified Alan Whint as one of the smooth, snooty type, and hoped that there was not going to be trouble with him.

It could be, indeed, it was, a matter of opinion who made the trouble when it boiled up some three months later. There had already been several occasions when it had lurked uneasily near. Very likely it would have come into the open long before had Whint's work not taken him out of the dome so much. The moment of touch-off came when Lellie lifted her eyes from the book she was reading to ask: 'What does "female emancipation" mean?'

Alan started to explain. He was only half-way through the first sentence when Duncan broke in:

'Listen — who told you to go putting ideas into her head?'

Alan shrugged his shoulders slightly, and looked at him.

'That's a damn silly question,' he said. 'And, anyway, why shouldn't she have ideas? Why shouldn't anyone?'

'You know what I mean.'

'I never understand you guys who apparently can't *say* what you mean. Try again.'

'All right then. What I mean is this: you come here with

your ritzy ways and your snazzy talk, and right from the start you start shoving your nose into things that aren't your business. You begin right off by treating her as if she was some toney dame back home.'

'I hoped so. I'm glad you noticed it.'

'And do you think I didn't see why?'

'I'm quite sure you didn't. You've such a well-grooved mind. You think, in your simple way, that I'm out to get your girl, and you resent that with all the weight of two thousand, three hundred and sixty pounds. But you're wrong: I'm not.'

Duncan was momentarily thrown off his line, then:

'My *wife*,' he corrected. 'She may be only a dumb Mart, but she's legally my wife: and what I say goes.'

'Yes, Lellie is a Mart, as you call it; she may even be your wife, for all I know to the contrary; but dumb, she certainly is not. For one example, look at the speed with which she's learned to read – once someone took the trouble to show her how. I don't think you'd show up any too bright yourself in a language where you only knew a few words, and which you couldn't read.'

'It was none of your business to teach her. She didn't need to read. She was all right the way she was.'

'The voice of the slaver down the ages. Well, if I've done nothing else, I've cracked up your ignorance racket there.'

'And why? – So she'll think you're a great guy. The same reason you talk all toney and smarmy to her. So you'll get her thinking you're a better man than I am.'

'I talk to her the way I'd talk to any woman anywhere – only more simply since she's not had the chance of an education. If she does think I'm a better man, then I agree with her. I'd be sorry if I couldn't.'

'I'll show you who's the better man –' Duncan began.

'You don't need to. I knew when I came here that you'd be a waster, or you'd not be on this job – and it didn't take long for me to find out that you were a goddam bully, too. Do you suppose I've not noticed the bruises? Do you think

I've enjoyed having to listen to you bawling out a girl whom you've deliberately kept ignorant and defenceless when she's potentially ten times the sense you have? Having to watch a *clodkopf* like you lording it over your "dumb Mart"? You emetic!'

In the heat of the moment, Duncan could not quite remember what an emetic was, but anywhere else the man would not have got that far before he had waded in to break him up. Yet, even through his anger, twenty years of space experience held – as little more than a boy he had learnt the ludicrous futility of weightless scrapping, and that it was the angry man who always made the bigger fool of himself.

Both of them simmered, but held in. Somehow the occasion was patched up and smoothed over, and for a time things went on much as before.

Alan continued to make his expeditions in the small craft which he had brought with him. He examined and explored other parts of the satellite, returning with specimen pieces of rock which he tested, and arranged, carefully labelled, in cases. In his off times he occupied himself, as before, in teaching Lellie.

That he did it largely for his own occupation as well as from a feeling that it should be done, Duncan did not altogether deny; but he was equally sure that in continued close association one thing leads to another, sooner or later. So far, there had been nothing between them that he could put his finger on – but Alan's term had still some nine months to go, even if he were relieved to time. Lellie was already hero-worshipping. And he was spoiling her more every day by this fool business of treating her as if she were an Earth woman. One day they'd come alive to it – and the next step would be that they would see him as an obstacle that would be better removed. Prevention being better than cure, the sensible course was to see that the situation should never develop. There need not be any fuss about it. . . .

There was not.

One day Alan Whint took off on a routine flight to prospect somewhere on the other side of the satellite. He simply never came back. That was all.

There was no telling what Lellie thought about it; but something seemed to happen to her.

For several days she spent almost all her time standing by the main window of the living-room, looking out into the blackness at the flaring pinpoints of light. It was not that she was waiting or hoping for Alan's return – she knew as well as Duncan himself that when thirty-six hours had gone by there was no chance of that. She said nothing. Her expression maintained its exasperating look of slight surprise, unchanged. Only in her eyes was there any perceptible difference: they looked a little less live, as if she had withdrawn herself further behind them.

Duncan could not tell whether she knew or guessed anything. And there seemed to be no way of finding out without planting the idea in her mind – *if* it were not already there. He was, without admitting it too fully to himself, nervous of her – too nervous to turn on her roundly for the time she spent vacantly mooning out of the window. He had an uncomfortable awareness of how many ways there were for even a dimwit to contrive a fatal accident in such a place. As a precaution he took to fitting new air-bottles to his suit every time he went out, and checking that they were at full pressure. He also took to placing a piece of rock so that the outer door of the airlock could not close behind him. He made a point of noticing that his food and hers came straight out of the same pot, and watched her closely as she worked. He still could not decide whether she knew, or suspected. . . . After they were sure that he was gone, she never once mentioned Alan's name. . . .

The mood stayed on her for perhaps a week. Then it changed abruptly. She paid no more attention to the blackness outside. Instead, she began to read, voraciously and indiscriminately.

Duncan found it hard to understand her absorption in the books, nor did he like it, but he decided for the moment not to interfere. It did, at least, have the advantage of keeping her mind off other things.

Gradually he began to feel easier. The crisis was over. Either she had not guessed, or, if she had, she had decided to do nothing about it. Her addiction to books, however, did not abate. In spite of several reminders by Duncan that it was for *company* that he had laid out the not inconsiderable sum of £2,360, she continued, as if determined to work her way through the station's library.

By degrees the affair retreated into the background. When the next ship came Duncan watched her anxiously in case she had been biding her time to hand on her suspicions to the crew. It turned out, however, to be unnecessary. She showed no tendency to refer to the matter, and when the ship pulled out, taking the opportunity with it, he was relievedly able to tell himself that he had really been right all along – she was just a dumb Mart: she had simply forgotten the Alan Whint incident, as a child might.

And yet, as the months of his term ticked steadily away, he found that he had, bit by bit, to revise that estimate of dumbness. She was learning from books things that he did not know himself. It even had some advantages, though it put him in a position he did not care for – when she asked, as she sometimes did now, for explanations, he found it unpleasant to be stumped by a Mart. Having the practical man's suspicion of book-acquired knowledge, he felt it necessary to explain to her how much of the stuff in the books was a lot of nonsense, how they never really came to grips with the problems of life as he had lived it. He cited instances from his own affairs, gave examples from his experience, in fact, he found himself teaching her.

She learnt quickly, too; the practical as well as the book stuff. Of necessity he had to revise his opinion of Marts slightly more – it wasn't that they were altogether dumb as he had thought, just that they were normally too dumb to start using the brains they had. Once started, Lellie was a regular vacuum-cleaner for knowledge of all sorts: it didn't seem long before she knew as much about the way-load station as he did himself. Teaching her was not at all what he had intended, but it did provide an occupation much to be preferred to the boredom of the early days. Besides, it had occurred to him that she was an appreciating asset....

Funny thing, that. He had never before thought of education as anything but a waste of time, but now it seriously began to look as if, when he got her back to Mars, he might recover quite a bit more of the £2,360 than he had expected. Maybe she'd make quite a useful secretary to someone. ... He started to instruct her in elementary book-keeping and finance – insofar as he knew anything about it....

The months of service kept on piling up; going a very great deal faster now. During the later stretch, when one had acquired confidence in his ability to get through without cracking up, there was a comfortable feeling about sitting quietly out there with the knowledge of the money gradually piling up at home.

A new find opened up on Callisto, bringing a slight increase in deliveries to the satellite. Otherwise, the routine continued unchanged. The infrequent ships called in, loaded up, and went again. And then, surprisingly soon, it was possible for Duncan to say to himself: 'Next ship but one, and I'll be through!' Even more surprisingly soon there came the day when he stood on the metal apron outside the dome, watching a ship lifting herself off on her under-jets and dwindling upwards into the black sky, and was able to tell himself: 'That's the last time I'll see that! When the next ship lifts off this dump, I'll be aboard her, and then – boy, oh boy ... !'

He stood watching her, one bright spark among the others, until the turn of the satellite carried her below his horizon. Then he turned back to the airlock – and found the door shut....

Once he had decided that there was going to be no repercussion from the Alan Whint affair he had let his habit of wedging it open with a piece of rock lapse. Whenever he emerged to do a job he left it ajar, and it stayed that way until he came back. There was no wind, or anything else on the satellite to move it. He laid hold of the latch-lever irritably, and pushed. It did not move.

Duncan swore at it for sticking. He walked to the edge of the metal apron, and then jetted himself a little round the side of the dome so that he could see in at the window. Lellie was sitting in a chair with the spring-cover fixed across it, apparently lost in thought. The inner door of the airlock was standing open, so of course the outer could not be moved. As well as the safety-locking device, there was all the dome's air pressure to hold it shut.

Forgetful for the moment, Duncan rapped on the thick glass of the double window to attract her attention; she could not have heard a sound through there, it must have been the movement that caught her eye and caused her to look up. She turned her head, and gazed at him, without moving. Duncan stared back at her. Her hair was still waved, but the eyebrows, the colour, all the other touches that he had insisted upon to make her look as much like an Earth woman as possible, were gone. Her eyes looked back at him, set hard as stones in that fixed expression of mild astonishment.

Sudden comprehension struck Duncan like a physical shock. For some seconds everything seemed to stop.

He tried to pretend to both of them that he had not understood. He made gestures to her to close the inner door of the airlock. She went on staring back at him, without moving. Then he noticed the book she was holding in her hand, and recognized it. It was not one of the books which the Company had supplied for the station's library. It was a book of verse, bound in blue. It had once belonged to Alan Whint. . . .

Panic suddenly jumped out at Duncan. He looked down at the row of small dials across his chest, and then sighed with relief. She had not tampered with his air-supply: there was pressure there enough for thirty hours or so. The sweat that had started out on his brow grew cooler as he regained control of himself. A touch on the jet sent him floating back to the metal apron where he could anchor his magnetic boots, and think it over.

What a bitch! Letting him think all this time that she had forgotten all about it. Nursing it up for him. Letting him work out his time while she planned. Waiting until he was on the very last stretch before she tried her game on. Some minutes passed before his mixed anger and panic settled down and allowed him to think.

Thirty hours! Time to do quite a lot. And even if he did not succeed in getting back into the dome in twenty or so of them, there would still be the last, desperate resort of shooting himself off to Callisto in one of the cylinder-crates.

Even if Lellie were to spill over later about the Whint business, what of it? He was sure enough that she did not know *how* it had been done. It would only be the word of a Mart against his own. Very likely they'd put her down as space-crazed.

. . . All the same, some of the mud might stick; it would be better to settle with her here and now – besides, the cylinder idea was risky; only to be considered in the last extremity. There were other ways to be tried first.

Duncan reflected a few minutes longer, then he jetted himself over to the smaller dome. In there, he threw out the switches on the lines which brought power down from the main batteries charged by the sun-motor. He sat down to wait for a bit. The insulated dome would take some time to lose all its heat, but not very long for a drop in the temperature to become perceptible, and visible on the thermometers, once the heat was off. The small capacity, low voltage batteries that were in the place wouldn't be much good to her, even if she did think of lining them up.

He waited an hour, while the faraway sun set, and the arc of Callisto began to show over the horizon. Then he went back to the dome's window to observe results. He arrived just in time to see Lellie fastening herself into her space-suit by the light of a couple of emergency lamps.

He swore. A simple freezing out process wasn't going to work, then. Not only would the heated suit protect her, but her air supply would last longer than his – and there were plenty of spare bottles in there even if the free air in the dome should freeze solid.

He waited until she had put on the helmet, and then switched on the radio in his own. He saw her pause at the sound of his voice, but she did not reply. Presently she deliberately switched off her receiver. He did not; he kept his open to be ready for the moment when she should come to her senses.

Duncan returned to the apron, and reconsidered. It had been his intention to force his way into the dome without damaging it, if he could. But if she wasn't to be frozen out, that looked difficult. She had the advantage of him in air – and though it was true that in her space-suit she could neither eat nor drink, the same, unfortunately, was true for him. The only way seemed to be to tackle the dome itself.

Reluctantly, he went back to the small dome again, and connected up the electrical cutter. Its cable looped behind him as he jetted across to the main dome once more. Beside the curving metal wall, he paused to think out the job – and the consequences. Once he was through the outer shell there would be a space; then the insulating material – that was okay, it would melt away like butter, and without oxygen it could not catch fire. The more awkward part was going to come with the inner metal skin. It would be wisest to start with a few small cuts to let the air-pressure down – and stand clear of it: if it were all to come out with a whoosh he would stand a good chance in his weightless state of being blown a considerable distance by it. And what would she do? Well, she'd very likely try covering up the holes as he made them – a bit awkward if she had the sense to use asbestos packing: it'd have to be the whoosh

then. . . . Both shells could be welded up again before he
re-aerated the place from cylinders. . . . The small loss of
insulating material wouldn't matter. . . . Okay, better get
down to it, then. . . .

He made his connexions, and contrived to anchor himself enough to give some purchase. He brought the cutter
up, and pressed the trigger-switch. He pressed again, and
then swore, remembering that he had shut off the power.

He pulled himself back along the cable, and pushed the
switches in again. Light from the dome's windows suddenly
illuminated the rocks. He wondered if the restoration of
power would let Lellie know what he was doing. What if it
did? She'd know soon enough, anyway.

He settled himself down beside the dome once more.
This time the cutter worked. It took only a few minutes to
slice out a rough, two-foot circle. He pulled the piece out
of the way, and inspected the opening. Then, as he levelled
the cutter again, there came a click in his receiver: Lellie's
voice spoke in his ear:

'Better not try to break in. I'm ready for that.'

He hesitated, checking himself with his finger on the
switch, wondering what counter-move she could have
thought up. The threat in her voice made him uneasy. He
decided to go round to the window, and see what her game
was, if she had one.

She was standing by the table, still dressed in her space-
suit, fiddling with some apparatus she had set up there. For
a moment or two he did not grasp the purpose of it.

There was a plastic food-bag, half-inflated, and attached
in some way to the table top. She was adjusting a metal
plate over it to a small clearance. There was a wire, scotch-
taped to the upper side of the bag. Duncan's eye ran back
along the wire to a battery, a coil, and on to a detonator attached to a bundle of half a dozen blasting-sticks. . . .

He was uncomfortably enlightened. It was very simple –
ought to be perfectly effective. If the air-pressure in the
room should fall, the bag would expand: the wire would
make contact with the plate: up would go the dome. . . .

Lellie finished her adjustment, and connnected the second wire to the battery. She turned to look at him through the window. It was infuriatingly difficult to believe that behind that silly surprise frozen on her face she could be properly aware what she was doing.

Duncan tried to speak to her, but she had switched off, and made no attempt to switch on again. She simply stood looking steadily back at him as he blustered and raged. After some minutes she moved across to a chair, fastened the spring-cover across herself, and sat waiting.

'All right then,' Duncan shouted inside his helmet. 'But you'll go up with it, damn you!' Which was, of course, nonsense since he had no intention whatever of destroying either the dome or himself.

He had never learnt to tell what went on behind that silly face – she might be coldly determined, or she might not. If it had been a matter of a switch which she must press to destroy the place he might have risked her nerve failing her. But this way, it would be he who operated the switch, just as soon as he should make a hole to let the air out.

Once more he retreated to anchor himself on the apron. There must be *some* way round, some way of getting into the dome without letting the pressure down. ... He thought hard for some minutes, but if there was such a way, he could not find it – besides, there was no guarantee that she'd not set the explosive off herself if she got scared. ...

No – there was no way that he could think of. It would have to be the cylinder-crate to Callisto.

He looked up at Callisto, hanging huge in the sky now, with Jupiter smaller, but brighter, beyond. It wasn't so much the flight, it was the landing there. Perhaps if he were to cram it with all the padding he could find ... Later on, he could get the Callisto fellows to ferry him back, and they'd find some way to get into the dome, and Lellie would be a mighty sorry girl – *mighty* sorry. ...

Across the levelling there were three cylinders lined up,

charged and ready for use. He didn't mind admitting he
was scared of that landing: but, scared or not, if she
wouldn't even turn on her radio to listen to him, that
would be his only chance. And delay would do nothing for
him but narrow the margin of his air-supply.

He made up his mind, and stepped off the metal apron.
A touch on the jets sent him floating across the levelling
towards the cylinders. Practice made it an easy thing for
him to manoeuvre the nearest one on to the ramp. Another
glance at Callisto's inclination helped to reassure him; at
least he would reach it all right. If their beacon there was
not switched on to bring him in, he ought to be able to call
them on the communication radio in his suit when he got
closer.

There was not a lot of padding in the cylinder. He
fetched more from the others, and packed the stuff in. It
was while he paused to figure out a way of triggering the
thing off with himself inside, that he realized he was beginning to feel cold. As he turned the knob up a notch, he
glanced down at the meter on his chest – in an instant he
knew. . . . She had known that he would fit fresh air-bottles
and test them; so it had been the battery, or more likely,
the circuit, she had tampered with. The voltage was down
to a point where the needle barely kicked. The suit must
have been losing heat for some time already.

He knew that he would not be able to last long – perhaps
not more than a few minutes. After its first stab, the fear
abruptly left him, giving way to an impotent fury. She'd
tricked him out of his last chance, but, by God, he could
make sure she didn't get away with it. He'd be going, but
just one small hole in the dome, and he'd not be going
alone. . . .

The cold was creeping into him, it seemed to come lap-
ping at him icily through the suit. He pressed the jet control, and sent himself scudding back towards the dome. The
cold was gnawing in at him. His feet and fingers were going
first. Only by an immense effort was he able to operate the
jet which stopped him by the side of the dome. But it

needed one more effort, for he hung there, a yard or so above the ground. The cutter lay where he had left it, a few feet beyond his reach. He struggled desperately to press the control that would let him down to it, but his fingers would no longer move. He wept and gasped at the attempt to make them work, and with the anguish of the cold creeping up his arms. Of a sudden, there was an agonizing, searing pain in his chest. It made him cry out. He gasped – and the unheated air rushed into his lungs, and froze them....

In the dome's living-room Lellie stood waiting. She had seen the space-suited figure come sweeping across the levelling at an abnormal speed. She understood what it meant. Her explosive device was already disconnected; now she stood alert, with a thick rubber mat in her hand, ready to clap it over any hole that might appear. She waited one minute, two minutes... When five minutes had passed she went to the window. By putting her face close to the pane and looking sideways she was able to see the whole of one space-suited leg and part of another. They hung there horizontally, a few feet off the ground. She watched them for several minutes. Their gradual downward drift was barely perceptible.

She left the window, and pushed the mat out of her hand so that it floated away across the room. For a moment or two she stood thinking. Then she went to the bookshelves and pulled out the last volume of the encyclopaedia. She turned the pages, and satisfied herself on the exact status and claims which are connoted by the word 'widow'.

She found a pad of paper and a pencil. For a minute she hesitated, trying to remember the method she had been taught, then she started to write down figures, and became absorbed in them. At last she lifted her head, and contemplated the result: £5,000 per annum for five years, at 6 per cent compound interest, worked out at a nice little sum – quite a small fortune for a Martian.

But then she hesitated again. Very likely a face that was not set for ever in a mould of slightly surprised innocence would have frowned a little at that point, because, of course, there was a deduction that had to be made — a matter of £2,360.

Compassion Circuit

By the time Janet had been five days in hospital she had become converted to the idea of a domestic robot. It had taken her two days to discover that Nurse James *was* a robot, one day to get over the surprise, and two more to realize what a comfort an attendant robot could be.

The conversion was a relief. Practically every house she visited had a domestic robot; it was the family's second or third most valuable possession – the women tended to rate it slightly higher than the car; the men, slightly lower. Janet had been perfectly well aware for some time that her friends regarded her as a nitwit or worse for wearing herself out with looking after a house which a robot would be able to keep spick and span with a few hours' work a day. She had also known that it irritated George to come home each evening to a wife who had tired herself out by unnecessary work. But the prejudice had been firmly set. It was not the diehard attitude of people who refused to be served by robot waiters, or driven by robot drivers (who, incidentally, were much safer), led by robot shop-guides, or see dresses modelled by robot mannequins. It was simply an uneasiness about them, and being left alone with one – and a disinclination to feel such an uneasiness in her own home.

She herself attributed the feeling largely to the conservatism of her own home which had used no house-robots. Other people, who had been brought up in homes run by robots, even the primitive types available a generation before, never seemed to have such a feeling at all. It irritated her to know that her husband thought she was *afraid* of them in a childish way. That, she had explained to George a number of times, was not so, and was not the point, either: what she did dislike was the idea of one intruding upon her personal, domestic life, which was what a house-robot was bound to do.

The robot who was called Nurse James was, then, the

first with which she had ever been in close personal contact and she, or it, came as a revelation.

Janet told the doctor of her enlightenment, and he looked relieved. She also told George when he looked in in the afternoon: he was delighted. The two of them conferred before he left the hospital. 'Excellent,' said the doctor. 'To tell you the truth I was afraid we were up against a real neurosis there – and very inconveniently, too. Your wife can never have been strong, and in the last few years she's worn herself out running the house.'

'I know,' George agreed. 'I tried hard to persuade her during the first two years we were married, but it only led to trouble so I had to drop it. This is really a culmination – she was rather shaken when she found that the reason she'd have to come here was partly because there was no robot at home to look after her.'

'Well, there's one thing certain, she can't go on as she has been doing. If she tries to she'll be back here inside a couple of months,' the doctor told him.

'She won't now. She's really changed her mind,' George assured him. 'Part of the trouble was that she's never come across a really modern one, except in a superficial way. The newest that any of our friends has is ten years old at least, and most of them are older than that. She'd never contemplated the idea of anything as advanced as Nurse James. The question now is what pattern?'

The doctor thought a moment.

'Frankly, Mr Shand, your wife is going to need a lot of rest and looking after, I'm afraid. What I'd really recommend for her is the type they have here. It's something pretty new this Nurse James model. A specially developed high-sensibility job with a quite novel contra-balanced compassion-protection circuit – a very tricky bit of work that – any direct order which a normal robot would obey at once is evaluated by the circuit, it is weighed against the benefit or harm to the patient, and unless it is beneficial, or at least harmless, to the patient, it is not obeyed. They've proved to be wonderful for nursing and looking after children – but there is a big demand for them, and I'm afraid they're pretty expensive.'

'How much?' asked George.

The doctor's round-figure price made him frown for a moment. Then he said:

'It'll make a hole, but, after all, it's mostly Janet's economies and simple-living that's built up the savings. Where do I get one?'

'You don't. Not just like that,' the doctor told him. 'I shall have to throw a bit of weight about for a priority, but in the circumstances I shall get it, all right. Now, you go and fix up the details of appearance and so on with your wife. Let me know how she wants it, and I'll get busy.'

'A proper one,' said Janet. 'One that'll look right in a house, I mean. I couldn't do with one of those levers-and-plastic box things that stare at you with lenses. As it's got to look after the house, let's have it looking like a housemaid.'

'Or a houseman, if you like?'

She shook her head. 'No. It's going to have to look after me, too, so I think I'd rather it was a housemaid. It can have a black silk dress and a frilly white apron and a cap. And I'd like it blonde – a sort of darkish blonde – and about five feet ten, and nice to look at, but not *too* beautiful. I don't want to be jealous of it. . . .'

The doctor kept Janet ten days more in the hospital while the matter was settled. There had been luck in coming in for a cancelled order, but inevitably some delay while it was adapted to Janet's specification – also it had required the addition of standard domestic pseudo-memory patterns to suit it for housework.

It was delivered the day after she got back. Two severely functional robots carried the case up the front path, and inquired whether they should unpack it. Janet thought not, and told them to leave it in the outhouse.

When George got back he wanted to open it at once, but Janet shook her head.

'Supper first,' she decided. 'A robot doesn't mind waiting.'

Nevertheless it was a brief meal. When it was over, George carried the dishes out and stacked them in the sink.

'No more washing-up,' he said, with satisfaction.

He went out to borrow the next-door robot to help him carry the case in. Then he found his end of it more than he could lift, and had to borrow the robot from the house opposite, too. Presently the pair of them carried it in and laid it on the kitchen floor as if it were a featherweight, and went away again.

George got out the screwdriver and drew the six large screws that held the lid down. Inside there was a mass of shavings. He shoved them out, on to the floor.

Janet protested.

'What's the matter? *We* shan't have to clear up,' he said, happily.

There was an inner case of wood pulp, with a snowy layer of wadding under its lid. George rolled it up and pushed it out of the way, and there, ready dressed in black frock and white apron, lay the robot.

They regarded it for some seconds without speaking.

It was remarkably lifelike. For some reason it made Janet feel a little queer to realize that it was *her* robot – a trifle nervous, and, obscurely, a trifle guilty. . . .

'Sleeping beauty,' remarked George, reaching for the instruction book on its chest.

In point of fact the robot was not a beauty. Janet's preference had been observed. It was pleasant and nice-looking without being striking, but the details were good. The deep gold hair was quite enviable – although one knew that it was probably threads of plastic with waves that would never come out. The skin – another kind of plastic covering the carefully built-up contours – was distinguishable from real skin only by its perfection.

Janet knelt down beside the box, and ventured a forefinger to touch the flawless complexion. It was quite, quite cold.

She sat back on her heels, looking at it. Just a big doll, she told herself; a contraption, a very wonderful contraption of metal, plastics, and electronic circuits, but still a contraption, and made to look as it did simply because people, including herself, would find it harsh or grotesque if it should look any other way. . . . And yet, to have it looking as it did was a bit disturbing, too. For one thing, you couldn't go on thinking of it as 'it' any more; whether you liked it or not, your mind thought of it as 'her'. As 'her' it would have to have a name; and, with a name, it would become still more of a person.

' "A battery-driven model",' George read out, ' "will normally require to be fitted with a new battery every four days. Other models, however, are designed to conduct their own regeneration from the mains as and when necessary." Let's have her out.'

He put his hands under the robot's shoulders, and tried to lift it.

'Phew!' he said. 'Must be about three times my weight.' He had another try. 'Hell,' he said, and referred to the book again.

' "The control switches are situated at the back, slightly above the waistline." All right, maybe we can roll her over.'

With an effort he succeeded in getting the figure on to its side and began to undo the buttons at the back of her dress. Janet suddenly felt that to be an indelicacy.

'I'll do it,' she said.

Her husband glanced at her.

'All right. It's yours,' he told her.

'She can't be just "it". I'm going to call her Hester.'

'All right, again,' he agreed.

Janet undid the buttons and fumbled about inside the dress.

'I can't find a knob, or anything,' she said.

'Apparently there's a small panel that opens,' he told her.

'Oh, no!' she said, in a slightly shocked tone.

He regarded her again.

'Darling, she's just a robot; a mechanism.'

'I know,' said Janet, shortly. She felt about again, discovered the panel, and opened it.

'You give the upper knob a half-turn to the right and then close the panel to complete the circuit,' instructed George, from the book.

Janet did so, and then sat swiftly back on her heels again, watching.

The robot stirred and turned. It sat up, then it got to its feet. It stood before them, looking the very pattern of a stage parlourmaid.

'Good day, madam,' it said. 'Good day, sir. I shall be happy to serve you.'

'Thank you, Hester,' Janet said, as she leaned back against the cushion placed behind her. Not that it was necessary to thank a robot, but she had a theory that if you did not practise politeness with robots you soon forgot it with other people.

And, anyway, Hester was no ordinary robot. She was not even dressed as a parlourmaid any more. In four months she had become a friend, a tireless, attentive friend. From the first Janet had found it difficult to believe that she was only a mechanism, and as the days passed she had become more and more of a person. The fact that she consumed electricity instead of food came to seem little more than a foible. The time she couldn't stop walking in a circle, and the other time when something went wrong with her vision so that she did everything a foot to the right of where she ought to have been doing it, these things were just indispositions such as anyone might have, and the robot-mechanic who came to adjust her paid his call much like any other doctor. Hester was not only a person; she was preferable company to many.

'I suppose,' said Janet, settling back in her chair, 'that you must think me a poor, weak thing?'

What one must not expect from Hester was euphemism.

'Yes,' she said, directly. But then she added: 'I think all humans are poor, weak things. It is the way they are made. One must be sorry for them.'

Janet had long ago given up thinking things like: 'That'll be the compassion-circuit speaking,' or trying to imagine the computing, selecting, associating, and shunting that must be going on to produce such a remark. She took it as she might from – well, say, a foreigner. She said:

'Compared with robots we must seem so, I suppose. You are so strong and untiring, Hester. If you knew how I envy you that. . . .'

Hester said, matter of factly:

'We were designed: you were just accidental. It is your misfortune, not your fault.'

'You'd rather be you than me?' asked Janet.

'Certainly,' Hester told her. 'We are stronger. We don't have to have frequent sleep to recuperate. We don't have to carry an unreliable chemical factory inside us. We don't have to grow old and deteriorate. Human beings are so clumsy and fragile and so often unwell because something is not working properly. If anything goes wrong with us, or is broken, it doesn't hurt and is easily replaced. And you have all kinds of words like pain, and suffering, and unhappiness, and weariness that we have to be taught to understand, and they don't seem to us to be useful things to have. I feel very sorry that you must have these things and be so uncertain and so fragile. It disturbs my compassion-circuit.'

'Uncertain and fragile,' Janet repeated. 'Yes, that's how I feel.'

'Humans have to live so precariously,' Hester went on. 'If my arm or leg should be crushed I can have a new one in a few minutes, but a human would have agony for a long time, and not even a new limb at the end of it – just a faulty one, if he is lucky. That isn't as bad as it used to be because in designing us you learned how to make good arms and legs, much stronger and better than the old ones. People would be much more sensible to have a weak arm or leg replaced at once, but they don't seem to want to if they can possibly keep the old ones.'

'You mean they can be grafted on? I didn't know that,' Janet said. 'I wish it were only arms or legs that's wrong with me. I don't think I would hesitate. . . .' She sighed. 'The doctor wasn't encouraging this morning, Hester. You heard what he said? I've been losing ground: must rest more. I don't believe he does expect me to get any stronger. He was just trying to cheer me up before. . . . He had a funny sort of look after he'd examined me. . . . But all he said was rest. What's the good of being alive if it's only rest – rest – rest. . . ? And there's poor George. What sort of a life is it for him, and he's so patient with me, so sweet. . . . I'd rather anything than go on feebly like this. I'd sooner die. . . .'

Janet went on talking, more to herself than to the patient Hester standing by. She talked herself into tears. Then, presently, she looked up.

'Oh, Hester, if you were human I couldn't bear it; I think I'd hate you for being so strong and so well – but I don't, Hester. You're so kind and so patient when I'm silly, like this. I believe you'd cry with me to keep me company if you could.'

'I would if I could,' the robot agreed. 'My compassion-circuit –'

'Oh, *no*!' Janet protested. 'It can't be just that. You've a heart somewhere, Hester. You must have.'

'I expect it is more reliable than a heart,' said Hester.

She stepped a little closer, stooped down, and lifted Janet up as if she weighed nothing at all.

'You've tired yourself out, Janet, dear,' she told her. 'I'll take you upstairs; you'll be able to sleep a little before he gets back.'

Janet could feel the robot's arms cold through her dress, but the coldness did not trouble her any more, she was aware only that they were strong, protecting arms around her. She said:

'Oh, Hester, you are such a comfort, you *know* what I ought to do.' She paused, then she added miserably: 'I know what he thinks – the doctor, I mean. I could see it. He just thinks I'm going to go on getting weaker and weaker until one day I'll fade away and die. ... I said I'd sooner die ... but I wouldn't, Hester. I don't want to die. ...'

The robot rocked her a little, as if she were a child.

'There, there, dear. It's not as bad as that – nothing like,' she told her. 'You mustn't think about dying. And you mustn't cry any more, it's not good for you, you know. Besides, you don't want him to see you've been crying.'

'I'll try not to,' agreed Janet obediently, as Hester carried her out of the room and up the stairs.

The hospital reception-robot looked up from the desk.

'My wife,' George said, 'I rang you up about an hour ago.'

The robot's face took on an impeccable expression of professional sympathy.

'Yes, Mr Shand. I'm afraid it has been a shock for you, but as I told you, your house-robot did quite the right thing to send her here at once.'

'I've tried to get on to her own doctor, but he's away,' George told her.

'You don't need to worry about that, Mr Shand. She has been examined, and we have had all her records sent over from the hospital she was in before. The operation has been provisionally fixed for tomorrow, but of course we shall need your consent.'

George hesitated. 'May I see the doctor in charge of her?'

'He isn't in the hospital at the moment, I'm afraid.'

'Is it – absolutely necessary?' George asked after a pause.

The robot looked at him steadily, and nodded.

'She must have been growing steadily weaker for some months now,' she said.

George nodded.

'The only alternative is that she will grow weaker still, and have more pain before the end,' she told him.

George stared at the wall blankly for some seconds.

'I see,' he said bleakly.

He picked up a pen in a shaky hand and signed the form that she put before him. He gazed at it awhile without seeing it.

'She'll – she'll have – a good chance?' he asked.

'Yes,' the robot told him. 'There is never complete absence of risk, of course, but she has a better than seventy-per-cent likelihood of complete success.'

George sighed, and nodded.

'I'd like to see her,' he said.

The robot pressed a bell-push.

'You may *see* her,' she said. 'But I must ask you not to disturb her. She's asleep now, and it's better for her not to be woken.'

George had to be satisfied with that, but he left the hospital feeling a little better for the sight of the quiet smile on Janet's lips as she slept.

The hospital called him at the office the following afternoon. They were reassuring. The operation appeared to have been a complete success. Everyone was quite confident of the outcome. There was no need to worry. The doctors were perfectly satisfied. No, it would not be wise to allow any visitors for a few days yet. But there was nothing to worry about. Nothing at all.

George rang up each day just before he left, in the hope that he would be allowed a visit. The hospital was kindly and heartening, but adamant about visits. And then, on the fifth day, they suddenly told him she had left on her way home. George was staggered: he had been prepared to find it a matter of weeks. He dashed out, bought a bunch of roses, and left half a dozen traffic regulations in fragments behind him.

'Where is she?' he demanded of Hester as she opened the door.

'She's in bed. I thought it might be better if –' Hester began, but he lost the rest of the sentence as he bounded up the stairs.

Janet was lying in the bed. Only her head was visible, cut off by the line of the sheet and a bandage round her neck. George put the flowers down on the bedside table. He stooped over Janet and kissed her gently. She looked up at him from anxious eyes.

'Oh, George dear. Has she told you?'

'Has who told me what?' he asked, sitting down on the side of the bed.

'Hester. She said she would. Oh, George, I didn't mean it, at least I don't think I meant it. . . . She sent me, George. I was so weak and wretched. I wanted to be strong. I don't think I really understood. Hester said –'

'Take it easy, darling. Take it easy,' George suggested with a smile. 'What on earth's all this about?'

He felt under the bedclothes and found her hand.

'But, George –' she began. He interrupted her.

'I say, darling, your hand's dreadfully cold. It's almost like –' His fingers slid further up her arm. His eyes widened at her, incredulously. He jumped up suddenly from the bed and flung back the covers. He put his hand on the thin nightdress, over her heart – and then snatched it away as if he had been stung.

'God! – NO! –' he said, staring at her.

'But George. George, darling –' said Janet's head on the pillows.

'NO! – NO!' cried George, almost in a shriek.

He turned and ran blindly from the room.

In the darkness on the landing he missed the top step of the stairs, and went headlong down the whole flight.

Hester found him lying in a huddle in the hall. She bent down and gently explored the damage. The extent of it, and the fragility of the frame that had suffered it disturbed her compassion-circuit very greatly. She did not try to move him, but went to the telephone and dialled.

'Emergency?' she asked, and gave the name and address. 'Yes, at once,' she told them. 'There may not be a lot of time. Several compound fractures, and I think his back is broken, poor man. No. There appears to be no damage to his head. Yes, much better. He'd be crippled for life, even if he did get over it. . . . Yes, better send the form of consent with the ambulance so that it can be signed at once. . . . Oh, yes, that'll be quite all right. His wife will sign it.'

Wild Flower

NOT Miss Fray. Not Felicity Fray.

Let others jerk awake to an alarm, scramble from bed, scrub away the clinging patina of sleep with a face-flannel, hunt out the day's clothes, watch the percolator impatiently, urge the toast to pop up more quickly. Let them chew briskly, swallow gulpily, and hurry, arms and legs reciprocating briskly, on their ways. Let these automata, with batteries regenerated, respond with spry efficiency to the insistent eye of the new day's sun, and let them greet the morning with resolution in heel and toe, a high-tensile gleam in the eye, and set off to make their new deals, new conquests...

But not Felicity Fray.

For today is part of yesterday. And yesterday and today are parts of being alive. And being alive is not just an affair of the days going clonk-clonk-clonk like the pendulum of a grandfather clock: being alive is something continuous, that does not repeat; something that one should be aware of all the time, sleeping and waking...

It may not last much longer.

There is no savour in hurry; so Miss Fray did not hurry; she did not jerk or bounce into the beginning of her day. About dawn she started to drift from dream through half-dream to day-dream, and lay unmoving, listening to the birds, watching the sky lighten, becoming aware of the day as it became aware of itself.

For more than an hour she lay hovering this and that side of the misty edge of sleep. Sometimes the sounds in her ears were real birds singing, sometimes they were remembered voices speaking. She enjoyed them both, smiling in her half-sleep.

By the time the day began to win her certainly from the night the birds were almost silent. They had done with the greeting, and started on the business of looking for food.

She was quite abruptly aware that the world was almost noiseless.

There was an alarming feeling of unreality. She held her breath to listen for some reassuring sound. Supposing it had all stopped, now? – As it might do one day.

Perhaps, even at this moment, there were in some parts of the world great columns of smoke writhing upwards in Medusan coils, swelling out at the top into cerebral convolutions that pulsed with a kind of sub-life, marking the beginning of the silence that meant the end of everything.

For years now, when she was off her guard, those pillars of smoke had been likely to start up in her mind. She hated and feared them. They were the triumphant symbol of Science.

Science was, perhaps, wonderful, but, for Miss Fray, it was a wonder of the left hand. Science was the enemy of the world that lived and breathed; it was a crystalline formation on the harsh naked rock of brain, mindless, insensitive, barren, yet actively a threat, an alien threat that she feared as un-understandingly as an animal fears fire. Science, the great antibiotic.

So Felicity listened unhappily.

A bird called, and was answered.

That was not enough.

She went on listening for more reassurance.

In the farmyard several fields away, a tractor coughed, stuttered, and then ran more steadily, warming up.

She relaxed, relieved to be sure that the world was still alive. Then she faintly frowned her ungrateful contempt for the tractor, and pushed it out of her consciousness.

It, too, was a manifestation of science, and unwelcome.

She withdrew among her thoughts. She resurrected stored moments and magical glimpses, and remembered golden words. She landscaped her own Arcady which knew no Science.

The tractor throbbed more briskly as it trundled out of the yard, the sound of it diminished to a purr as it crossed the fields, unheard by Felicity.

There was plenty of time. Enough to take the field-path way to school, and not to hurry over it.

The sun was climbing, a medallion pinned on a deepening blue cloak. Later on, the day would be hot, but now it was fresh, with a touch like a cool, white-fingered hand. Refractile gems still trembled on the leaves and stalks.

Beads from the shaken grass ran down her legs, showered on the white canvas shoes, fell like kisses on her feet.

Cows, coming out from the sheds with their udders relieved, but still slow and patient, stared at her with incurious curiosity, and then turned away to tear the grass, and munch in thoughtless rumination.

A lark, high up, trilled to mislead her from its nest.

A young blackbird, looking puffy and overfed, eyed her cautiously from the hedge.

A light draught of summer wind blew through her cotton frock, caressing her with cobweb fingers.

Then there was a muttering in the sky; then a roaring that rumbled back and forth in the vault; then a shrieking over her head, a battering at the ears and the senses, not to be shut out. The present assaulting her, bawling unignorably, frighteningly through its jet-mouths; Science on the wing.

Felicity put her hands to her ears and rocked her head. The outrage hurtled close above, sound-waves clashing together, buffeting, and reeling back.

It passed, and she uncovered her ears again. With tears in her eyes she shook her fist at the fleeing shriek of the jets and all they represented, while the air still shuddered about her.

The cows continued to graze.

How comfortable to be a cow. Neither expecting nor regretting; having no sense of guilt, nor need for it. Making no distinctions between the desirable and undesirable works of men; able to flick them, like the flies, aside with the swish of a tow-ended tail.

The shriek and the rumble died in the distance. The

shattered scene began to re-integrate behind it, still for a while bloom-brushed and bruised, but slowly healing.

One day there would be too much bruising; too much to recover from.

'Imitations of mortality,' said Miss Fray, to herself. 'So many little deaths before the big one. How silly I am to suffer. Why should I feel all these pangs of guilt for other people? I am not responsible for this – I am not even much afraid, for myself. Why do I have to be so hurt by fear for all and everything?'

A thrush sang in the spinney beyond the hedge.

She paused to listen.

Unguent, sweet notes.

She walked on, becoming aware again of the silk-fringed zephyrs on her cheeks, the sun on her arms, the dew on her feet.

As Felicity opened the door the hive-murmur beyond sank into silence.

The rows of pink-cheeked faces framed in long hair, short hair, plaits, some of it morning-tidy, some of it already waywardly awry, were all turned towards her. The bright eyes were all fixed on her face.

'Good morning, Miss Fray,' they all said, in unison, and silence fell as completely as before.

She could feel the suppressed expectation in the air as they watched her. There was something she must respond to. She looked for it. Her glance went round the familiar room until it reached her desk. There it stopped, where a small glass vase held a single flower.

The rows of eyes switched from her to the desk, and then back again.

She walked slowly across and sat down in her chair, her gaze never leaving the flower.

It was something she had never seen before; she was quite unable to classify it, and she looked at it for a long time.

It was more complex than the simpler field flowers, yet

not sophisticated. The colours were clear, but not primaries. The shape was comely, but without garden-bred formality. The ground-colour of the petals was a pale pink, flushing a little at the over-rolled edges, paling to cream further back. Then there was the flush-colour again, powder-stippled at first, then reticulated, then solid as it narrowed into the trumpet, but split by white spurs of the centre veins. There was just a suggestion of orchis about it, perhaps, but it was no kind of orchis she had ever seen, alive or pictured. The petal curves were sweet natural roundings, like limbs, or water cascading, or saplings bent in the wind. The texture was depthlessly soft.

Felicity leaned closer, gazing into the velvet throat. Little crescent-shaped stamens faintly dusted with pollen trembled on green, hair-like stalks. She caught the scent of it. A little sweetness, a little sharpness, a little earthiness, blended with a subtlety to make a perfumer's art vulgar and banal.

She breathed in the scent again, and looked into the flower hypnotized, unable to take her eyes from it, loving it in its brave delicacy with a sweet, longing compassion.

She had forgotten the room, the eyes that watched her, everything but the flower itself.

A fidgeting somewhere brought her back. She lifted her head, and looked unhurriedly along the rows of faces.

'Thank you,' she said. 'It's a beautiful flower. What is it?'

Seemingly, no one knew.

'Who brought it?' Felicity asked them.

A small, golden-headed child in the middle of the second row pinked a little.

'I did, Miss Fray.'

'And you don't know what it is, Marielle?'

'No, Miss Fray, I just found it, and I thought it was pretty, and I thought you'd like it,' she explained, a trifle anxiously.

Felicity looked back to the flower again.

'I do like it, Marielle. It's lovely. It was very kind of you to think of bringing it for me.'

She loitered over the flower a few seconds more, and then moved the vase decisively to the left of the desk. With an effort she turned her eyes away from it, back to the rows of faces.

'One day,' she said, 'I'll read you some William Blake – "To see a World in a Grain of Sand, And a Heaven in a Wild Flower ..." But now we must get on, we've wasted too much time already. I want you to copy out what I write on the board, in your best handwriting.'

She picked up the chalk and thought for a moment, looking at the flower. Then she went over to the blackboard, and wrote:

'Their colours and their forms were then to me an appetite; a feeling and a love ...'

'Marielle. Just a moment,' Felicity said.

The child paused and turned back as the others streamed out of the room.

'Thank you very much for bringing it. Was it the only one?' Felicity asked her.

'Oh, no, Miss Fray. There were three or four clumps of them.'

'Where, Marielle? I'd like to get a root of it, if I can.'

'On Mr Hawkes's farm. In the top corner of the big field, where the aeroplane crashed,' the child told her.

'Where the aeroplane crashed,' Felicity repeated.

'Yes, Miss Fray.'

Felicity sat down slowly, staring at the flower. The child waited, and shifted from one foot to the other.

'Please, may I go now, Miss Fray?'

'Yes,' said Felicity, without looking up. 'Yes, of course.'

Feet scuttered out of the room.

Felicity went on looking at the flower.

'Where the aeroplane crashed.' That had been almost a year ago – on a summer's evening when all the world was quietening and settling down for the night. 'Now fades the glimmering landscape on the sight, and all the air a solemn stillness holds.' Then the aeroplane, wheeling its droning flight, destroying the peace. It was a silver-paper cross up in the sky where the sunlight was still bright. Unusually, Felicity looked up. She tried to ignore the noise and her prejudices, for the craft had, undeniably, a silver-moth beauty of its own. She watched it turn, the sunset glistering the undersides of the wings as it tilted. Then, suddenly, amid the silver there had been a flash of rose-red fire, and the silver moth ceased to exist. Pieces of glittering foil were spreading apart and falling. The largest piece trailed smoke above it, like a black funeral plume.

A great crack slapped at her ears.

The pieces twisted and flashed in the sky as they came, some fast, some slower. The biggest of all seemed to be falling straight towards her. Perhaps she screamed. She threw herself on the ground, arms clutched over her head and ears, willing to sink herself into the earth itself.

There were interminable second-fractions of waiting while the silver wreckage came hurtling down the sky, and Felicity and all the world about her held their breath.

The solid ground bounced under her; then came the crash, and the shrieking of metal.

Felicity looked up, biting fearfully on her hand.

She saw the silver body, a crumpled fish-shape, less than a hundred yards away, and in that moment petals of flame blossomed round it.

Something else fell close by.

She cringed close to the earth again.

Something in the main body blew up. Bits of metal whirred like pheasants over her, and plopped around.

Presently she risked raising her head again. The wreck was a cone of flame with black smoke above. She could feel the warmth on her face. She did not dare to stand up lest something else should explode and send jagged metal fragments slicing into her.

She had been still there, clinging to the earth and crying, when the crash-parties arrived and found her.

Shock, they had said, shock and fright. They had treated her for that, and then sent her home.

She had cried for the destruction, for the fire and smoke, the noise and confusion of it; and, too, for the people who had died in it, for the wanton futility of it, for the harsh, mindless, silliness of a world that did these things and kept on doing them and would keep on doing them until the last two sub-critical masses were brought together for the last time.

They kept her in bed a few days, with instructions to rest and relax; but in was difficult to relax when things kept on going round and round in one's head.

'Oh God,' she prayed, 'won't You stop them? It isn't *their* world to do as they like with. It's Your world, and mine – the heart's world that they are destroying with their brain's world. Please, God, while there is still time – You destroyed their presumption at Babel, won't You do it again, before it's too late?'

Felicity remembered the prayer as she sat at her desk, looking at the beautiful flower.

They had put a fence round the place where the aeroplane had crashed, and set guards, too, to keep people away. Inside it, men in overall suits prowled and prowled, searching, listening, watching counters.

Cobalt was the trouble, they said. She had wondered how that could be. But it was not the artist's cobalt they wanted: the scientists had taken even the deep blue colour of the sea, and had done something deadly to that, too, it appeared.

Though not altogether, not necessarily deadly, Miss Simpson who taught science at the High School had explained to her. The aeroplane had been carrying some radio-active cobalt intended for a hospital somewhere in the Middle East. In the crash, or perhaps in the first explosion, the lead box that kept it safe had been broken open. It was extremely dangerous, and had to be recovered.

'How? Dangerous?' Felicity had wanted to know.

And Miss Simpson had told her something of the effects of gamma rays on living matter.

Several weeks had passed before the searching men were completely satisfied, and went away. They had left the fence, no longer guarded, simply as a mark to indicate the piece of ground that was not to be ploughed this season. The ground had been left free to grow what it would.

And out of the noise, the destruction, the fire, the deadly radiations had sprung the lovely flower.

Felicity went on looking at it for a long time in the silent room. Then she raised her eyes, and glanced along the rows of desks where the bright faces had been.

'I see,' she said, to the emptiness and the unseen. 'I'm weak. I have had too little faith.'

She had a disinclination to revisit the site of the crash alone. She asked Marielle to come with her on Saturday and show her where the flowers grew.

They climbed by a cool path through the woods, crossed a stile and the pasture beyond it. When they came to the enclosure, its fence already pushed flat in several places, they found a man already within it. He wore a shirt and blue jeans, and was engaged in unslinging a heavy cylinder from his back. He laid the thing carefully on the ground and pulled out a large spotted handkerchief to wipe his face and neck. He turned as they approached, and grinned amiably. Felicity recognized him as the farmer's second son.

'Hot work carrying three or four gallons on your back this weather,' he explained apologetically, wiping the handkerchief down his arms so that the golden hairs stood up and glinted in the sunlight.

Felicity looked at the ground. There were five or six small clumps of the flowers growing in the weeds and grass, one of them half crushed under the cylinder.

'Oh,' said Marielle, in distress. 'You've been killing them – killing the flowers. They're what we came for.'

'You can pick 'em, and welcome,' he told her.

'But we wanted some roots, to grow them,' Marielle told

him woefully. She turned to Felicity unhappily. 'They're such pretty flowers, too.'

'Pretty enough,' agreed the man, looking down at them. 'But there it is. Can't have this lot seeding all over the rest, you see.'

'You've poisoned them all – every one?' Marielle asked miserably.

The man nodded.

' 'Fraid they're done for now, for all they still look all right. 'F you'd've let me know . . . but it's too late now. But they'll do you no harm to pick,' he explained. ' 'Tisn't poison in the old way, you see. Something to do with hormones, whatever they are. Doesn't knock 'em out, as you might say, just sends 'em all wrong in the growing so they give up. Wonderful what the scientific chaps get hold of these days. Never know what they'll bring out next, do you?'

Felicity and Marielle gathered little bunches of the doomed flowers. They still looked as delicately beautiful and still had their poignant scent. At the stile Marielle stopped and stood looking sadly at her little bunch.

'They're so lovely,' she said mournfully, with tears in her eyes.

Felicity put an arm round her.

'They are lovely,' she agreed. 'They're very lovely – and they've gone. But the important thing is that they came. That's the wonderful thing. There'll be some more – some-day – somewhere. . . .'

A jet came shrieking suddenly, close over the hill-top. Marielle put her hands over her ears. Felicity stood watching the machine shrink among the scream and rumble of protesting air. She held up her little posy of flowers to the blast.

'This is your answer,' she said. 'This. You bullies, with your vast clubs of smoke – this is greater than all of you.'

Marielle took down her hands.

'I hate them – I hate them,' she said, her eyes on the vanishing speck.

'I hate them, too,' agreed Felicity. 'But now I'm not afraid of them any more. I have found a remedy, an elixir:

> *It is a wine of virtuous powers;*
> *My mother made it of wild flowers.*'

FOR THE BEST IN PAPERBACKS, LOOK FOR THE

In every corner of the world, on every subject under the sun, Penguin represents quality and variety – the very best in publishing today.

For complete information about books available from Penguin – including Puffins, Penguin Classics and Arkana – and how to order them, write to us at the appropriate address below. Please note that for copyright reasons the selection of books varies from country to country.

In the United Kingdom: Please write to *Dept E.P., Penguin Books Ltd, Harmondsworth, Middlesex, UB7 0DA.*

If you have any difficulty in obtaining a title, please send your order with the correct money, plus ten per cent for postage and packaging, to *PO Box No 11, West Drayton, Middlesex*

In the United States: Please write to *Dept BA, Penguin, 299 Murray Hill Parkway, East Rutherford, New Jersey 07073*

In Canada: Please write to *Penguin Books Canada Ltd, 2801 John Street, Markham, Ontario L3R 1B4*

In Australia: Please write to the *Marketing Department, Penguin Books Australia Ltd, P.O. Box 257, Ringwood, Victoria 3134*

In New Zealand: Please write to the *Marketing Department, Penguin Books (NZ) Ltd, Private Bag, Takapuna, Auckland 9*

In India: Please write to *Penguin Overseas Ltd, 706 Eros Apartments, 56 Nehru Place, New Delhi, 110019*

In the Netherlands: Please write to *Penguin Books Netherlands B.V., Postbus 195, NL–1380AD Weesp*

In West Germany: Please write to *Penguin Books Ltd, Friedrichstrasse 10–12, D–6000 Frankfurt/Main 1*

In Spain: Please write to *Longman Penguin España, Calle San Nicolas 15, E–28013 Madrid*

In Italy: Please write to *Penguin Italia s.r.l., Via Como 4, I-20096 Pioltello (Milano)*

In France: Please write to *Penguin Books Ltd, 39 Rue de Montmorency, F-75003 Paris*

In Japan: Please write to *Longman Penguin Japan Co Ltd, Yamaguchi Building, 2–12–9 Kanda Jimbocho, Chiyoda-Ku, Tokyo 101*

BY THE SAME AUTHOR

THE DAY OF THE TRIFFIDS

The Day of the Triffids is a fantastic, frightening, but entirely plausible story of the future when the world is dominated by triffids, grotesque and dangerous plants over seven feet tall.

THE KRAKEN WAKES

The title is taken from a poem by Tennyson. and the book tells of the awakening and rise to power of forces from beneath the surface of the sea. The almost imperceptible beginnings and the cruelly terrifying consequences of this threat to the world are seen through the eyes of a radio script-writer and his wife.

THE CHRYSALIDS

A thrilling and realistic account of the world beset by genetic mutations. 'Jolly good story, well-conceived community. characters properly up to simple requirements. Better than the *Kraken* perhaps even the *Triffids*' – *Observer*

TROUBLE WITH LICHEN

'If even a tenth of science fiction were as good, we should be in clover' – Kingsley Amis in the *Observer*

THE MIDWICH CUCKOOS

This is the book from which the film *The Village of the Damned* was made.

CONSIDER HER WAYS
and Other Stories

CHOCKY

THE SEEDS OF TIME

WEB